A Plague a' B(

MW00411726

By

Dan Jammal

Edited by Sue Rasmussen

Designed by Dan Jammal

Cover Art By Kristen Hart

Thank you Jason Daniel Bryant and Melissa Constantine for being my second set of eyes once again. Thank you family and friends who support me on this path.

Steven Manchester, deepest appreciation for your knowledge and guidance, from one writer to another.

Sue Rasmussen, my humblest thank you for your keen eyes and hard work.

Kristen Hart, deepest thanks for your inspiring art to make my work shine.

Above all, for your life changing literature, thank you Mr. William Shakespeare

To those known and unknown

lost in my love's dream,

within the chambers of my heart

A Plague a' Both Your Houses

A Novel

Chapter One

I have broken my own moral code and, for that and that alone, I must cease to be. These many years of my life, I have watched Lord knows how many souls fly to His high kingdom well before their calling.

Desperation would cry out from the eyes of the unwell, of both physical health and of the soul, to be healed and returned to their natural state from the confines of their bed. And I, a man of rich wisdom, a trained and experienced apothecary, would give them juices so empowered with cure, that not two days would pass and they would be at my door to thank me for my remedies of life.

Though, like the sun that doth rise in the eastern sky and travel its long and steady path, my years have passed to see the setting of my youth, as the stars have colored my hair white with their falling dust. In these never-ending years, others have practiced in this art of combining herbs and like substances into medicinal tinctures and done well, yet well call I it, as they have healed as I have. Thus, I have lost many a family to those who would offer the same medicines, but at a fee that would be unforeseen and unimaginable to support their own life and health. My aging years could not keep in the chase of these younger men who would even travel to learn more of their art. I had fallen poor, and inevitably my own health had lost its fight, as famine and hopelessness covered my bones. What was I to do?

From Verona he came, of an age where decisions were still new and un-thought-out, and I, a man of experience in the workings of the world, especially that of the mind and body, should have directed his judgment and desire to gain more logic and settle it to a steady place. Even as only a fortnight, or so, has passed since this boy from Verona came to me, I remember his words as clear as my own.

"Let me have a dram of poison, such soon-speeding gear as will disperse itself through all the veins that the life-weary taker may fall dead…" he said. Even as I informed him of Mantua's law, the passion within him, as deep as to the heart that I have ever seen, called to me from my own youth. It was not in violent acts against another that this lad sought to obtain this poison, but for something even more rich and pure…for love. I may myself never have known love, but I have seen it in the eyes of those that I have saved from death's door as they embraced their families and loved ones. This boy's love was more powerful than all those I have saved, united together, as the glare in his eyes was as steady and sure as a captain in the royal fleet steering his ship into a storm of war. I am not fully sure if it was the forty ducats that truly persuaded me to give him the poison or the realization that he would stop at nothing to achieve his final goal. Though his words did pull at the strings of my heart and poverty, that I, in my weakest state, allowed for my deepest heart's emotion to take hold of my will and lead me to the unlawful contract.

In my purse now are the same forty ducats, unspent. How can I, in all my thoughts of righteous acts, spend one solitary ducat to save my own life when I have taken his? It was only two days ago that late word from Verona struck my soul, hearing of the death of a boy by such same poison and that of his love, who stabbed herself to take her own life at his loss. There can be no other but the boy that I had sold the poison to. Thus, it was only within hours after my assumptions were confirmed when I learned of his name. My confusion at first puzzled me, as his final words before we parted ways convinced me that the deep love he held was the cause for the poison's desire.

"Come, Cordial and not poison, go with me to Juliet's grave, for there must I use thee" he said. True love's words called to him to be where his love was, and my poison would send him to be with her once again. Though, I dread upon the airy knowledge that this love of his, this Juliet, stabbed herself upon his own life's ending. It was only through further reports, of more reliable story, that informed me of her plan of deception to leave her family to be with him. She had consumed a distilling liquor that made her appear as if death had called upon her. She was to awake from this appearance of the grave and leave her city of birth and her family, to be with her love. What transpired that the connection was not made, and he did not have knowledge of this act, I will never know. In the end of this all, the result is the same. My poison traveled through his body and ended the flow of blood that would have kept his strong heart beating for years to come. O', that the world never conjured such poisons to place such ill fate upon the souls of men. Nonetheless, it is the very same such poison I carry in my pocket with me, to seal my fate for all that I have done. It is the same poison, from the same natural material that removed the first person of its usage, that I will let course through my own veins and join the poor boy, wheresoever his soul has ended. Upon heaven's eyes, I have tried to drink of it before, even just days ago. I held the small bottle to my lips but could not summon the courage to punish myself for my wrongs. Was it God's hand reaching down, halting my efforts, or that of other supernatural callings? It is of no matter now, as I have finally discovered why my arms could not lift it to be consumed and allow my spirit to spin into the sky. It was within the church that both their lives ended, and it will be within the same church that I will ask for their forgiveness and end my own. My resolve is as steady as the wind, as my questioning hand has found purpose and will allow me to take the action needed.

Yet, before I send my soul to the darkest of places, where the devil himself will shake my hand for what I have done, I will look to God to forgive this boy, the dear and sweet Romeo, as he knew not of what he did. Never are the thoughts of youth as clear as the night's sky full of stars, when love shows her face and leads hearts like the warm summer wind. Thus, I travel now, and see that I am only within a short distance away, if not closer, from this same church, in the city of Verona. I will speak out to God, and to the friar of this unfortunate church where the bodies were discovered, to ask forgiveness for the blood that covers my hands. I have done an ill deed to the world; I have done wrong to a youthful boy and his family's hopes and dreams. Let my prayers plead to God to save both of their souls; let these forty ducats from the boy be used by the church however these rounds of poison, as the boy called them when given to me, seem fit to use. O' Romeo, O' Juliet, what have I done? These tears fall, pouring from my soul, to plead for your forgiveness.

"May these actions I will soon perform allow for their souls to be free, as ever is the blame in this matter pointed solely at me." Looking to the heavens as I speak these words in the open air, I hope for a reply, but the clouds pass unknowingly ignorant of my existence, and no streams of light gleam down upon my being, in recognition of my entreaty. I know God is there, and I place my life in his hands to do as he sees fit. I can only hope and pray he has set His forgiving touch upon these children.

Children; what do I know of them? That I was never a father, I did not hold the wisdom to stop such acts and capture the light of the path that was lit for you, dear boy. O' bloody deed! It is as if I handed the poison to you not a day ago, unfortunate, unknowing boy. What shall I do but to follow my course?

At the church in Verona, I will plead to God, ask for forgiveness, leave the friar these forty ducats, and then in a peaceful and hidden corner within the walls of the holy place, I will drink of this poison and call my life's story to an end. I see no other purpose in my aged existence. Two and fifty years have long been enough for these cracked bones and drooping curtains of flesh. God had given me a purpose long ago and I did all that I could within it. Now, those years have passed on this life and I have failed Him in that purpose. As he has not presented me any other reason to be, it appears the time has come that I should no longer be.

Stepping one foot in front of the other, as my mind's purpose has clouded the time spent on this long road, I see that I have reached Verona and that my end is nearer than it was from when I awoke this morning. The time is mine. So shall I find one last reprieve, one last ounce of liquid spirits that may assist my sure and steady hand to lift the poison to my mouth, lest the pleading of some fear were to show its face and attempt to hold back my driven purpose. Thus, to my word and my decision, as no force on this earth will stop me.

If it is furthermore possible to learn of any additional news of the tragedy that I have caused, I will include these such findings into my prayer. May Verona forgive me for handing their youth a tragic ending. O' most foul soul, most repenting nature, carry me to my action. That I may find peace, which I do not deserve, will be a miracle upon itself. I am not worthy of such peace. Nor am I worthy to enter such a place as this, the beautiful city of Verona, where my hand played such a role. Up strength of will, carry me into your just hands, that the blackness of my thoughts will hold firm and not be removed once I have found my resting place.

Entering the city, there is an initial sense of calm both from the buildings as well as those that walk from one place to another. It would seem that the veil of woe still hangs on the faces of its citizens, mourning the loss of these two lost souls. Even as several weeks, if it be not more than three, have passed and the death of these two children, if not others, still rests heavily on their souls. It may be well advised that I not inform any that I speak with that it was I, the Mantuan apothecary, that brought death to this place and the frowns that have painted the expressions of these once happy faces.

Though, as I enter further and look around closer, deeper and sharper, I see that of those that I cross the path of, fear is more present on their shoulders than that of misery. In my profession there is no emotion that I have come across more than that of fear. In the eyes of a dying father, or that of the same father watching his dying child, fear is similar to waves of the ocean drowning the shore as the tides swell and swallow the land. It is here, on every face that I see. What is it that brings this blanket of sadness to such a fair city as this? Stopping the present movement of my legs, my own fear comes to the shore of my eyes, as I wonder if Verona has been struck by the plague.

"Good Madam," I ask, as a woman rushingly passes me, holding herself tightly together it seems, as if to protect her spirit from a demon. "Good Madam, if I may be allowed to pause your eager pace and ask if the plague has rested here on sweet Verona?"

"The plague?" she asks, as if I have given her more to protect herself from as her hands further constrict their grip. "There is a plague that stays within this city, but it is not that dreadful disease that makes the lives of men fall."

With these few words, she moves her feet once again and is out of my sight and into a building with the firm closing of the door. My thoughts of this mission's safety are within the edge of my mind entering the fair Verona, knowing that even as some plague roams these streets, it is not one that willingly looks to harm my life. Though, even as the plague is not traveling rampant to the bodies within this loving place, I still must be wary of whatever it is that she was meaning. My soul has its calling. My life is coming to its end, but it must be as I have planned it or my purpose and the desire that traces to my roots will be lost.

"My life may have its end in sight, but the plague is not a thing I would care to suffer through" I say to the sky, committing my mind and actions to my deed with this verbal contract. Gathering my thoughts, I see that only a few doors from where I stand there is a tavern that offers shelter and spirits. This place shall be my last air of peace, the final moments of whatever joy I may gather on this land. One drink, maybe two, and then I will most assuredly make my way to the church to end all that I have known.

Chapter Two

With several very sure and somewhat ease-of-nature steps, I walk to the door of 'Il Nascondiglio', which has a feel of darkness about the name that I did not consider until I was so close that I could not change my approach. The ease of nature that I held in my depths was gone rather quickly once I arrived at the door, but as some very murky gentlemen were following me closely in from behind, I did not want to seem out of sorts by changing direction to bring any attention to myself.

Entering what might very well be my resting place, if I am not careful, I look with steady eyes and quite quickly, too, at the inner surrounding of this tavern and lodging place. The bar is straight ahead, with tables scattered to the right. More tables are gathered together to the left, placed randomly about the open space, and the stairs to the upper level where the overnight rooms are, make the distant and awkward far corner where the stairs begin seem rather too dangerous for my likings. As the bar provides a resting place for only a few men, and the tables house more randomly seated visitors, I settle myself to the farthest right of the bar, allowing for a view of the entire room. Well, except for whoever may come from the level above, until they are already in the lower dining place, I am fully aware.

"Signor, may I get you something?" the bartender asks, as I seat myself and wear a disillusioned eye upon me. He uses a formality I would not expect in such a dark and unwelcoming place, but one he seems to desire to enact.

"Yes, please, something of liquor that will carry my thoughts far away from all the pains of the world." He nods, smirks his lips and points a finger in the air, acknowledging the request and seeming to know what it is that I will want. Whichever liquor he will choose to bring to me will very much gratify my nerves, even if it will likely pass harshly through my mouth, the passage to my soul. The effects it will have on my brain will be quite welcoming though.

The air in the room still captures the dark clouds from the sky within the level of our eyes. I cannot clearly see the faces of many of these men, but the words float well around and are welcomed into my observant ears. I have been alone far too long, and the speech of others, especially within this quantity, is as if I have walked into a gathering of birds eating bread left for them on the ground in winter.

"Good man, I hope this will be to your liking," he says, placing the drink before me. "If it be not, let me know straight, and I will try once more."

"I am sure it will be to my liking." I nod to him, grab the beverage, and take a quick sip to offer him the satisfaction of a smile that will allow me to be alone. The harshness of the liquid burns my throat as I force it into my body. Gathering all the strength within my old bones holds my face firm to not show the pain it is putting me in. O', that I believed that in my many years of being an apothecary, I have seen all the conjuring of liquids that were known to man. The times, they change ever yet without my being aware.

Once I find my clarity again, I continue to look around, gathering what kind of place this is and who it is that finds this dwelling pleasing for the soul. As this establishment offers rooms above, many of those that are here are only passing through on their way to another destination. Yet one may never know the kind of place that others would find appealing to their desires. Nevertheless, it is within these darker places that one would hear the darker stories of a city as well. For here are the men who commit the acts, or at least the men who think that they can and gather to hold within them the feeling that they have. I am thankful for my choice of placement, as the two men seated to the middle of the bar talk at just the right tone that I may hear everything they are speaking. And if I am not mistaken, I have gathered in the few words shared with my senses that they are not talking of happy events. My ears now become my instrument.

"Are you sure that your words are correct? If this be the case, then that will make one dead on each side. This will bring the war between the two families to the streets once again, and with even more blood spilled." The man speaking, that is closer to me, is in shock at what he hears from the other fellow that sits with him and speaks of a war between families.

"Yes, it will bring about the war between the two families, where peace had been in the air by proclamation of the prince. Yet, as the prince is away on affairs of the government, it seems to the citizens of Verona as if the families have once again struck down on the other, does it not? Death once again hangs on Verona!"

This second man speaking openly, wearing a ring on each of the fingers on his right hand, every one a different metal, confirms what I believe the woman had said to me in the streets. The war between the two families is once again raging. This war of the families is known by all, across cities both far and wide. Have they not learned from the death of the two most dear children, slain by their own hands, stemming from the conflict of their elders? I wish that I could blame this old strife for their deaths, but as much as I would wish to place the charge on their bloody hands, it is my own that finished the lives of the young lovers.

These men now laugh as whispers fly between them, and I cannot make out what they speak to each other. Do these laughs bend toward the war of the families or some other matter that may direct them to their more immediate night? I may never know, as the second man farthest from me bearing the hand of rings, who seems to know the wealth of the knowledge, finishes his drink and heads to the stairs to the upper level to call an end to this night. Time has walked upon the day and now brings upon the blackness of the sky, as darkness is behind the door that now allows entrance for others who have finished their day and look to find peace within their final waking hours. The more people that enter, the greater the desire I have to leave. This shall be it, my last sip of liquor on this earth. As I empty the contents into my mouth, and allow it to burn me one last time, I leave what I feel is the correct worth for the drink and a bit more, as this dealer of spirits was beyond courteous and fair, even in a place as mysterious as this.

Up from my seat, the whispers still fly around, as their words are the wind's gust blowing through the air, and brushing only bits of language into my ear. I hear of the foolishness of death once again and the start of the war. It is good that I will not be upon this world much longer, as this war looks to carry on until the end of the bloodline of the families, if not the end of the planets that make us all one.

Out of the door I walk, and night is welcomed and has bid farewell to the day that ran from sight. It seems even the sun does not want to watch the death that hangs upon this city. However, you up there, old moon, you are one that has seen the blood shed more than the sun, and you come for more with the craving of men's souls as your only desire. You have seen the villainous man kill and steal in the night. You have seen tragedy upon tragedy, but you call the stars and the black of night your home. How is it that you shine so bright and white, with centuries of blood coursing through your soil of skin? You are one that could tell a thousand tales and still have more to share.

"Well, my good friend, you bright beacon of the night, prepare yourself for my spirit's heavenly ascent. But if it be not heaven that opens its gates for my soul, then observe the ground tremble by the devil who will begin conjuring the great fires to burn me to dust and sweep me below."

It is a small walk to the church; I see the holy steeple high in the night sky, as the white of its top reflects the light of the moon so that all will see where God lives when on earth. This holy dwelling is where my last breath will take place, and the battle for the possession of my soul will begin. Though, that is only if God himself cares to call for me. Will the goodwill that I have done in my many years outweigh the deeds of sin that I have recently done or the even more sinister deed that brews in my mind that I am about to commit? Do heaven and hell fight for every soul that leaves this majestic place, to satisfy their own need of an army for when the rapture begins? I have never been the most religious of men, though I have spoken to God I know not how many times. Do I believe that He is up there, somewhere in the sky watching down on us? Yes, I firmly do. Though it is said that when a man comes close to his end, he once again finds the way of God and prays like never before, in fear that the heavens are there and will not welcome him into paradise. As I live now, I see that I may be the shadow of that man, as to the church I go, to ask forgiveness of my sins. Nevertheless, I am not a shadow of the same sun, as the sins I seek to purge are as real as the air and weigh down on me with the recognized imperfection of my innocence.

These streets are dark. I can see why it is that Death walks in Verona as frequently as he does. Sounds echo from the alleys that I pass. Voices travel in the air from I know not where. I hear unnamed men call out to me speaking the words 'old, kind sir', as I pass the darkness of doorways and roads, asking me for help, or for as many ducats as I can spare. There may have been a day where I would offer them what I could, but the remaining ducats I possess have a meaning that is greater than my own worth. For look, the church grows near, as does the growing pulse of my fear. Steady feet! Hold me to my course and see me through to the action of the action.

Nearer, within the short distance of time, the church doors are ahead to my right. Though, looking immediately to my side, beyond the black metal fence that appears as vertical spears holding back the sky, is a graveyard of Verona's faithful. Here is the history of families that once lived and breathed in the city walls. Their bones, covered with dirt and stone, weighed down to not allow for the visitation once again by way of evil possession on these roads. I feel the calls for my soul, in the darkness of the graves. It is as if they know I will be joining them soon. The mystical world beyond this realm of flesh holds secrets that we only learn once we ourselves attain the right of passage. O', how the weight of the soil already rests lightly on my bones. Even there, nearest to the church walls, are two freshly covered graves, lit only by the vision of the moon. There rest two that are children to the netherworld, newly born into the haziness of eternity. I can only wonder if these are the two that I overheard the men speak of, the fallen soldiers in the war of the families.

"I will pray for your souls as I enter these sacred walls, hoping that you will walk with your fathers in heaven's great paradise."

Chapter Three

The door opens slowly, as the weight of the wood is greater than it seems it should be, even with a massive size such as this. My thoughts allow me to believe that doors as large as these were placed here to allow the proportion and greatness of God to enter the church. Twice my person could walk into this passageway without bending at the knee. I close the door even more slowly behind me, as this late time of night is when the darkest of spirits will walk the earth. As I am in a church, where apparitions are said to roam, and even more so being close to this graveyard that I passed, my worst fears bring me to worry about coming into the evil favor of a demon. The darkness inside of me must be a welcoming place for an evil spirit that would want to feast on the fresh shame and sorrow that I carry within my heart.

This small lobby is poorly lit, but I can still see the bowl of holy water in the center on the room within arm's reach and the paintings of God's holy family on the walls. That ever I healed one of these saints to place me in God's favor to enter heaven.

Walking through the next entranceway, as large as the door openings at the front, I am struck by the grandeur of the church. Candles are stronger at the altar ahead, but there are scattered candles against the walls as well, defining the area of this room and enlightening images of scenes from the Bible itself. I walk slowly down the main aisle, peering at each painting on the bordering walls, recalling the context of the image and what the event means. There are some, if not most, that I do not well understand. I am very hopeful that I am not questioned of these images, if I am fortunate enough to make it to the gates of heaven, as my knowledge may persuade the saint at the gate from allowing me in.

The front row of the pews is far too close; I will seat myself several aisles back. I want God to hear my prayers and grant me pardon, but the benches nearer the altar are for those that God has personally invited to come into his earthly realm. These first four rows are for those families that make the church their second home, attending mass as much as the priest himself. I would not dream to think I am as devout as they, and thus, I will take my place in the fifth row. In front of me, row-by-row, will be the Father, the Son, and the Holy Ghost, and one more row in between for respect. I perform the sign of the cross and shuffle slowly into the row, kneeling on the ground, placing myself in proper position to begin my prayer.

"O' God, O' Heavenly Father, I am here to ask your forgiveness for my sin. I know not how one should do this, and I know not where I should even commence. My mind houses darkness and my soul doth feel the weight for what I have done. Yet, from these choices that I have made, I know there is no other place where I can appeal for forgiveness for my soul. Please grant me your mercy, even as I prepare to sin my very last sin. I place my soul in your hands, as my body will lay at the doorstep of your kingdom."

Does he hear me? Is God within this room, with me in this moment, touching me now though I cannot feel his hand? This questioning is a show of disbelief, for which I am committing, and prevents the truth of my words. I know he is here, watching and listening to my every word. I do not lie nor do I look to trick him, and yet as he is God, he would read me as if I were an open book within his hand. I will say on, pray for the souls of the two I have wronged, and then find my place inside these walls where these bones will for their last time lay.

"O' God, most powerful, heavenly Lord of might, I pray for the souls of the two young children that I have sent into worlds beyond this one. To the young and beautiful Juliet, whom I have never seen, I send her all of my soul's energy wherever her distressed spirit may be. Then thus, the sweet boy, Romeo, so young and full of passion. I sent him from this world well before the time mapped out for him. In his eyes was life's bountiful possibility, which flowed to his heart. The vastness of his ever-loving nature was the greeting at his door. That door is now closed, as his life is no more, and never will this world see such a flame. All his undoing, the shallow air of an empty presence; such greatness that was yet to be discovered."

Tears fall, as my soul achieves a point where it cannot stand to feel such pain within its chamber. This ache that consumes my organs' proper functions, weakens every artery, as even my blood begins to refuse its purpose. O' cursed nature, O' broken will to live. I am at my body's end. Soul, prepare yourself for a journey that may never see the same such ending, traveling within the eternity of hell. If God allows, I may see the light of the heavens, but if he does not, then may the souls of the two most wronged children find their own path there, if they have not already.

I hear voices coming, quite faint, but the echo increases in volume, informing me that within moments I will no longer be alone. I must get myself out of sight so that I will not be seen and so that no attention shall fall upon me, preventing me of my will.

My hands grab the bench in front of me, as I look to assist my legs to stand. Yet, kneeling as long as I have, there is a weakness that is either from my body giving up all hope or from my age, which does not welcome such stationary positions that remove strength. Fear comes to my present moment as I see a man enter from a door behind the altar and stand to the far right. It is the friar of this church. From what I have heard in Mantua of this bloody event, he was the one who discovered the bodies of Romeo and Juliet. If I remember well, his name is Friar Laurence. He does not see me yet, but walking any farther toward the front and I will be an image he will not miss as I am the only person within his church. As I stand, my legs gain the ability to move as the blood re-establishes its course, but I do not budge so I do not attract attention. When the time is right, I will back away and hide within the confessional to my left. It will be there that I will drink the poison and end my world. O', Romeo; sweet boy, Romeo. I come to replace thee.

"Romeo. Romeo."

I hear his name spoken, but it was not from me. Does the voice in my head echo out into this church chamber and test my own will?

"Romeo! Please stop what you say."

Yet, as I hear his name once again, I hear that it is the friar that is saying it aloud. Does he pray for the souls of Romeo and Juliet as well?

My heart jumps into my throat, depriving me of air, and my eyes look to deceive my every sense of sanity and wit, as I see Romeo enter the room and stand in front of the friar. It is Romeo himself, in form and shape, speaking with the friar. How can this be? He was said to be dead. I heard the story as clear as the chirping birds in the early morn. He and Juliet, dead by their own hands. Was this all a trick? Can it be so? If it be so, then I have repented for nothing and was at such a point where my own life was to be taken for theirs. O' what a fool am I, where I allowed myself the thought of ending my beating heart. Many feelings rage within me, but with composure that I have groomed myself to present, I will keep my blood cool and not rage like a storm on the sea.

The friar walks to the altar and stands in clear sight. Romeo joins him, but before any other words can be exchanged, the friar looks to me and, with wide eye, pauses his every movement and sound. A smile slowly appears on his face, but the look of shock is still painted in the glance of his eyes. My presence was clearly not expected, especially this late in the day, but that I have caught him in the act of such amazing treachery explains his face's expression, as this must undoubtedly be the cause for this unmoving reaction.

"Hello, my son. What brings you to God's church so late in the evening," he asks of me, as he looks to not acknowledge what is in clear sight.

"Good friar, I came to repent and pray for the souls of those recently lost in Verona and to find peace for myself, but it seems that my prayers and repenting have been for those who are not actually dead." He looks at me still, confusion dressed as his appearance, not acknowledging my words.

"Friar, that is the apothecary who sold me the poison," Romeo says. Yet, the friar waves his hand within Romeo's direction, eyes still affixed on me, his astonishment apparently preventing him from saying anything further. It seems being caught within a wrongful act has also relieved the good friar of his manners toward others.

"Friar, speak to him. Ask him for your help, if this is the fortunate reason to why the apothecary is all of the sudden here," Romeo says, but yet once again the friar waves at him to quiet his speech. To not appear as he is waving off the boy, he flows his hand in the air as if he waves away a fly.

"Good son, who is it that you pray for and what do you mean? One can still pray for not only those that are dead, but also for those that are still living."

"Friar Laurence, if I am correct in assuming you are he, why is it that you wave away his words? Are you so ashamed that you cannot answer him in front of me?" I speak this and he glances quickly and lightly toward Romeo, but looks around as if to find someone else to address that may be within the room.

"Friar Laurence am I, you are in the right thought my son. Yet, of whose words do I not properly address that you say float within this room? You are but alone."

"You may play the part to those who have not seen what I am seeing now, but as he stands next to you, I pray you, do not lie. For God's sake, you are a man of the cloth." He looks around again, but pretends to see no sight of another person within the room. He then looks to Romeo, finally acknowledging the body standing within reach of him. No words are exchanged, but I know that he sees him as I do. I will not allow this game to carry on any longer. I will speak to the boy and end this play of deceit.

"Romeo, my boy, I thought you to be dead. As much anger as I feel for the deception that has occurred, I am happy to see you alive and well." I move to the main aisle now and stand open to their view. The friar stares at me and then looks back again to Romeo. How can he still be in shock over this? I walk toward them and climb the two steps to the altar to be opposite them, across this large, marble table where the friar performs his mass.

"Apothecary, you can see me and hear me?" Romeo speaks with much joy, as his face unfolds. I am very glad that he is happy to see me, but does he understand what foolery that he has put himself in? I do not think he has considered the outcome of his actions with others.

"Yes, dear boy, your sight is present to me, though my eyes grow tired, as your image is not as clear as I wish it to be. This long day and late hour have evidently weakened my spirit, as well as my sight, as you appear as more of a haze."

"Apothecary, if I may understand you more, please forgive my distress and wonder, but have you addressed Romeo?" The friar has amazement about him, yet it should not be amazement that pauses him so, as this hidden show would have been discovered within time enough. Word of his death travels the land, so that wherever Romeo would ever go, he would cause outrage for the deception when finally seen.

"Yes, good friar, I spoke to him such word, where you would wave him away for speaking plainly. As he entered this room, I was much amazed, but quickly gathered my wits about me. No longer will my mind be puzzled with these false stories." The joy on Romeo's face is very clear, and he has a bliss that looks to have not been in him for some time. As I desire to be free of indecisive meaning, this once again makes my old mind perplexed.

"How can this be, how can this be? Of all those who have entered this church, I am the only person that has had the ability to perceive his sight, let alone speak with him." The friar, as puzzled as a man of God can be, looks up to Him now to attempt to find some way to share what he has been holding inside of him, as the relief on his face is easily received.

"Good friar, those that would not address him directly may feel the same sting that I feel right now, as this trickery of faked death will not heal an already damaged soul." I look at them now and know that as this night goes on, I will not be able to defend myself, either by word or action, due to my weakness. I must be careful with what I choose to say if they decide that I must be silenced.

"Apothecary, what trickery do you speak of? There is no illusion of story that we look to fool you with," Romeo says, as he is clearly siding with the friar and has learned to twist his words just as strongly. It is sad when a boy as young as he is corrupted by misguided elders.

Once again, from the far door behind the altar, where these two came about, another voice calls out, of a female tone, but this time enters to the room in the middle of some speech.

"Romeo? How shall we move our wills to stop this violent flood of family rage? We cannot allow this war to go on, as our own lives and our loving union have started this falling blood." As she now enters and stands next to Romeo, her beauty alone verifies that she must be the fair Juliet. The stories I have heard of her, not only through Romeo's mouth when he visited me that one time, but that of those carrying the news of their death, were true. Her beauty and show of innocence is a beacon to a troubled ship searching for shore. She stands, looking at Romeo, and then in sudden motion, sees me standing across from them and no longer places her eyes on him.

"I see we have company visiting in the holy pews before us. No matter, as this man, like the rest, will never acknowledge us and cannot assist us with ending what is between our families." She frowns, as she looks at me, but her eyes widen in shock as mine own two white globes connect with hers.

"Juliet," Romeo says quickly. "He can hear me and see me, which only means that he can hear and see you as well. This is the apothecary from Mantua, my love." Romeo makes an obvious statement, but one that brings the same joy he found in himself within her eyes by the same depth and speed.

"He sees us?" she asks, and the excitement is even clearer in her young eyes. Though, my eyes seem to still be within their haze, as her image is just as unclear as Romeo. The friar presents true color to me, but that he stands behind the altar drenched in the light of the candles, gives me reason as to why.

"O' good and fair apothecary, you must help us," Juliet says. "The blood that spills in the streets of Verona must stop so that it does not fill all the hollow graves." She seems desperate, but still affixed in a passion that flows from her eyes. Does she not feel the same foolishness for this trickery? I will not allow their words to be spoken any longer.

"I ask you all, please do not beg of me to help you in this dishonesty. You may have deceived many people of Verona with your act of false death, but you cannot talk me into your counterfeit story. So it be better that you hold your breath and find some other foolish knave with a dirtier soul than mine to take part in this." My statement is as clear as the shows of confusion on their faces. They will not deceive me any longer. They insult me to the core if they believe they will continue to have such power over me.

Again a noise is heard, but this time from a door to my left. In walks a nun of this church, who will now join me to catch the friar in his act of deceitfulness and straighten his lying ways. I am sure of it. Nuns are the holders of truth and laws within the church. There is a reason why most children fear them.

"Good friar," she says. "Will you be in need of anything else this evening? O', my word, I am very sorry. I did not know you were meeting with someone so late," she says, as she looks at me falling into a blush and lowers her eyes to the floor for intruding on our conversation.

"We are well, and you have been splendid in your tasks this day, goodly sister. You may find rest in your evening." The friar nods to her and she returns the gesture with a light curtsy.

"Thank you. I will leave you two alone, as you were." She says, and then turns.

"You mean you will leave us four alone?" I ask of her before she begins to walk away. She turns back and looks at me kindly.

"O' my heavens, are there more guests here that I have not seen?" She looks around and then back to me once more. "I am not sure who you speak of, good sir, but I only see you and the friar."

"Good heavens above, are you in on this deceitful affair as well?" I say, as my clear and loud voice moves her settled soul to fear of a growing anger from another.

"Apothecary, you know not what you do. Peace," Romeo says, hoping to calm me. I may be old, but I am not easily manipulated.

"Romeo, my boy, you have fooled me once, but it shall not happen again." In the conclusion of my words, he walks to the nun and stands next to her, waving his arm in front of her eyes. She does not budge by his movement, nor act upon noticing his presence in front of her.

"That she does not move, dear lad, only verifies her role in this falsehood," I say, to show him I am no fool. As the nun looks at me, Romeo lifts his arm, preparing to strike her. "Good boy, Romeo, do not hit a nun!" I yell, but as his arm travels down, it passes through her body as if the mass of his arm's structure became instant smoke. He swings again and again, and every movement of his arms waves through her, not touching her person, nor creating a wave of air that would move a touch of her clothing. Have I gone mad? Are these late hours deceiving my eyes, calling for movement to pass through her when he must clearly be striking her? But thus, she stands untouched.

"Friar Laurence, who is it that this man speaks to? I hear him pronounce the name Romeo, but there is only one by that name that I know of, who is now sadly dead." She looks at the friar and then at me, unmoved from the waving arms of Romeo, that continue to pass through her body like the fog through a forest. "If that will be all," she says, and then turns and leaves the room.

"My eyes deceive me, as I cannot speak to what I have just seen. Your arms, like the clouds that pass above, block images of objects that are behind you and yet you move through them without altering their course." I am myself now housed within the shock that the friar himself earlier displayed upon seeing my presence. I have gone mad; there is no other explanation than this.

"Kind apothecary, you are not deceived. These are but the spirits of our loved ones, still shown in their original form, as you are seeing them now before you. I know not how, or why their souls have not passed on, but they are here, presently in front of us." The friar walks around the altar table and stands next to me now, placing his hand on my shoulder. It seems he has felt the same confusion that he witnesses on my face.

"How is it that their souls have not transcended to the world beyond our own? Once their lives have come to an end, their spirits, to the heavens, should have gone." This being my understanding of the world and realm far away from this, I pause in fear that if I am incorrect in the meaning of the afterlife, then the depth and mystification of this great beyond is far more trivial than I will ever conceive.

"Good friend, in the weeks since they lost their lives, they have been dwelling within this church together. It seems that they have not been called above, or below, and are somehow stuck within our world. But that you can see them, as I presently do, brings me much joy. It allows me to rest in the comforts of my own mind, that I am not going mad myself. Others have entered my church and yet, not one has seen what I have seen—not one. Even as others have stood next to me and pass by these two as close as to touch them, not one person has seen their sight. Yet, how is it that we have this power where never before have I been able to see such spirits walk the earth? Unless it is that I have seen spirits roam but have not understood that they are the same as these two. This is too much." He poses a question that moves our minds to distant thought, as I myself cannot imagine what gifts seeing spirits as this I have ever possessed.

"Not one ghost in the night, nor lurking soul during the day, has come across my path in the many years I have lived," I say, agreeing with his statement. "Though, as I had a hand in their death, which brought them to this state, I understand now why this is. Thus, I witness them walk this earth, as it is punishment for what I have done. It was my poison that Romeo consumed, bringing about his death. So thus, God has cursed me to see Romeo's tortured spirit walk the globe, as punishment for what he has done and my action, or shall we say, my inaction." My words terrify me, but the truth in my last chosen few positions me with a sense of reality of this situation and my punishment.

"Apothecary, it was I that did much of the same, as I gave dear Juliet the distilling liquor that made her body seem as if it were dead," the friar says. "I was only looking to make her death appear real in the eyes of her family, so that when she awoke, Romeo would be by her side and, being newly married, they could be together. Yet, these two conjuring drugs consumed by them, created by you and I, have tied our souls all together." The friar looks at each of them, and then down to the earth. He feels pain greater than I myself could have imagined he would bear.

"Gentle apothecary, you are not to blame for my life, as I am the one who forced you into selling me the mortal liquor," Romeo states. "I would have taken my life in some other way, if it were not the poison itself that killed me. Yet here we are, fair Juliet and I, and we believe that we have not been called to either resting place for one sole purpose."

Romeo comes around from the altar, as Juliet follows him closely. Side by side they walk toward me, and as two so close would be, they should contact or bump into each other's flesh, yet this cursed smoke of image they embody prevents even their touching each other. They do not make words of this, or notice by offering a glance to their sides, but of all things active in their thoughts, this they must know. As they stand before me, Romeo continues to inform of the cause of their situation.

"Juliet and I took our lives, and then appeared here in this church, within the brief time following our last waking moment. This much is true. We do not know how it is that we came to such a fate to be locked within this world, but even worse, within these walls we are trapped." Romeo looks around at the walls and ceiling, as if searching for a way out. I look around with him, even as I don't understand how it is that they are still on these grounds.

"Apothecary, you must believe us," Juliet speaks. "Our deaths did not bring the same end to us, as those before us have all passed on to other worlds greater than this occasion. We are not only trapped in this world, but also within the church walls. Within our homes our families' war has once again begun, as the friar here informed us when he was last out speaking with many citizens of Verona. It is not clear who drew the initial strike to release the first drop of blood, but that they once again mercilessly kill each other only means we must find a way to stop them." She pauses and collects herself, as her sadness consumes her and she cannot continue to speak, being that any further mention of the war between their families will likely drive her mad as well. It appears we are all mad, whether it is my perception of seeing these ghosts, or that I am being deceived well beyond my comprehension. Romeo turns to her, and stands in front of her, trying to connect his eyes with hers, but as her head is lowered to the ground and he cannot raise her glance with the touch of his hand, he must lower his body in order to appropriately reposition himself to achieve her attention.

"Apothecary, there have already been lives lost in our families' foolish battle," Romeo states, returning focus to the conversation with me. "Of my family, Abram has been murdered not one week ago, left sliced by a sword in an alley. His sword was drawn, but there was no blood on his blade, and no other show of a struggle between he and someone else when he was found. Of the Capulets, Gregory has been murdered just two days ago, in very much the same fashion. His sword was drawn the same, but the only blood appearing to be found on the ground was his own. Juliet and I have spoken about these murders, and to us this seems very strange." Romeo, looking to make sure Juliet is of healthy mind, turns his attention to her once again.

How strange, indeed, as these two spirits still show signs that they are real, by showing emotion and purpose. I have always heard that spirits walk the night, in a manner to haunt those that have wronged them in their lifetime. Though, before me now are two spirits that show emotion and a calmness that allows me to believe that all the written word documented of the afterlife cannot be as it seems. With all the braveness that I can muster in my weakened state, I reach out my hand toward Romeo, and as I look to place each of my fingers on his shoulder, they pass through as if the image, as present as it is before me, were not real, but a smoky image cast to air.

"Apothecary, believe it to be true. They are but the shadows of their former selves. I have myself attempted to place my hand on them to console the sadness they carry so clearly through normal human actions and words. I have learned to no longer try, as each time, as you have discovered, my hand passes through as if I were reaching for my reflection within water." The friar instructs me well, as the lessons he has recently learned agree with my own experience. It is so very hard to understand, but even as I search for explanation to this situation, there is no other reasoning. They are lost spirits, trapped between this world and the next. They are unable to live here, and yet unable to move to the next phase of their existence. The torture their souls must be experiencing, even in their ghostly state, must be immensely terrifying, compared to this harsh world. Here, we have limitations to our pain, as even in my age, as I have experienced much pain and sadness, I have been through almost every distressing situation one can name, but the other world must have more frightening encounters that are unknown to our humankind.

"Romeo and dear Juliet, I am very sorry for all that has happened, and even for the fact that you are trapped, contained by our world, and within these walls," I say, hoping to offer some comfort for their young minds. "I have heard what I need, but more so, I see the pain that still rests within your ghostly beings. This cannot be. I cannot allow your spirits to be trapped in this world, especially since I had taken part in their being seized from reaching the next territory for the soul, wherever that may be. The friar and I will both do what we must to give your souls the passage from this world they most certainly deserve." I look to the friar, whose eyes are filled with fear when he looks back at me, after hearing my statement. My firm look to him verifies that he understands that our part in all this is crucial, since we hold much responsibility that assisted in their fate, perhaps more than any other persons. As his face changes demeanor, I see that he agrees to my words.

"Good sir, speaking for both Romeo and myself, as we are one, we thank you so deeply. As much as we wish to leave this world, it is the intention of stopping the war between our families that matters most. No more bloodshed can occur on our behalf. Why should others die because we chose to love?" Juliet looks to Romeo, and as they now stand, face to face, I can see the love they still hold for one another, and if they were living beings, I know they would be within each other's arms even now.

"The friar and I are very much pleased to do all that we can. It is getting quite late, so we should call an end to this night shortly and start fresh tomorrow. Yet, before we part, Romeo, what is it again that you said which makes these killings that have recently happened, strange to you both?" I ask, as receiving some understanding of it this evening may allow me to prepare myself tomorrow for whatever it is that I will have to do.

"Sir, what we have found to be strange is the manner of death. I do not mean strange that they died from the sword, as that is very common in Verona, especially between our families. What is beyond understanding is that each of our loved ones was found with their swords drawn. Yet, there were no shows of blood, except for the blood they themselves shed. Even the tips of their swords did not show one color of red that would present a strike upon the person they had come across. Is this correct in the information the apothecary is looking for, good friar?" Romeo looks from me to the friar, and startles the friar a little, as he was not focused on us and was not expecting to be involved in the conversation.

"Yes, yes, this was the instance. I spoke with several of the officers who reported to the scene of each man. They investigated each showing of evidence, but it was concluded that the murderer was not even scratched by their swords. He evaded the conflict untouched it would appear." The friar nods, and looks us all in the eye, one by one, verifying what he had discovered when questioning those in Verona.

"Each person within our families are trained on the sword, but none, on either side, have such talent that would battle so well that they would come from the fight without a scratch. Those with such abilities, that being Tybalt and Mercutio, are already gone from this world. The rest, as good as they allow themselves to believe they are, could not walk from a fight without a touch or the loss of one drop of their blood." Romeo informs me well, and this does add some mystery to these murders. Again, he returns his gaze to Juliet.

"Come, apothecary, let me show you to a room here within the church that you may stay and find your rest. It is not as large as this hall here, but it will suit you well. Come," the friar says, as his warm invitation is a welcoming one at that.

We walk from the altar and begin heading to the door that they had entered through. As I step down, I look back and see Romeo and Juliet still standing in the same place, facing each other, eyes locked as if nothing else around them, or within the world itself, mattered. I pause, as the deep connection makes much sense. The word that reached Mantua spoke of their undying love that would last from this world to the next. Seeing them now, I do not doubt it. It is then that I hear some words spoken.

"My love, how does it that your magnificent attraction pulls me toward you like that of the sun within the universe of no other planet but one?" Romeo speaks his words of love, and Juliet looks at him with the same depth of affection. It is not my nature to watch such intimacy between two as so, but they continue to amaze me with each experience.

"My sweet Romeo, you speak such words that would make a flower wilt from jealousy from their most tender scent."

"Juliet, you are the only sun that I see and I spin around you in the twirling night sky, wishing to be brought closer and closer, so that I may burn in your love. Not even the stars in the sky would reflect their light, if they knew it would take away from your radiant beauty." Juliet looks at Romeo after he speaks these words, but no longer reflects the same sweetness in her eyes.

"You speak of the stars, that guide our direction and allow the ancient gods to receive the respect of their sacrifice. If they do not burn, then how will we know north, or how will speedy comets in the night know which way they travel to find their own home? Do not banish their eternal flame for the sake of my love." She speaks as wise as an ancient one herself, placing the good Romeo on his best behavior, balancing his words with their meaning.

"Juliet, how can I even care to see a star when my eyes only gaze at you? I need not follow a comet to know that you are the center of where nothing else need exist."

I am amazed at this, as never have I seen such wit and love shared between two so young as they. They are the balance, that in my mind would have the power to bring two feuding families to a truce, but in this harsh world, it was not the case.

"Gentile apothecary, shall we go, for the night only passes along faster the longer we stay?" the friar asks, knowing that I should have followed straight.

"Yes, yes, my apologies. I was admiring the church one last time."

As we walk through the door, the friar leads me down several long halls, to a door that stands open. He waves his arm into the room, directing to me that this will be my resting place for the evening.

"Very kind of you sir, for this offering of a bed. It is much appreciated for these old bones." I bow my head, enter the room and then turn back to him. "A good evening to you sir. Until tomorrow, where we will look to right the wrongs and spare heaven a few lives for a little while."

"Yes, that does seem the plan for us. I just pray that a friar and an apothecary can find the skill to talk two feuding families, who have found such dueling abilities within several of their generations, to lay down their swords and find peace for the sake of their ghostly children. My prayers are powerful, but I am not sure they can part such seas as this. My words will have to be as strong as those from the Bible to calm their waves of war. Maybe your skills as an apothecary may persuade them otherwise."

"Friar, you are wise beyond your years, even as they are thankfully not as far behind mine. Until the morn."

He closes the door and leaves me to my room. Taking a closer look, I gather the surroundings and see a humble space, with a bed and a chair. It will serve fine for my evening of rest. I am so tired that even the stone streets that cover this city would have been a welcome retreat. Though, through God's good graces, here I am.

Walking to the bed, I seat myself and gaze at the burning candle on the small table next to me. This flame lights the room well enough. When it is time for me to sleep, I will blow it out and rest my head, to awake in a new day and challenge the world to change. What a turn of events has presented itself on my arms. I entered this goodly church to pray for the souls of those I spoke with just moments ago. I knelt and pleaded with God to forgive them. I asked for God's forgiveness upon my own soul, as I have sinned as deep and very much entangled myself in the bloodshed that has traveled across time and place. Though, of all these newly engaged events, I was to find a small, hidden place in some dark corner, and drink from the same poison I sold to the young Romeo. I wonder if he could sense or smell that the same poison he drank was here, in my pocket, awaiting my lips? Is it not strange that I come to the house of God, to pray and repent, and find myself now suited with a new cause and now no longer engaging upon the immediate ending of my life as I had planned? Would this be His will, speaking to me, helping me to save myself, from myself? With all of the things that I have done in these recent weeks, I must look at this as no other thing than His will upon me. I have agreed to assist these young lovers in ending the bloodshed their families cannot end on their own. My true abilities are with my trained profession as an apothecary. If I can use my knowledge to apply words like healing liquids, then this will be a fruitful task that will have a healing end. If I cannot, then blood will continue to fall, and these lovers may spend an eternity trapped within this church.

Now to bed, to another night of sleep. I pray that my bones allow me a night of rest so I can use all that I have within me to do what looks to be more of a fight than the fight itself.

As my weary head reaches a place where I will greet my dreams, a welcoming warmth covers my mind. The presence of the world around me fades slowly, as I am engulfed within tenderness and love. This is the place where my mind enacts the fantasies that my life could not complete. Two and fifty years have been lived, and none have known love, except for this world of dreams.

A knocking at my door startles and awakens me harshly. This sudden noise disrupts my attempt at sleep, as I know not how long my head has even rested in my post of confusion.

Chapter Four

"You may enter," I say, as I shuffle myself from lying down to being seated in the bed to greet this unexpected guest.

"I am very sorry to bother you, dear apothecary, but as the immediacy of our situation is best sought upon the result of an action, I thought it best we involve ourselves at this newly horrid event." The friar says this as he enters the room and lights the candle next to my bed to fill the room with light once more.

"What hour is this?" I ask to ready my mind for this day's start.

"It is the unchanged night. The moon still works to brighten all the darkness but has failed to work in everyone's favor." He backs away to the door to allow space for me to collect and prepare myself for this calling of ours.

"My lack of instant awareness agrees that night is still in pulse and the moon is still hard at work. What calls us to action when all others sleep?" Placing my shoes on each foot, and correcting the clothing that hangs in awkward positions on my body, prepares me enough to be ready for such a response as this.

"I will speak ever so lightly, as I do not want Romeo and Juliet to hear what I am about to tell you. There has been another murder. Much of the dark side of Verona stirs in the night, and fear flies over the city as this war continues to take lives from us." The friar looks to the heavens as he gathers the strength to pray for another soul. I watch as his lips silently move, as he hopes to guide and soothe the recently released soul that may still be floating in the air above.

"Another has fallen? O', most harsh deed. Who is it that has lost their life?" I ask. I see now why it is that he awoke me. The families will be in hot fire over another fallen soul. The more blood that falls, the greater the tragedy that will ensue.

"Another from the house of Montague. This one will touch Romeo deeper to his heart. His close friend and servant, Balthasar, has met his end," the friar says as the emotion enters his throat making speech more difficult. "This is the same boy that traveled to Mantua to inform Romeo of Juliet's death, when he was banished there. It also was he that accompanied Romeo to the church, unknowing that he would take his life. His death will spur more action upon both sides. How it is that they allow this hate to brew so deeply and take such actions as this, I will never know. Meet me at the front of the church, good apothecary. I will inform Romeo and Juliet that we have awoken early to begin our discussions."

He leaves the room and I rest in the thoughts of this boy that has now been taken from the living world. How foolish it is that they strike each other down, when peace would be the more rational choice in these short lives that we live. There is more land, far greater and richer, outside these walls that either family could safely move to and occupy. Yet, due to pride beyond reason, they stay and strike down upon each other like hawks to a field of mice. I am not sure what it is the friar believes we will be able to achieve in the middle of the night, while most of the city sleeps and dreams of their next day. Nevertheless, if he feels that it is time to act upon this evil deed within short moments of the action, then the importance must be of the utmost.

Walking through the church, I hear the friar's voice in the distance informing them that we are early to rise, so that we can discuss how it is that we will approach the families.

As I do not hear yelling or crying, the friar did well to not enlighten Romeo of his man's fate. For now, it is still unknown, but when the body comes to the church for its final rites of passage, it will be more than known and the scene shall not be as calm.

I am not sure if the friar meant to meet outside or inside, but as my desire calls me to be out of doors, I will wait in the air and lose myself in the stars. Hearing these young lovers speak of the stars earlier in this evening allows me to appreciate them all the more now, knowing that they shine down history and direction and not so much the aging dust that colors my head.

Walking out of the door, I breathe in deeply, as the evening air is crisp and follows a trail through my lungs, renewing the life where old air and smoke had settled. There was a time when I would walk in the evening, around the streets of Mantua, just to greet my neighbors and move my legs so they would not lock up in my solid stance while I worked. One must be quite still when mixing liquids, as the wrong amounts could kill those I am meaning to heal.

Hearing a sudden cough, I turn to see a man lying on the ground, his back against the church wall, covered in clothes that would not carry the same name by their appearance. This is one of the unfortunates, where his life did not go the direction that brought happiness and wealth. His age seems similar to mine, though, as the years that have passed, being less opportune than mine own, perhaps they have left harsher effects on his face. He looks up to me, eyes unchanging of their sad demeanor. His mouth slowly moves as if words are the next things he hopes to conjure.

"From ancient…grudge break to new mutiny…where civil blood…makes civil hands unclean."

He stops with a sudden shock, as if his mind was instantly wiped clean; his head lowers, as he coughs more, and then falls back into a trance of sleep.

What is it that he said? He spoke of mutiny and death. Yet, it is fairly well known that both love and death exist in Verona more than any other thing. Love brings forth happiness, but happiness is masked over by the intensity of love. It is even the emotion of love that will keep two souls together even if it were to appear that they dislike each other more than their own enemy.

The doors open and the friar comes walking out, prepared to be on our way. The poor man on the ground coughs once again, bringing awareness to the friar of his presence. I wonder how the good friar treats men like this? As a man of the church, I would assume he would show compassion for their ill state, and as any child of God, give them the care they would need to survive.

"Hello Christian," the friar says to him and then approaches me steadily. "Shall we go?" he asks of me, and then lifts his arm to show which way we are heading. I have not traveled to Verona often enough and, even if he were to tell me where it is that we are going, I would not have the knowledge or direction to get there.

As we walk, I cannot help but to contemplate the exchange between him and this unfortunate, Christian.

"Good friar, the man outside the church, on the ground, the one you addressed as Christian, do you know him well?" I ask him as he shows a look that affirms my question, but also one that I would expect from a friar, as his eyes hang heavily to the ground.

"Yes, I see him quite often. More nights than I could count these many a year. I know him only through sight, as he has never spoken a word to anyone. I call him Christian, as I would hope and pray that he comes to the church to sit outside its walls, like a good Christian would, even if he could not contribute to the church." He grins in joy seemingly from the thought that Christian's soul still follows God.

"Yet, you said he never speaks? Are you sure of this?" I ask in amazement.

"Why, yes. I have addressed him many a time. Each nun that has closed the church doors at night has spoken to him, but they say he never replies. If the man does speak, it is not to us or any that have crossed his path that I have met. Come, it is not far from here that the body was found. If we make good time, we may even see the body within the position and state of death that it was found."

My eyes return to the stars, and then the ground, as I know by more than the beating of my heart that I heard the man speak to me. This Christian, thus being his given name, spoke words I could not clearly understand, but they were very much words referring to love and death. I will speak with him again when we return, hoping very much that he will still be there. He shall speak with me once more; as he is the one who opened the door to our conversation, I feel sure that he would do it again.

After walking through several streets, and with the ease in my heart that they were ones that were well lit by the moon in the night, I see the attentive bodies of the officers standing in the distance. Knowing that murder is now in the streets, even as I have no relation to any of the families involved, I still fear that this family conflict may spill over to those who are simply living their lives and are in the path of a swinging sword.

The officers, in numbers I cannot confirm, as some move around as if they are fish within a river changing course against the current, see that we are nearing them and prepare to address us by the movement of their stance. If we were any other men, I believe we would have been approached well before we neared their location. As I am accompanied by the friar, we are welcomed to come forth by a wave of the arm from one of the officers. It may very well be common within Verona to see the friar come to the place where men have lost their lives so that he may pray for their souls to pass on to the worlds beyond our own. As we approach, one of the men begins to address us, yet their eyes seem to stay firm on me.

"Friar, you have come too late. The body has been moved, as the morning is upon us. He will be brought to you shortly," he says. The officer, stern in look, and very well trained to be so, still has a softness of speech to the friar. This friar may very well have been the man to baptize this officer. As I look around further at these men, the friar may very well have baptized most of these officers. Their youth shows in their faces, but the harshness of what they do for work shows in their eyes, in the deep and vacant glance that intercepts the evil intentions of any man that walks near them. They must always be prepared, with arms, to defend the city and its laws. I am envious of these men, as I in my youth never had such power in my will to hold something so strong that I would die for it. This task, even now, is one that will hold a memory in my library of knowledge, as I feel the risk I am about to take to stop this war will be greater than any I have ever thought to accept.

"I thank you for the information, but may I ask, how was the body found? In speaking to his soul, to assist him in passing on to the heavens of God, if I could know how he died, I can ease the spirit to see the light." The friar, as smart as a man of his authority must be, spoke very well and cunning to ask for the information that we came here in search of.

"Good friar, he was found just the same as the last two. This one, Balthasar, of the house of Montague, now the second of that house, laid the same. Mortal strikes that were precise to the goal of ending his life. His sword was drawn, but not one show of blood on the blade or elsewhere, other than his own that spilled from the mortal strikes. This is most strange, but we officers will find the murderer, as we look to speak with the families this very same day. These murders must end before the prince returns, or it will be our heads on the ground presenting death's message of mortality for all of Verona to see."

"My good son, I thank you for your help. I will look to go back to the church to await the arrival of the body and to pray for his soul. This knowledge will most definitely allow me to ease his spirit into the afterlife. By God, please be safe yourselves, and be swift in finding out the cause of these murders. We most assuredly know the reason and very well how they fall. This war between the families will end, whether it be by the truce so desperately desired or by the last body that will fall and end the history of their bloodline. Peace to you all."

The friar is precise in his words and knows what to say to these men to keep them from asking any questions within our direction. As we turn to walk away, the friar grabs my shoulder to hold me from going any farther and turns back to the officers one last time.

"My son, one last thing. Which house do you visit first today?" he asks, as he inquires for the same reason I would hope he would.

"We go to the Capulets, good friar. Then we will visit the Montagues. As they have already received the news of this death, we will allow them time to grieve before we question them."

"Very well. That is very well thought out and decided upon. This city is blessed and graced to have officers such as you to protect us. God bless you all," the friar says, as he turns back to me to begin our walking away. He is a clever and cunning man. Either he has been around death often enough where this has become habit, or he has worked magic words of deception to spin this malleable world into the grasp of his control and that of the church.

"Very well, my friend," he says, as he looks around to make sure we are alone. "We have the information we sought to gain. Another murder, just the same. It seems to me the families are murdering each other in the same fashion, showing that if one can kill one precise way, so can the other. This is not faring well, as in these same such situations, they will begin to make their shows of death greater, so that fame can be absorbed and celebrated. This will have to end soon. Apothecary, please do not be so shy as to not offer your thoughts. This will take more than one mind, ever so much in this present situation."

"Good friar, I will make my voice known if thoughts or actions that may help to end this war come about. If I may ask, as my observations are not the best, especially with limited sleep and the darkness of the streets, but we do not seem to be heading back to the church." I say this and he looks at me with a glare in his eye, showing that he knows this and has made a decision that changes our course.

"You are correct, we do not head back to the church. Even as I said that we would, I have thoughts that making our way to the house of Montague would be more in the profit of our mission than heading back to the church. Their blood will be in full rage, and if a friar can calm them from taking any immediate action against the Capulets, then that is the destination we will have to plot a course for. And the body will be safely placed at the church in the care of the nuns, so I am not worried about being there for its arrival."

The friar uses his mind well, thinking that this would be the time when the Montagues would look to execute upon the act of revenge. Blood for blood, as most would think it to be a common reaction, is engraved upon the family crests of each household. From the first sword that sliced through the wind and struck down on one of their ancient ancestors, revenge has been sought after and seems to be the only thing that feeds the desire to breed and to arm more hands for battle. These are the tales I have heard in Mantua and every word has been verified and justified since my arrival. One does not need spend much time here to know of this ancient strife.

Verona is a large city, with many homes scattered both on the outer edges, and encompassing the city streets. There is much beauty here, from the houses that show of color and class, to even the homes in the more poor area of town that still make Mantua appear as a land of dust and dirt. The one sight that brings the most joy to my eyes is the flowers and the trees that drench every home and government building. Even in the darkness of the night, the colors are vibrant by the light of the moon. I pray for energy and awareness when the sun does rise, as the splendor that will erupt from these beauties may overwhelm my eyes and blind me. Though, there is not an image more beautiful than these such things that I would prefer my eyes to remember, as my sight would burn away.

Romeo would not agree with my statement, as Juliet is all he can focus on when she enters a room. Their love is sweet and, as their affection is more uncommon than most that live, I enjoy every show of passion and tenderness that they offer each other. If one drop of love and delight that Romeo possesses entered my will, I would have a lifetime filled with everlasting love. I believe that to this moment, as the sun has almost risen, surely they still stand near the altar, gazing within each other's eyes, sharing words so dear that their own family strife that shows matter to their awareness would be deciding who would love the other more.

"We are almost there," the friar states, as light from the sky beckons the birds to sing. Lost in my own thoughts, I did not pay much attention to the way we have walked. I very much hope I do not need to find my way back to the church. Though, if I could find the steeple in the night, I am very sure I could find it in the day.

Turning a corner from one road to another, facing us some many steps away is a large gate. At the top of the gate, made from black, all metal bars, as if this were a prison for the wealthy, is a large, iron 'M'. I cannot help but to think that we have reached the house of the Montagues. The closer we near the gate, the more the presence of the guards at the gate make themselves known. As the walls surrounding the estate themselves are made of stone, the iron gate allows us to see within and watch as swords begin to be drawn. Yet, the nearer we get, the swords return to their sheaths as the friar is recognized. As we are upon the gate itself, it does not open, as I feel eyes gaze upon me in obvious wonder as to who I am. Not much time passes until they make their actions known.

"Good day, friar," one of the men says, as we stand at the gate.

"Good day to you, my son. May we please gain entrance and speak with the lord of the house? We are here to pay our respects to the family."

"Friar, our gate will always open for you, but who is this that is with you? All must be identified before entering these walls."

"Yes, that is very well advised. This is my friend, visiting from another church." The friar does not seem to tell them more of who I am. What is to hide with my gaining access to this home? Am I not one that the friar would care to associate with if they knew my profession? O', the shades of men when the light is cast upon them.

"Does this friend of yours have a name?" the guard asks. It is a goodly question. I would not allow some strange, unknown person into my home with the events that are transpiring in their world. I pause as he stares at me, wondering if the friar has made an answer for this question as well.

"Why, yes. His name is, uh, Paul. His name is Paul. Isn't that right, Paul?" he says, looking at me and nodding his head so that I will agree with him and join in on this ruse. As he has been in charge since this adventure began, I find that I must trust in him.

"Yes, that is correct. My name is Paul. Pleasure to meet you, sir." I say this, bowing my head and attempting to show the same effects that the friar would show upon meeting someone. I am not a man of faith, as he, but that does not mean I cannot show the same visage.

I am upon a watch as if I were entering a place where the prince himself would live. It is as if no other things or beings exist with the intensity of their gaze on me. The gate opens, and we enter, slowly, thanking each man as the friar blesses each one with a bow.

"God be with you gentlemen," he says, as we walk toward the main door of the grand estate. Looking over to me, the friar has the easing of eyes that captured fear only moments ago.

"Friar, might I ask why you offered a name of me that is not mine? Is it not respectable to be seen with an apothecary from Mantua? We are men of an honorable profession, healing those that knock on the door of heaven against their own desire."

"My dear friend, you are a fine man, with more honor than leaves across a forest as far as the eye can see. But if you will remember, the young Romeo did die from a poison given to him by an apothecary from Mantua, that being you. So, as we enter this boy's home, it would be ill advised to bring back such memories of grief, as we ride upon another. Moreover, Romeo's death has been the greatest loss the family has ever experienced. It is best to leave all that pain and hurt in the cavern of their memories."

"My good heavens, I did not even think upon such a thought as that. You are very wise." I cannot believe that I would not recall such information as this. Here, to Verona, I have traveled for this one reason and yet, I enter the home of the family that I shattered through the loss of their cherished son. Where has my memory gone? Is it age that slows my wit that would have conjured the same response and offered a name that is not my own? O', how time makes fools of men.

Nearing the door of the home, my nerves react to the situation I am about to enter. How will I keep myself as calm as a day without the mighty wind, as I enter a place that I myself have removed the heart and soul from? This shall not fare well for me. I am not of the age where I am able to hold my bones strong and keep calm the force of guilt that will charge against my walls.

Arriving at the door, the friar grabs the knocker and pounds the ball against the door, so loud that my soul almost crumbles from the noise. My eyes are heavy and my shoulders seem to be attempting to drag me closer to the earth and lay me at rest. As wise as the friar is, to grab the emotion by the throat and prevent more bloodshed, I am not sure it wise that I attended.

"Hold strong, good apothecary. This shall be a test of our will. We must remember Montague has lost much these passing weeks: Romeo, the lady Montague, and now two more in the week that has brought us to this day. He shall be filled with much emotion, and I cannot think what state of mind he will be in. I am also aware of the situation for you and all that you may be feeling, but the raw nature of your emotion will work well for you here. You will see." The friar is wise, but how it is that my emotion that suffers regrets as much as ten men locked in the prisons, will be useful at this moment and within this place, puzzles me.

The door opens and a servant invites us in. As we enter, I wish that there were less pain in me that blinds my light of the day, as the pieces of vision I allow myself to witness show a place with much wealth and color. We are escorted quickly to the first room on the right and asked to wait here while the lord of the house attends to other matters. We both offer a warm and thankful gesture and walk into the room. What matters are there to attend to this early in the morn? Does business by men get completed at this time in the day? I am not a man of business, but at this early hour, most sleep, or look to nourish their bodies and souls with food and prayer.

My mind changes thought quickly, as I gather the sights of the room we are in and am instantly amazed. The room is not large, nor the ceiling that high, as one would think when being in such a grand estate. But what makes this room surprise my eyes, are the books that are on every wall, with not one small breath of space for anything else. There may be two windows on the wall straight ahead as we walk in, but as I turn completely around, there is no other show of wall itself that is not covered by the spines of books. The desk before us, and a chair to each far corner, represent all that occupy the floor. I have never seen this many books in one place before. The friar walks to the desk, as papers are scattered about, but what seems to draw him closer is the large map that lay open. I walk closer myself, as I do not know this map very well.

"Friar, what is the map of? Some foreign land that they are looking to travel to?" I ask, as reading a map was never a strong ability I did possess. A man cannot be great at all things.

"My good friend, this is a map of Verona. They have placed markings on the map as well. Each one looks to be at the place where the lives of this family have been lost. It must just be of the recently dead, as the years of conflict would have placed more markings that would make this map more of a parchment to write on than show of the land."

What is the usage of this map? Do they just mark their dead to know where each has fallen? Or is this a map to plot against the Capulets to gain advantage in this war? How deeply the hatred flows where they go to such measures as this. I have heard that great battles by the royal armies have plotted with maps such as this that show the land and ways to surround the enemy for their annihilation. Has this conflict between the families come to such a place where extinction is more desired than life?

"Back away, my friend, I hear the lord of the house approaching from outside the door. It is best not to be too close to the desk where he would believe we are looking upon his business matters. No need to anger a man that carries anger like a guard carries a sword."

I remove myself from looking at the desk and walk to the side wall to leaf through the many books that could be the base structure of any home, by their quantity and mass.

"Friar, have you seen such quantity of books? Even more amazing is the selection within them as well. There are books of literature, of poetry, of the sciences, and even books on the philosophy of the Greeks. Simply marvelous." Being so taken by all before me, I was unaware that Montague himself had walked into the room.

"There are even books on the ancient war tactics of the Romans," Lord Montague states. "You will not find them there, as they are on the shelf behind the desk. Good day, friar. Good day to you as well, sir. I believe I was told your name is Paul?" Montague is quite straightforward and direct, with not a smile that would penetrate the wall of winter's face, which freezes emotion from coming about.

"Yes, sir, it is rightly that. My name is Paul. It is my honor to meet you, sir." I say this as he shakes the friar's hand and then comes to me to shake mine as well. Once completed, he walks around to the back of the desk and seats himself, instantly folding the map in half, to reveal more layers of papers and books.

"Good friar, I am sure you are here due to the circumstances of the morning. That you come to pray for Balthasar's soul, I much thank you for your service. Balthasar was a goodly boy, honest and fair, as he was one that cared for this house deeply and even more for my son, Romeo. It is most unfortunate that he was taken from this world, as he would have shown to be a loyal and loving companion one day and increase the name of this house, as I was hoping Romeo would also accomplish." He staggers his vision off upon the shelves of books, as one would think that he were deep in thought. Yet, I have seen strong eyes as his, and they use muscle that will hold back the tears and emotions that would flow like a river for most. That he is the lord of the house, and under much duress for the present matter of the battling families, he must hold himself as strong as ice in the winter season.

I could not have been blinder to this affair. The friar was correct to not name me at the door as the Mantuan apothecary. I would have entered this home but never given the right to leave, as my final days would have been in the dungeon receiving whips and slashes for each drop of pain I caused this family. As there are many Montague still upon the living earth, I would not have survived a single night.

The friar approaches the desk, slowly and with much ease, as any sudden or awkward movements would startle the good lord and agitate his present calm demeanor. No need to wake the spirit of a demon when they are at rest.

"My lord, you are beyond right in your thoughts. I have come to pray for his soul, as these deeds of death are most tragic and against the will of God. Balthasar now walks with Jesus in His kingdom upon the clouds of heaven, and watches over this house from above, and attends to the other Montague that rest by the side of the Lord." As the friar states his words of peace, I instantly think of Romeo, as he does not sit by God or walk with Jesus. He rests in the church, held captive by his actions, but also in the company of the one he loves. I wonder what would be the reaction of his soul if Lord Montague knew Romeo were at the church? As much as my eyes would desire to see his eyes upon being told such a fantasy as that, I would not want to be there if he were also one of the many that could not see or speak to Romeo's ghost. O' how my emotions build and suffocate the air from my lungs, bringing thickness to my neck, taking away my ability to openly speak.

As I gaze back at Lord Montague, his eyes are affixed on me, with a look that is colder than the top of the icy mountains.

"And why is it that you are here, Paul?" he asks of me, with a gaze that strikes me so deep that the emotions that I have built, now pour from me as if Noah's great flood started through the doors of my eyes. Even my voice is taken a-back by the sudden question and attention, that I cannot for the life of my spirit answer him. I look to the friar, who equally has is eyes upon me, and seeing that I cannot form words and stop the flowing of my eyes, nods and faces to address Lord Montague.

"Lord Montague, Paul is my companion, learning of the ways of attending to families that struggle with grief through the loss of their loved ones. He is not yet a friar, and to be sure, with shows of grief as clear as this, may not have the ability to perform such tasks it seems. Nonetheless, he is here to offer support for your loss."

Well said, as I myself would have used words that come nowhere near this. As he looks back to me, I now nod at him, agreeing upon what he has said, especially in that the Lord Montague would hope to find comfort in my being here.

Lord Montague rises from behind the desk and walks around to me. Still speechless, I begin to panic even more, as being as wise as he is, perhaps he has figured out that this is a lie and will instantly punish me for my dishonor during these trying times. He stands close to me, directly in front, eye to eye. Still his face is frozen emotion, which would allow the wrath of hell to strike on me by his command. His arm rises to me, and I can already feel the essence of his fingers around my throat, as he would strangle the little life I have within me from my soul within seconds. But the hand comes down and rests on my shoulder.

"My dear old man, I am thankful for your show of grief upon the loss of members of my family. This is most kind of you to offer emotion as strong as this and to show it as openly as you do. Most men I know hide their grief and do not allow for such woes to be seen in their eyes. I believe you to be more than these men, as I respect this release of truth. Good friar, you have chosen your companion wisely. Now, to my day. If you will excuse me gentlemen, I have much to attend to. I thank you for your prayers and concern."

"My lord, there is another reason I have come," the friar states. "These matters you will attend to, as you say, I pray that they are matters of peace. These deaths must stop. The fallen children, that take away from the future of this fair city, will only leave vacant homes and unused air."

"Friar, this present war between our families is not of my working. I did not strike first, but I will be the man that strikes last. Never will a life be taken where it will not be avenged. How foolish are they that believe me to be of weakness, as my house has lost more than theirs. But I assure you, your prayers will come ten thousand times more after I have cleansed my soul from the anger that has rested there from my loss."

I listen as they speak, and as truthful as the friar is in arguing his case for peace, this lord will not hear of it. Death is all his mind holds and the constant coldness of emotion toward peace and flames that spark from fury in his eyes, reassures that he will not release the anger from his grip until the house of Capulet burns to the ground. Such ancient hate— how fresh and alive it is.

"Lord Montague, to strike any further would bring the hate back to your door, as revenge is not an emotion felt by your single soul. Each action causes another action. Where shall this bloodshed end?" The friar now showing more emotion than I have witnessed, holds strong in his plea.

"Good friar, I did not order the attack on their fallen man, Gregory, but that they believe that I did causes more hate for their dishonor in thought. With their foolish determination to falsely avenge a death not marked on our table, they have restarted a war that had no hint of Montague involvement. If you want to plead for peace and mercy, speak with them, if there be any Capulet left when I am through with them. Now, away. I am in much thanks for your prayers, but that is the most of what I can accept my ears to hear from you. Good day to you both." As he concludes his words, with balanced rage, I am sure that there will be no stopping this man from his task of eliminating the Capulets. He has seen much death, and due to this vision, it is all that he sees. He walks out the door of the room, and we listen as he walks away, each step a lost opportunity to bring the peace. The friar looks down at the floor, with disappointment heavy on his shoulders. I know this feeling, as I have felt it for myself many weeks now.

"We have failed to calm his rage. Nay, more precisely, I have failed. Am I able to understand the shoes this man wears, with a son, a wife, and now those under his house, dead and removed from this world? Are these the same actions that I, a friar, would have taken if I were not a friar? O', woe is our state of affairs. This is only half of the war. We must to the Capulets to uncover what mind they are in, so that we may find a way to prevent this destined bloodshed."

"I wish that I were able to help you more, friar, but the magnitude of the past events overwhelmed my soul, and as you predicted, it erupted from me. I believe you hoped that it had more of an effect on him, but it did not stir one authentic emotion of compassion or calm one nerve in him."

"My good man, you are an apothecary, not a friar, as I, who is trained to calm men from such thoughts of war and blood. Did I see such a response as this? Never. Montague has always been on the shore of calm waters. Even as their families share hatred beyond compare, in the brief moments of harmony there is no more peaceful a man in Verona than he."

"And now, good friar, what is it that we do?" I ask this, and whether it be my old age or the ending of this meeting, I am more than sure that I will not be able to be the peacekeeper and allow others to live. My hand, reaching into my pocket once again, surrounds the vial of poison. I hold it firm. It is my security of knowing that I can exit this world whenever my time has come, by the decision in my mind. Yet that is a distant thought, as my word has been writ to do what I can to end this war. But what power do I have?

"Now? Now, we leave this house and make our way to the Capulets. There cannot be another direction on our course. The battlefields are being prepared, and the soldiers are arming themselves. Unless we sacrifice our bodies, and place them in the way of the next sword, we must make our words our weapons and disarm their fury in their minds."

A knock at the door of the library startles our nerves, and as the door opens, we are alerted that time has passed enough and we should find our way out of this house. I do not argue a moment with the request and lead the way for the friar to follow my quick step. As we exit the house, I keep my lips toward the ground and my eyes to my person, walking calmly to the gate, so our safety is more in our hands and not that of this family.

Walking out of the gate, the same guards watch every movement we make, as I believe they hope we do something that will allow them to step in and leave their mark on our souls, if not our flesh. If I were not with the friar, I wonder what actions they may have taken. As two peaceful men we are, peacefully we leave, and exit the gate safely.

"Pleasure to see you once again, friar. And pleasure to meet you, Paul," the guard states, as through his tone, it is clear he does not believe this to be my name. Though, how does one question a friar, when a friar is not meant to lie, under oath to God?

"Friar, more than any other feeling I have ever had, I would never choose to return there. I fear I would not be seen alive stepping through those gates once more." The friar smirks in understanding and nods his head to empathize where it is my statement comes from. He is wise, there is no question, and very hopeful he has the will and strength to see this event through and prevent bloody streets.

As we reenter the streets of the city, there is more for me to now see, as the sun has risen and the buildings wear the rays on their stone faces. Even a home that has seen better days looks loved with the sun shining down on it. I am happy to see another day of my life in moments like these. This day was not on my calendar of existence.

Walking and still holding the vial of poison in my hand, I release it slowly and lightly, to fall back into the well of my pocket, and allow my arms to swing in the newly given hour. So close I was to dying, to tasting the fires of hell, and receiving a formal escort by the devil himself to my purgatory. These rays of light are the sources of heat that welcome my heart, as I could now not imagine what the raging fires of hell would have felt like as they would have consumed every bit of flesh. It is said that old men find God once again before death takes them. I may have proved this to be correct, yet accompanying the friar on this mission, as lacking in a worthy outcome as holding back the tides of the mighty ocean, is my answer to finding God.

"Well, well, well, it seems we have not allowed enough time to pass. Good apothecary, up ahead, in the distance, you will see several officers standing watch outside another great estate of wealth. That is the house of Capulet. I will very much prophesize that our entrance will not be granted whilst the officers and other officials are speaking with the lord of the house. We will pay our own visit later this evening, around dinnertime, as food and talk are common, but together one rarely shows the acts of violence themselves. Our word will be kept to our ghostly visitors, as we will head back to the church to pray for Balthasar and offer more words of love and support for them, which will be needed once Romeo sees Balthasar's body. It will be a study within itself to see how a ghost deals with such tragic events and what this will do to their airy figure."

I am not upset that we will not visit the Capulets, as more hate is not what I would prefer my soul to feel. Two Montagues and one Capulet have fallen in recent events. If the balance of death will play the act, a Capulet will be next. Lord Montague spoke that this would also be the case and, with the rage he captures in his soul, I doubt it not.

As we near the church, we can hear screams coming from inside. They can be none other than Romeo's and even that of Juliet, by the pitch and volume. I feel the pain unleashed through the painted glass of the church, as the images in their frames show the terror for what is in there. It is good that others cannot hear or see their ghostly selves, as the sounds I hear would bring much attention upon the church.

"Good apothecary, will you leave me as we enter and allow my conversation to be with Romeo alone? He will need much support, and even as Juliet is one that can give him this, he and I have shared a bond in times such as these that allows me entrance into the softest places of his heart and mind. This grants him the ability to speak truth to me on his heart's pain. We will enter together, so that we do not appear to show that we are avoiding the tragedy, but I will gather his will and escort him to safer emotional ground."

The friar cares much for Romeo. If Lord Montague were not Romeo's father, then the friar would clearly have raised him. Being that he baptized the boy, and many other children in Verona, the attachment to most is far greater than the butcher who prepares the meal or the blacksmith who arms the youth with their first sword. I would even go so far as to say that his investment is far greater and thus, his concern toward the outcome of each life must be deeper than any other, not including the parents.

We walk in through the church doors and as we pass through the entrance room, we stroll into the church itself and see Romeo and Juliet at the altar. I wonder if they have been there this entire time that we were gone. Though, the demeanor is not what it was. Romeo is on his knees, facing the large cross that hangs on the back wall. His head is lowered. Juliet stands behind him, very close in what shows to be in full support, as she understands that he is grieving the death of Balthasar. Even I, in this moment, feel his pain from where I stand in the church.

"Good sir, if you take this door immediately to your right, it leads you down a side hall and will take you back to the rooms. I will call upon you shortly to discuss our next plan, for, as we know that we will go to the house of Capulet, I feel we must have more of a plan in mind on how to convince them to walk away from this war. Be still and rest yourself."

The friar then walks down the main aisle, and as he approaches, Juliet turns and faces him, in a show of clear grief. This is the punishment that most affects their being in their current state. Juliet cannot console Romeo, as she cannot touch him, and he is suited with the same fate as she. Even the friar is troubled, though he has flesh and blood about him, that he cannot respond in a way that he would prefer, wrapping his arms around the boy, showing love the boy most desperately needs.

I see him kneel at Romeo's side and whisper words to him. Romeo is unmoving, his head still facing the ground as he kneels, his shoulders so heavy that even as a ghost he may never release such weight from him. As the friar rises, and stands above him, his voice increases so that I can finally hear him. With this, I walk to the door to my right, which I was advised to go to, that will lead me to my room. Though, I cannot coerce myself to walk entirely through and go to my room, for my much needed rest. My own heavy heart desires to hear what is being said. I feel compelled for my part to offer words of support, but as I am the one who placed Romeo in his ghostlike state, regardless of his words allowing the blame to fall on himself, I am full of guilt still. I am not sure this guilt will have time to remove itself from my body with the lingering time that remains of my life. My time on this earth is not long.

"Romeo, rise good boy. Come with me below and pray with me over Balthasar's body, to assist with guiding his soul to entering heaven. Let us show the love to him that you show now."

"Good friar," Romeo begins to say, attempting to hold back the grief that is in his body, pouring out of him. "I will meet you there shortly. I thank you for the show of love that you have given me through all my years. This death, like that of Mercutio, touches me deeply. These men were the brothers I was not given by my mother and father. They held my love as I held theirs. Were it not for my foolishness in failing at holding Mercutio within a realm of peace and slaying Tybalt, much of this blood would not have fallen, leading men to their graves. Good friar, go first. I will follow shortly."

With these words, the friar agrees through gesture, and walks slowly to the back door that has so commonly been used by them as the exit from the stage of God. After his exit, I push my door forward slightly preparing for my departure, but as I do, Romeo stands, still facing the cross, though his body has changed its posture. His wind has returned and filled his spirit with reason to fight. If he were allowed to leave this church, released from the grips of God, he would undoubtedly alter the history of this great city with his passion to stop this war.

Juliet approaches Romeo and stands next to him firmly. She raises her hands to try and touch his arm, but it goes through. Still, no connection allows them to fortify each other in love.

"That I could embrace you, my love, I could make you feel the sorrow and grief that I bear with you and for you. Fie on this ghostlike state! How false a prison this sentence is, to allow us to be together and yet not be allowed to be together. How cursed are we to share these days under the roof of this church, not able to touch, and not able to speak with our loved ones. You were banished to Mantua, yet you could fight the word of the prince and come back to Verona, as you did. However, we are banished to a worse fate, where we spend this eternity together, but our souls banished from loving each other. God tells us to look upon a flower, but do not smell, do not touch. It is as if we are once again the first two that have walked on this earth. I am the daughter, Eve, and you are the son, Adam. Speak upon me not, as once again, woman has forced man to eat upon the apple and be placed into a hell for their existence."

She turns away and faces the back of the church, but does not look to my direction or see that I still stand within the earshot of their words. That I am partially standing within the door, prepared to exit if they looked within my direction, I will hope they do not gaze upon me. This much learned state of death, one that I have never seen, enriches my soul, seeing where our spirits may end and how so very similar they are to our flesh covered bones.

Romeo turns, in what looks to be grief encompassed by tears, and faces Juliet. It is as if he recognizes that her own tortured soul has reached its limit of pain, and knows that now is when he must place his pain in a deep well within him and attend to his love.

"Juliet, do not speak so harshly on the history of man. Such moments from the past allowed us to learn and develop into the glorious beings that we are today. Hold yourself, my love, in the thought that all that we are, is only within the control of our hands. I cannot change the path of the sun to follow me when I am cold. I cannot move the trees to shade me in summer when the heat has overwhelmed my flesh. Yet, I can love thee in every movement of my lips, when they speak with you, and did once lovingly kiss you. I can walk each step wherever it is that I go, as each touch of the ground is a touch upon you, so light and cunning to caress each beauteous curve. I will follow you until the end of our time, and if our end may never come, I will follow you to the end of that end and one day more, fighting against any decision to part us from our eternal union."

"O' Romeo, you speak of the unnatural world, one beyond our own, that neither you nor I, nor the friar or that of the angels themselves, can amend and hold within the grasp of their hands. That my love is as rich and as deep, there is not question in the Bible that will prove otherwise. But that God himself would allow his will to be changed by two lovers, or any other empowered soul, is a fantasy that I care not to think, for it will only sadden me more than I can withstand."

"Juliet, you are as rich in love, that I would not need dream of wealth of any other kind."

"Am I like the purse of ducats you look to place in your pocket, attaining a value that you would lock away and not make use of?" she says, changing her inspired tone.

"Fair Juliet, you know better than this, that wealth is nothing to me, as your return of love is the food for my table, it is the air for my lungs…"

"Will you look to consume me, my love, for use to keep you alive? Is love not two that feed from each other, nourishing each others souls with bountiful enrichment?"

"That I could touch you now, I would feed my love to you and nourish every artery within your temple, giving you a feast that you have never seen," he says, still passion filled.

"O' cursed, damned state of smoke and air. That I could touch you now. But let us not speak of this anymore. To your kinsman we should go and pay our respects with prayers that will keep his soul far from this punishment we live today."

"You are wise, my love, my Juliet. You steer the course of my thoughts and soul wisely, my captain. Let us go to Balthasar, and do as you have said. There is nothing worse than allowing his soul to be on this tortured earth, as is our own fate."

My heart pounds and the uncontrolled pains verify that I am alive and have never lived or loved like this. How deep, into what is a shallow frame, their love still fills and embodies two beings greater than any that live today. As they walk away from the altar, through the door, without the door itself moving, I stand and wait several moments so that I do not make a sound or call attention to myself, alerting anyone that I heard the interaction. There is nothing to be ashamed of in their words, but that I listened without permission does not rest well with me. In spite of that, in the case of my study upon their ghostly adventures, this was more rewarding than watching those that live today and yet do not live as this. Two and fifty years, I have never lived as this. How regret fills me, as fear consumed my will when I ever thought to marry. There were women I did love, but none I could offer a life to. My work as an apothecary took up much of my time. Though, that is not an excuse for not choosing one that would have had me the same. Fear of the other seeing the deep secrets of my soul, prevented me from sharing even my likes toward the weather or soup.

Here, two most young and fresh souls, love deeper than ten men and their wives. Nay, a thousand men and their wives. But I could not offer enough love for one. Why else hold existence on this mighty planet but to love those around us? Heavy burden of guilt, I must put you to rest and lay my head in hopes of removing you from my core. It has been on my soul far too long. That ever I said that I would love. Of what I have within me, there is no better time to complete this calling of love than now, but not for the sake of my reward, but for the souls of the two who show the world what love truly is or was. Now do I find more energy and willingness to use these bones to change the course of history and take hold the fate of others in my hand. Once again will I be the apothecary, though not for the body, but for the soul.

Through the door I pass, down the hall and to the room, where light from the corridor shines in to offer me a path to the bed. I will rest myself a little while, and when the friar has finished his prayers for the fallen Balthasar, I will consult with him on what it is we will do to stop the war between these families. Until then, I will rest my eyes and replenish my strength so I will be able to focus all my energy on this rejuvenated mission that God has positioned me on.

Placing my head down, as my mind at rest allows peace to enter, I begin to hear faint cries and screams. It does not last long, only but a moment, but this is the result of one who loves deeply, losing someone that they loved to their heart's core. I see why the boy wanted the poison. If he received word that his one and only love, Juliet, was dead, then there would seem no other solution but to take his own life. Through him, I feel the impact of such a loss.

I have never allowed myself to care for anyone so deeply, as I was afraid to lose them and suffer the pains that he now holds. For a boy, he is as strong as a lion. Even in the state that he is in, as a ghost, his strength still shines from his eyes, as I see him love his Juliet so steady and constant, and still look to work a mission of peace as his life is no more involved in this world as is the fallen leaf from a tree. Shall I mirror this image and side with the friar to be pillars of justice in Verona? More than I would desire for such heights of ability, I am not such a man as that. I play my role on this earth, but as my time does come in my aging years, it is now that I must leave my mark.

Chapter Five

"My good son, I am sorry to interrupt you from your restful state, but the time has come for us to try once again and conjure words of peace as we go to speak with the house of Capulets. I will allow you to rise at your leisure, as I shall meet you in the main area of the church. I would like to pray before we leave and consult with God on my course of action."

"Yes, that will be well. I will be with you shortly, as it is my desire to do the same," I say as I lean myself up on my arm and smile at the friar to let him know that I am awake and responsive. He turns and leaves the room, calmly with even steps. He does not seem as covered in grief as he prepared himself for being whilst consoling Romeo, but his mind is still very much alive with thoughts of what to do; his eyes secretly speak this. Asking God for his guidance and wisdom sounds like a wonderful way to start this next undertaking. We did not fare so well with Montague, so this is our only other chance to calm the raging war.

Up from the bed, I rub the limbs of my body, as waking each time tightens my every muscle so that movement is not easy. I did not think much time had passed, but when my mind is elsewhere, it loses every hold time allows us to have. O' age, O' body of limited life, that I should think that eternal life would be a blessing, when each day I would awake to such chores as movement of my arms and legs. Would it were that Romeo was an older age; I could ask him if his ghostly frame called for the same such pains.

Purpose to my bones, I stand, shuffle my clothing so that I appear, to a point, well put together and make my way to the church to join the friar in prayer. Entering through the door behind the altar, I walk as close to the wall as I can, as I do not want to disturb God, being that the altar area is where he exists when he is here. Though, some may argue that God is everywhere and no matter where I walk, I walk next to him. This is a comforting thought, but yet, I would not like to disturb him as he walks the earth to heal its children.

Entering the seating area of the pews, I see the friar in the second row, and from the side aisle, join the same bench that he is on, but allow for space between us so that I do not interrupt him either.

Kneeling myself, I face the mighty cross behind the altar and gather the weight of our duty. It is not an easy position to be in, and any assistance from God could make all the difference in the course of the outcome.

O' God, heavenly father. With your servant, the goodly friar you see before you, I pray for our finding the words that will end this war between these two families, and allow for peace to rain down on Verona. This is a mighty commission, but with the strength of our will, and a blessing of your graces, there is no task that cannot be achieved.

From the corner of my eye, I see the friar raise his glance up and look over to me. A smile verifies he is pleased to see me next to him, kneeling before God, asking for the wisdom that he equally looks to attain so that together we will bring peace. As he stands, I stand as well.

"Well, my good apothecary, shall we proceed to the Capulets and offer them such deep love that they have no other choice but to end this war?"

"Yes, let us go dearest friar, for the night comes upon us and this is when it seems the families choose to strike down upon each other, in the blind eye and corner of the city."

"You are wise, good apothecary. Let us hope that as days pass between each murder, that they are still in the mind of planning, so we may intervene and change that plan of death into an extension of love."

I smile his way, as this would very much please me and bring a lighter feel to my burden of regret. I would prefer no other outcome between these two families that I do not know well, but for the sake of their lives, especially those of the young, there is no other greater purpose for the healing of my soul.

Walking into the aisle, we head toward the door, and there we see Romeo and Juliet standing in silence, facing us as we near them. There is matter in their eyes, as they do not stand there without purpose in mind. Walking toward them, we stop and stand quietly, allowing them to speak whatever peace they are preparing to offer us.

"Good friar and kind apothecary, you go to my house, that of the Capulets, where I, their loving daughter, have lived all my life. I pray you all the speed and love that God can offer you. My father is a good man, but his anger does overpower his kindness when grief enters his heart. Once, some time ago, a family member from some distant city went on a spiritual journey and was never seen again. This man was one that my father was very close to in his childhood. They shared many stories and moments together. My father almost killed a servant, after hearing the news of his cousin's death, for simply dropping a flower that had slightly wilted and was being replaced in the main entranceway. Please remember, there is love in his heart. You will find it if you have the skill to stay within these feelings. Though yet, my mother, well, you may want to bring God with you and all of His angels. If my father grieves, she is the outward emotion that enacts his grief. She will be the dagger that stabs the man that he would want to kill. I pray for you both."

Juliet, in wise words, prepares us well for what we will experience in her family home. These are informative and yet still loving words, but the knowledge that both her parents are united together, becoming a thought and action, does not rest well on my soul. If it were not for this friar, I would not be attempting to speak with the families, as I have not the courage to do this alone.

"We thank you for your knowledge. We shall be wary and sway their minds to peace and love," the friar says, as he bows his head to them, looks back to me and walks toward the door. I bow my head to them as well and follow him in his quick pace.

The light falls behind the distant sky, as the final clouds of the day blanket the sun for a calm night's rest. The colors that she leaves behind are marvelous. Brightness screams from her parting and the shadows begin to appear, as evil finds its way to be reborn in the night. The friar leads the way to the Capulets and I stay steady with his pace, as he is desperate to get there, not for fear of the night, but for fear of what the night will bring.

"So that you are in the same thought as I, we will continue the same introduction, as with the house of Montague, by assuming you are named Paul. God will understand this play on names, as we will want to stay equal to what is known or said about you. And that keeping the knowledge of who you really are hidden from their minds will allow for your life to remain on a constant path of living. Does this agree well with you, sir?"

The friar is a smart man. Staying consistent with who I am, may keep not only my life and heart beating, but his own trust alive in the minds of these families. They would want to strike me down for what I have done, and thus, spill more blood onto the already drenched ground. God only wants his children to fly to heaven when He calls for them, is my understanding.

"I am in full understanding and agree with you on this decision," I speak, to impart an agreeable tone to this preparation of the moment. He once again greets my eyes with his grin and nod of the head, in association with agreeing with me equally.

I enjoy that he and I have connected well in this new partnership. He could have been any other style of man that I previously have not received well into my life. I have seen many a friar who truly takes truth by the throat and suffocate all life from it, so that he can use it for his own. These are not men I would want to neither be around, nor include in my life. Dishonesty has bled into the souls of many men and taken them from the true path of living a good life. Even I have been swayed from my goodly path. A boy, with more wisdom than many his age, used words so convincing that I found justification in what he said to me. I believed him more than I believed myself. As he stated to me, he could have found many other ways to end everything that he was. I very well may have prevented an even worse death than the one I provided. I have never been struck by a sword or stabbed with a dagger, but my imagination convinces me it would be far worse and the death even longer with much more pain. My poison spared the intensity of pain and time of anguish and allowed his soul to be spared such an eternity of physical grief. It was very likely a similar version of love that I used when I gave him the poison. And it will be love once again, when this poison will be raised to my own lips, as I will drink from it as well. I may be on this course to end the war, but my own inner war may never be resolved until all sides are sent to their final rest.

"We are approaching, dear friend," the friar states. "Be sure of your step and confident in your words. We have only been given two chances to stop this war, and we have already lost the battle on our first opportunity."

As we near the gate, I am immediately struck by how similar it is, in style and form, that it would resemble the house of Montague so evenly. The stone walls are high, to the left and to the right, and the metal gate itself has bars of spears that reach for the heavens and will pierce the skin of any man that would look to climb over. The same struggle they have to survive offers the same protection from the other family. It is as if we approach the same gate, as guards round the walls and stand at the entrance watching as we walk closer. The friar, under the same soft tone, informs that he himself is here, with Paul, to speak with the lord of the house. As these men know him the same, and do not question me as deeply this time nor look to remove my life as easily, he offers them more prepared and convincing words, and we are allowed in and pointed to the main door ahead. Looking to the sky as we near the door, I see and feel that the stars are brighter here than at the house of Montague. This is where the lovely Juliet did live, and such stars should shine down brighter and sharper on such a girl as she. This must have been how Romeo fell in love with her, comparing her to the stars, yet informing her that they are far less alluring than her brilliant eyes. These are words I could never have prepared if I had a lover in my life, and yet this boy spoke them as if they were as common in his mind as air to the lung,

With one small knock, after reaching the door, it immediately opens, and we are shown into a room shortly after walking in. How is it that as we enter a new and separate home, being that of a family who cannot agree with the other, they nonetheless are so similar to that other family in design and function, and yet still wish to destroy them?

The door is closed behind us, and we stand within the office of Lord Capulet. This office does not make space for one book, as did the Montague's room, but every inch of the walls in this room are covered with paintings of the generations of Capulets. Every face, quite comparable to the next, all here, represented from one can only imagine how far back in history. The only resemblance this room has to the Montague room is the desk that sits in the middle.

"Good friar, this room, as amazing as of that from the house of Montague, brings wonder and even fear to my soul. I see the same expression of art, yet here, each painting of their elders looks upon me as if I should not be here. Does this not strike you as it does me?"

"I have been within this room many times. It is a show of family love to represent each person in their history, as far back as they can find." As he speaks, the friar moves closer to me so that we stare at the wall together, shoulders almost touching. "What I have always wondered myself," he continues "is, of all the eyes that look upon us as we stand and wait, how many are of the natural painting and how many are real?"

My heart jumps at this. Could it be that behind some of these paintings are men watching us and judging on all that is said between us and how we move within the room? I glare lightly across many of the paintings, watching for movement of the eyes, to see if any strike me as real. Each one seems just as real as the next. These paintings are so beautiful and realistic, that I cannot tell which are that of the artist's work and which are real eyes looking upon me. This unnerving feeling travels in my blood and makes my spine tingle in fear. I have said the name of Montague within this room, and if any were listening, they would know that we have been there already. The mask of confidence I did wear coming here has shattered and now all I encompass is fear.

Footsteps are heard coming and like a steady signal, the friar warns me that they will be here soon. The difference between this meeting and the previous is that we will have Lady Capulet here joining us. As Juliet warned, she will heighten each emotion that Lord Capulet will feel. As long as we can keep them under a veil of composed thought, we may walk away from here achieving our one goal. I look forward to leaving this estate without any more darkness and blood placed on my soul. There is energy given off by others that can find its way to our souls. There is enough within me that adding further doses will overwhelm my state of mind and escort me to eternal darkness.

The door opens and Lord Capulet awaits and holds it open, allowing Lady Capulet to enter and follows her in as he closes the door behind him quite loud and quickly. We turn from admiring the paintings and walk over to them for our formal greeting.

"Hello friar. We are thankful and pleased to have you here," Lord Capulet says, as he shakes the friar's hand. "And who is this?" he asks as he looks over to me.

"This is Paul," the friar says. "He travels with me to learn from my experience and gain knowledge of our church. I shall think that if he lives long enough, he might one day be a friar himself."

"Pleasure to meet you both," I say as I bow my head to Lord and Lady Capulet in formal duty. They walk behind the desk, and as Lord Capulet seats himself, Lady Capulet stands to his side, placing an arm on his shoulder. The dynamic that Juliet has mentioned to us seems very much word for word, as Lady Capulet's demeanor shows that she is only to speak when spoken to, but the fire in her eyes appears ready to strike when Lord Capulet himself opens the gates of hell.

"Gentlemen, you will have to pardon me, as I will begin by saying that I do not have much time to speak with you both. There are family matters that call, and I must meet with others this very night immediately following our engagement. Though, friar, as we will always have a moment to speak with you, and our love for the church knows no bounds, I could not turn away a man of the church when he arrives at my door."

"We are thankful for your time, and honored you would see us so late in your day. We would have hoped to come sooner, but prayers for a recently fallen boy took much of my time from me." The friar pauses gently as he does not want to show any emotion yet, but he could not speak an untruth.

"Yes, good friar, you pray for Balthasar," Lord Capulet states. "I have heard of his sad fate, and I am glad that you offer such prayers for his soul. But what is it that brings you hither? I am not of his house and cannot provide you information for his burial."

"Lord Capulet, it is not his burial that brings me here. Even as he is the matter and reason of conversation, it does not touch upon his arrangements of death." The friar still speaks softly, hoping to maintain the calmness that still hangs in the air.

"Then, goodly friar, why is it that you have come to my home? The only reasoning that I could apply to your purpose is that you are here to ask if we are that bloodied hand that struck him down. Am I correct, good sir?"

I feel his rage slowly beginning to peak in his body. His face turns shades of red but he has not reached the description that Juliet has spoken to us of. Let us pray it does not get that far. The friar clears his throat to continue his words of compassion.

"My lord, that Balthasar was a goodly lad, I am most certain. Trouble in this world was never of his doing. Peace walked with him as he lived within Verona and offered such love to his family and dear friends. Yet, as all of Verona knows, your house and that of the Montagues have never seen peace stay constant. I prayed days ago for the loss of Gregory, as you were there by my side, and days before that for the loss of Abram, another of the house of Montague. There is much blood being spilled on the streets of Verona." The friar reaches for the core of this man's heart and sensibility. Lord, let him take hold and cradle the emotions to stay within his control.

"My love," Lady Capulet says to Lord Capulet, even as she maintains her glare on the friar. "The good friar looks to place blame on our heads for a tragedy that Verona has seen fall on her streets. Is that what you are here to do, friar? Blame the Capulets for murder?" Lady Capulet speaks, in her efforts to fuel the rage that continues to build in Lord Capulet's appearance, as his reddening face grows even brighter, and the inner corners of his brows begin to point down to the gates of hell.

"I do not accuse any household but that these murders are only happening between the two, I must speak with each and ask for peace, as the prince himself proclaimed. Even with the prince not in Verona, we must still follow his rule and speak of peace together." The friar's voice moves its tone and strings of desperation are sounded.

I stand over the right shoulder of the friar, watching as things unfold, and wondering if I myself will add words that can calm the brewing storm in Lord Capulet, as dark clouds form over his mind.

"I have followed the peace, spoken by the prince himself, and even watched my own man be buried," Lord Capulet says, as he shifts in his chair to hold himself more upright. "Two from the house of Montague fall, but not upon my orders. If you would desire to see what orders I can speak, and gather my revenge for my fallen man, then just you watch. That dirty pig, Montague, as we stand here and speak useless words to my innocent cause, is home himself preparing to strike upon me, as he believes that I may be to blame for another of his household leaving this world." His rage brings him to a point where he stands and points a steady and fierce finger at the friar.

"I would bet my life that Montague even now plans a strike upon one of us," Lady Capulet follows with, stirring his rage as if brewing a tempest. "The foolish frenzy within him does harm against all of Verona. Who will be next in our house? My Juliet, of all the most loving and pure beings, was struck down by a Montague. Never again will my husband allow another Capulet to be handed to the gates of heaven, by the cruel and unnatural hand of a Montague."

The friar raises both hands toward them, hoping to calm the rage that erupts from Lady Capulet in the form of tears and from the straining mouth of Lord Capulet in the intensity of his anger, as hearing of Juliet's demise once again looks to prevent reason from being heard.

"My dear Capulets, we cannot speak of our fallen children, our mirror images of love, and how their fate brought them to their ending. We know that love did exist, and still very much does, between Juliet and her Romeo."

The friar, unknowing of what he just did, has seemingly ended all hope we had to turn the war from what it is, into a peaceful celebration of balanced calm. Lord Capulet comes around from the desk, with Lady Capulet fast on his side, keeping each step with his.

"Do not speak that name within this house ever again, friar, so help me that I do not strike down a man of God! That name, of most vile and despised disgust, will not be spoken to mine ear. It was he that brought my dear Juliet to her end. And he, of the house of Montague, met his end most proper, yet I would have shown him the pain that he caused my wife and myself, for what he did much longer and stronger than what he suffered. He should be thanking the poison that he consumed for what it did, as I would have brought him to the devil myself and plunged his soul into the fires of hell and held him there under the charred skin on my hand to burn for eternity!" His voice and tone is so loud that the house probably stirs in anxious nervousness.

"Even hell alone was not punishment enough for what he has done to us!" Lady Capulet adds, to quicken the winds of rage even more and call upon the end times of this world.

I stand behind the friar still, but if I could secretly drink this poison now to end these waves of crashing rage, I would, as I am more terrified than I have ever in my life been.

"My lord, please," the friar says, but Lord Capulet will have none of it.

Lord Capulet raises a hand to the friar, to stop him from speaking, but if he were not a friar, I am not sure what he would have done to him at this point with that hand. He seems to center himself and bring his awareness to his mind's focus.

"I will take my leave of you," Lord Capulet states, "for if I were to spend any more time with you both, I cannot promise God that I would be a just man and not strike a man of his house. Away with you both, and be very well warned that if you accuse me of such things as murder and not have merit to that statement to back your words, then I will not hold myself off the next time. Yet, gentlemen, I thank you. It has never been more clear to me how all this struggle between my house and the house of Montague should end. Friar, prepare yourself to pray for more souls than you have ever seen fly to God's heaven. Make room beneath the church for bodies that will fall like the heavy rains. Choose your path from here, good friar, for what is about to be writ in Verona's history will be spoken in bloody stories until the end of time."

In full rage, he storms from the room, Lady Capulet hanging on to his arm as he leaves so that she will not be forgotten. The door closes hard, like the strongest of winds were testing its hinges. I fall to a knee and breathe as I have never before. My heart aches, as I place my hand over it to pray that my own touch will slow its beat. I look up and see the friar standing without motion, his face angling towards the floor. I can feel the disappointment he swims in, as we have not only failed in our mission, but very likely stirred the fires of hell, giving Lord Capulet more will to strike than ever before.

"Good friar, I may need of you to help me to my feet. I cannot stand on my own, as fear has me held to the ground." Moments pass, and the friar eventually turns, moving toward me slowly with what looks to be pain in every step. As I look up at him, there are tears in his eyes. He lightly reaches for my arm and shoulder and gently helps me to my feet. As I've known him for only a short while, I know that his stages of emotions are all new to me, but this sadness that I witness must be one so deep that he may never have felt as low as he does now.

"We have failed. Nay, I have failed. I could not ask of you to step in and speak reason to a man that cannot see reason. Juliet was correct to inform us of his rage, but that rage, though not present in him as we arrived, brews so deeply, and very likely has been warming to a rage within him since her loss. Let us leave and go back to the church. There is nothing more we can do. I shall pray to every angel for help, as I feel the war that is coming will spill over to the heavens and pits of hell. Come, no more words, gentle apothecary. Let's away."

He turns and opens the door, and slowly walks out. I follow steady behind him, but as we are both at a loss, drained of energy and desire, we move slowly. Looking to my right, deeper into the house as I exit the room, I see a portly woman standing as still as a mountain, staring at us. She has sadness in her face as well. Grief hangs in her so deeply that a face as sad as this is not one I will likely ever forget. There are faces from my past which shared such an image of grief that still remain locked in my memory. Moreover, she does not look like one of the family members of this house; so thus, by her dressing attire I would assume she must work with some of the youth as a nurse. She must have known Juliet, I would dare to say. Friar Laurence does not notice her as his face looks to the ground, leading his path by grains of sand and dirt. I offer her my eyes, but that is all that I have to give. Even a smile from my lips would be false and easily understood as being so. I nod to her and turn my attention back to the friar.

Chapter Six

The many passing moments of this exit from the house of Capulets to the front door of the church are a mystery to my present mind, as I stand there, outside the large church doors with the friar, and we prepare ourselves to go in. We both know what is upon us. We have failed our mission and must convey such words to Romeo and Juliet, who will soak the sadness like a sponge and fall upon grief that we ourselves outwardly live.

Calling upon the will of the bravest soldiers that walk into a battle with no weapons in hand, we enter the church. Within this first room, all seems quiet. The friar walks to the holy water and dips his hand into the small pool that hangs on a monument on the wall. He blesses himself and then looks to me to do the same. Not ready to cease following his brave lead, I walk over and repeat the process. I very much understand the weight and severity of walking into the church and speaking with the children. Their hope lay in our hands and we failed in our mission. Their hope centered on peace within their families to end the useless death. It may have also played a part in the hope that peace may end their time on this world, trapped within the walls of the church. Though even upon these thoughts, there may have been other reasons for them to see peace handed out like plates of food at a grand feast. To inform them of this will be quite hard. As with the visitations to the family houses, I will allow the friar to use his words, even if those words have not brought us the outcome we have hoped for.

Walking into the main part of the church, our first sight is that of Romeo, standing on the top of one of the benches in the aisle, as Juliet is seated two rows in front of him. As we walk in slowly, we do not disturb them, as they are in conversation, with Romeo in full voice and motion.

"I am not saying how, my love, but when. The how of the matter will work itself out in such a way that fate will fly her wings to us, and upon her softest touch, will grant us this freedom. Is it not her demand to have us here, now, within this church, and not in the presence of the devil himself for what we have done? It is known by all, that those who commit self-slaughter are delivered to the dungeons of hell to work the devil's bidding for eternity."

"My Romeo, you are a gentle and loving soul, with all your dreams in your hands ready to be lived. Have you not ever listened at church when the friar spoke of matters such as ours, when those that sin meet their death? You speak of travels that will not happen, as all we can prepare ourselves for is the judgment of God in the decision of where we will end up."

"But as that decision is yet to come, there may be a new judgment being prepared for us. When has love ever been felt so deep that it did not have the power to stop the movement of the sun and kill every rooster from its morning cry to awake the day? My love, when we are free from this imprisonment, I will show you the land where you have never been. Beyond our city walls are places even greater than ours, where beauty, still unable to compare to thee, will amaze you even still. I will compare you to flowers almost as sweet and beautiful; I will show you foods your heavenly lips would find more delight in than the air you breathe; and I will kiss you upon mountain tops and by ocean shores where every heavenly body will position themselves to make our moment as sweet as the first kiss ever shared. This is the love you and I will entertain when we are free."

"My mind pictures these images of delight, and I am even more excited being with you and loving you as I have. I will dream of these places and the joys within each, but only when I am under night's cloak and my eyes have closed, will I look to place them within my mind. For as they are beauteous dreams, they are just that—dreams. I cannot place them in my hopes, as the thought alone will drive me mad to wish them to come true every day, and if they do not, the disappointment will without question send my soul further and deeper into the sadness that we already encompass. If you want to speak of the love we can share, think of the resolution of our families' war and the lives spared, as this alone will bring us closer in love."

After she replies to his loving gesture, he climbs down and walks in her direction, seating himself next to her. These moments are wondrous to witness, as two beings such as they, in the forms of ghosts, can still reflect upon the love they embodied in the living world.

I am an apothecary and I am well trained and educated in the body and mind. Blood flows from our hearts and circulates to every point of our bodies, carrying rejuvenation to each cell. As this sustains life, our bodies live and create such things as thoughts and actions. What brings me to pause and wonder is that they no longer have blood flowing within them, and yet they still create these words to bring forth actions. This world beyond our own is such a mystery, where events such as this happen before our eyes and yet cannot be explained. In the last of my days upon this world, I may look to study all knowledge on such questions of the world beyond our own, but I may sooner learn by experience before I will by my studies. I am drawn back to them, as Romeo speaks once again, yet softer than before.

"Well, my fair Juliet, may your mind be at rest when I tell you that in this moment, where all that exists is within the breath we share, that all my love and thoughts fall upon your feet so that you may step each stride with nothing but love carrying you along. If you slip, my love will support you; if you fall, my love will catch you; if your feet grow weary and tired, my love will be the strength that brings you safe to home."

"My love, my Romeo, I imagine nothing more. But what if I dance or run or walk upon fire? Will not your love be hazy or crushed or burned?"

"My love wears a shield that cannot be harmed, as every moment in your light makes it stronger. The only fare that hardens my will is the most excellent kiss of your lips to mine own."

He nears her, as their eyes are locked, and carries his lips to hers in a slow and passionate movement. As they have never touched within my presence, I wonder if this throwing of words of love will end as it should? The closer he gets, the more uncomfortable I become. Is it natural to watch such an event, whether from the living or the dead?

"Good friar," I whisper, as I need to awaken us from this trance we seem to be in. "Is this right by God, as we watch such supernatural events?" His hand rises to quiet my speech, as he does not want us to be heard, but the motion of his arm does exactly what he hoped our voices would not, as Juliet looks over to us and acknowledges our presence.

"Hold off your words my love. The friar and apothecary have returned. Shall we greet them and know of their news?"

Juliet quickly rises first, and walks like the wind to us, as Romeo, slumping his head down in sadness that they did not kiss, rises as well and follows her. As they make quickly their way toward us, they are gazing into our eyes and reading every body motion that they can to see what news we bring. I cannot speak, as the news is not what will offer any joy to the private moment they just shared. To see such love, so deep and complete, and then to compare it to what we have experienced at their households this same day, is just as it is, night and day.

"Gentlemen, your peace is not comforting. Not only are your stares as blank as unmarked parchment, but your eyes, the windows to your minds and souls, are as empty of love as our frames are empty of blood," Juliet says, as she loses her own joyous expression the longer we take to acknowledge.

"Juliet, I do not believe they need words to tell you what has transpired. There will be no peace. Our families cannot reason, and with that, blood will fall and we shall remain here until heaven is done with us and opens the ground to welcome us to our new home." Romeo says his peace and walks away toward the altar, looking up to God and then down below as he walks.

"Is this true? Have our families closed the door on peace, even from the request of a friar?" Juliet asks, as the wonder at the thought erupts sadness in her eyes.

"My dearest daughter, it is true." The friar keeps his words short. He is wise to not say more.

"Who was it that you spoke with at my house? Did you not speak with my father and my mother? Did they not gather reason? Is my death so soon forgot that they take up the sword in coldly distant memories?" Juliet embodies fear and disillusionment that her own family cannot elect the choice of peace, especially after her death.

"My sweet, it is so. The rage of your father was far greater than the love that may still exist in his heart, and yet that love may even fuel the fires of that rage. With as much mercy as the kindest angel, we did plead with him to end the hate and think of purely love. He would have none of it. All he could feel was revenge for the death that has fallen in your house thus far." The friar ends his words, but it does not satisfy Juliet. She looks to me for more answers, but I am not sure I will have more to offer.

"The friar is most correct," I say. "Your father's rage and your mother's dissatisfaction were hand in hand, as if they both would strike upon a fallen foe. There may have been sadness, but not in their eyes whilst we were there. I only witnessed such sadness when we were leaving, upon a woman who wore her grief all about her. She did not seem as if she were a member of your family, so I did not approach her to speak with her."

"Good apothecary, this woman you speak of that wore grief like a veil, was she of a more fuller size and less your age by some few years?" Juliet asks, as her energy seems to be regaining its wind of her.

"Why yes, this does seem to sound like the woman I saw. Know you this woman?" I ask, to see if there is something of her that may enlighten my experience with her.

"Why yes, most assured, I know her as comparably as you know your own mother. She was my nurse. She raised me from birth and cared for me like no other in my house. She still dwells in grief it seems, which saddens me as well. But this may be the power that will reawaken the cause. Romeo, return once more to us. My thoughts bring an idea that will need your mind." Juliet's eyes are full and wide. There is matter in them that would talk an army of men into diving off a cliff into rough waters to save a wounded fish.

"I have returned, so that I may offer you my mind my love, but the wit that I have will not budge my father or yours from their hatred of a name and its history." Romeo seems weary and returns only to satisfy her wishes. He is wise in this, as love will make a man do things that he cares not to do. Of course, these are actions that I can only speak to from sight and not by experience.

"My nurse did live for my joy and grieves now at my loss. I am saddened to hear this, but of all people who will act upon my name, it will be she," Juliet says, as she looks to form the ideas in her mind. "Good friar, you must return to my family house and speak with the nurse. Convince her to come here to the church, and when we have her here, I will give you words so personal from past events, that she will know that I am within these walls and trapped from leaving this world. There would be no other desire from her than to help us."

"Juliet, I am a friar and carry the word of God on this earth, but if I return to your family home, I will be sent up to God's side. I am not prepared to end my life just yet, as much as I do love thee."

"I understand," she says, but just as quickly, her light returns. "Then, to the market tomorrow you must find yourselves. The nurse goes every day to the market for supplies for the house. My mother instructs her to buy items of beauty that will keep her youth upon her skin. When she is there, you can approach her and ask of her to come. She will not deny a holy man."

"This can work. It is wise. I believe we can achieve such a thing," the friar says with moments of hope. The friar looks to me and I nod at him, agreeing that this may very well be a good plan. The nurse had more love in the one glance I had of her, than the entire house did otherwise.

"Juliet, the nurse did love thee, almost as deep as my love is for you. Yet, her actions alone will not be enough to persuade my father to lay down his sword. As like your father, mine has a will to obey only to history, and no one person from the enemy of my family can speak to him and change his mind." Romeo adds insight to reason that may not have carried with Juliet's thought.

"Then, my love, you will do the same as I," Juliet says, as once again her eyes open wide with thoughts in motion in her mind that would move the moon.

"Juliet, the nurse will not listen to words spoken from my mind, as I am the one who brought you to this fate. Let her support our love as we lived, but I can only imagine that she carries a hate for me in death," Romeo says, losing some power of wind.

"My silly love, bring your mind to mine. You will entreat one from your house to do the same. Someone that did love you as deep as the nurse did love me. Surely there must be one who you called upon to support you through all of your actions while you lived." Juliet, as wise as one twice her age, brings forth an idea once again that will shake the heavens.

"There was one, but he is dead. Even as Mercutio was not of my blood, he was a man I trusted with every part of me. Yet, as I understand what it is you speak, and look to my living family with a piece of your mind in mine, there is one, Benvolio, who will help in this matter. He did love me as deep as any other, and one word of purpose to bring into motion a desire of my own will fill his intentions with God's saving grace. Friar, if you care not to go to my house to speak with him, then I can tell you straight where he will be. There may not be as strong a motion than from the hand of our fathers to end this war, but that they will have a voice to them, this will be better than no voice at all."

"Then it shall be. We will speak more on this tonight, but for now, let us settle our spirits and welcome the night with a meal. Good apothecary, if you would like to retire to your room, I will have one of the nuns inform you when dinner is ready," the friar says with a powerful grin, as hope looks to brew within him once again.

"Thank you, good friar. That would be wonderful. My old legs do call for some rest. Romeo, Juliet, I pray that these ideas will give us new life to ending this war and sparing just that—life." With my brief words, I retire from their side and walk to my room. My body has seen more passion and hate in one day than I have ever experienced in my many years. I surely hope we will entreat these others to join our cause and help to end the war and complete this lifelong bloodshed. I feel the good graces of God on our side once again. If God did not want us to achieve the set-on goal, then these ideas would never have come about.

Entering my room, I sit on the bed and rest every muscle that needs a breath. Verona is a city that I could not have lived in, if this is what life here would be like. My mind could not hold all this confusion and allow me to perform my job as an apothecary. How any one person survives, both in body and profession, I will never know. Leave out the constant bloodshed in the streets by its own citizens, and a prince that holds a very tight rule, this city is still too much for me.

Enough of this thought. Now to a brief rest, in hopes I may gather some strength as dinner will surely remove all possible energy I have left of engaging in thought and speech this night. Tomorrow will be a battle of my own, as I will look to convince a nurse and another that the ghosts of their loved ones are here and ask of them to take on an ocean of trouble.

Mantua may be a quiet place, but at least I could lay my head down peacefully.

<u>Chapter Seven</u>

A knock at the door wakes me, and brings my heart to a quickened beat that reminds me that I am still alive. Has the day come? I pray that it has and this is not another nightly notification of another death.

"You may enter," I state, as the person behind the door has yet to announce himself or herself.

"Gentle apothecary, I bid you good morning on this newly risen day," the friar says, as he enters slowly. "The sun has shown its face in the east and our spirits must ascend as well and carry us upon the day as steady as our God-given bodies are able. If it pleases you, take your time rousing from your dream world. I will myself work on completing a few more necessities before we are off. Shall we say, within this half hour, at the front of the church, we shall meet?"

"Yes, that shall be more than enough time for me to rouse my spirits and gather my mind. I thank you for waking me, and I am even more thankful that it is within the morning of the risen sun and not well before."

"As am I, good friend; as am I," he says with a smile. He backs his way out, closes the door and I seat myself in the bed so that I do not fall back asleep. O' how many times I have awoken, stayed in bed, lying there peacefully, as I had when sleeping, and fallen back into the story of my dream only to reawake hours later with the day well started. It is far wiser to rest with my feet on the ground, so my body knows that sleep is over and the new day needs to commence.

Rising out of bed I move myself slowly, feeling the pains of my back and legs from such a long day. If today brings such events as the happenings of last evening, then I am not sure I shall endure one more day in this loving world. My aging heart barely survives the waking of my day, and I cannot imagine experiencing more hatred as I have already. I must prepare my soul and my body for all that may come about on this fresh day.

Leaving my room, I walk through the church halls, and do not catch a sight or sound of Romeo or Juliet. The friar must be preparing himself as well, as peace hangs like a fog in the morning fields. It is welcoming and comforting to be in the church when no one is in here. Sunday is almost come, and I know the friar will have his duties full in hand when his followers gather to be forgiven of their sins and show him how loyal to God they have been. Is it not strange that it is those that sin the most that enter these doors more regularly? My thoughts inform me that they must come this often to repent for what they have done, but is it not their job as well to learn from their sins to become a better person, a more devout and focused catholic? This may be high hope in this changing world, but I imagine there is no other correct process to make it to heaven than to be a good catholic.

Entering the main part of the church, I kneel on the steps at the altar, facing the large cross on the back wall, and bow my head. I have never been the best follower of the church, but I am not one that allows sin to get the best of me either. Regardless, my thoughts still bend toward prayer when my soul calls for it and in this situation, there is a screaming town crier making the announcement.

Motioning the sign of the cross on my body, I stand and walk to the front door, still wonderfully drenched in the silence. I marvel that my prayers are heard more clearly when it is this quiet in these walls.

As I walk out the front door, I feel the sun in the sky and welcome the beauty that it brings on a new day. The wind offers a light and gentle passing, making a pleasant, cooling sensation as I stand here absorbing nature's love.

Turning to look back at the structure of the church, I see Christian on the ground, several lengths farther away from where he was last. His gaze focuses on the ground in front of him. He does not move nor acknowledge my presence. I walk to and stand before him, silent, but hoping that my being there allows his lips to speak from his inspired place and pronounce more of his riddling words. I did not understand what he spoke our previous meeting, but I am of no other mind than to hear his voice enunciate. I wait, but he does not speak, nor look up to me.

"Hello there, Christian. It is I, the apothecary. Do you remember me, sir? You spoke words to me that I did not understand, but as I am prepared this time around, please open your lips again to share your wisdom." Not a sound comes from him nor a movement. I see his chest rise and fall upon each breath, so I am sure he is alive. The longer I stand, the more foolish I feel. Were his words just thoughts in my head, sounding from a voice I would have expected to come from him? If this be the case, then madness must be settling into my soul. I turn and face the world, and walk away several steps so that I do not concern this unfortunate to think I am looking to harm him. The friar should be here soon. To the market we will go and…

"Now old desire doth in his deathbed lie, and young affection gapes to be his heir. That fair for which love groaned for and would die…"

I turn in shock, as once again I hear the voice come from him. His head is up, and his face glares at me, firm and steady in sight. His lips slow their movement, as words are now complete. Again, and quickly too, his head lowers and he stares at the ground, the same way that I found him moments ago. Where are these words coming from, that erupt from his mouth and mind and then, like the end moment of the parting of the Red Sea, the waters come crashing and return to their natural state and he returns to his motionless silence?

"Good sir, speak again. I do not well understand your words, and cannot assist you with their purpose unless I am well informed. Speak once more. Offer me the meaning. I bid you, speak!"

Turning quickly again, I hear the church door open and the friar now stands outside, looking at me as if I have gone mad.

"Good apothecary, I have mentioned to you that this man does not speak. I pray you, leave him be."

"Friar, he very well speaks, but of a riddling nature. Upon my oath to God, this man has said such trivial words but none I can remember and none do I understand. I pray you, speak with him."

"My good son, he has never spoken, and in the many times that I have tried, I have never walked away with a result that had pleased my soul, as I no longer offer the time to test him in hopes that he will speak with me. Now come, shall we to our purpose? I will want to get within the good graces of the nurse and then look to come across Romeo's man as well."

"Yes, good friar. Let us go." I turn to walk toward him, but before my legs move, I take my last, deep glance at Christian, hoping he will speak once more and show the friar that I am not going mad. Nothing comes about from him, bringing me to walk away, and in pace with the friar as we make our way to the market.

I am dumbfounded by this situation, where I have now heard this man speak twice, and yet he will not utter one word before the presence of the friar. What is this choice he makes, to test my will and only speak his trivial words to me? I must write down the next thing he says to me so that I can document his words and inform the friar of what he is saying.

"My son, we are not so far away from the market as you would think, so ready yourself for this meeting with Juliet's nurse. I have spoken with Juliet this morning, and she instructed me as to the demeanor of her nurse. She is said to be wise, but more tough in will than removing a soul from hell to bring up to heaven. She will challenge us well and even cry out in madness if she feels threatened by our advance. She did love Juliet deeply, that I am sure, through my own knowing of her and her attendance at the church. Yet, I never knew the woman well enough, nor tried to move her and her will like we will attempt to do. I shall admit, there is a bit of fear in me, as actions of death are easier to accept by a man wielding a sword than the damage this woman has been said to administer to those she brews anger against. We will speak Juliet's name, which will touch upon her softest spots, but also conjure the rested lion into action to support our cause."

"Good friar, your words are sure to prepare me, but they also tempt me to run for my life upon meeting this woman and seeing her anger brew like a tempest. I will stand behind you and allow you to speak your peace. I am sure she will remember us, from our visitation yester-night, so we must also be prepared for her memory of that evening, but also the anger that she will remember the Lord Capulet expressing toward us as well."

"He did convey such anger that the entire household must have felt the foundation shake. I am sure that an event such as this, heard by all in the world without a doubt, would have locked the memory of our visitation in her memory as well."

"Good friar, she was there, and close enough to that room that I am certain every word must have been heard. I saw her myself as we were leaving, standing at the end of the hall. Unless her ears do not work or understand our language, she knows of our plight to end the war."

"Then glorious apothecary, be prepared to speak your words of memory to her if the situation calls upon it. If she begins to channel the same anger as the lord of the house, be also prepared to leave our entreaty and move on to other endeavors, of which I will inform you after this meeting. Look ahead, my good sir, as we have arrived at the grand market."

Once more, I have walked distracted from the church, while listening to the friar's words, lost within our conversation, and cannot speak to how we arrived at where we have just ended our march. Yet, for where we have arrived, there is no other place in Verona that I would ever care more to go.

The market is as grand as any open square I have ever seen. It is as if we turned a corner from the quiet and dark streets into paradise itself, the true and present Garden of Eden. All sorts of provisions border the large area, with endless tables and stands within rows, scattered throughout the middle. Comparably so, there are even more people in this one square than I have seen in all of Mantua. There must be hundreds of citizens gathered here. Yet, I would not doubt, by the offering that must be present that other surrounding cities come to trade and buy their goods at this affair.

"By God, friar, this is the largest market I have ever seen," I say, as I stop for a moment to take it all in.

"Yes, my dear son, it is the largest anywhere. Verona is known for their trade and commerce. If you believe this to be the busy time, then do not be here when the sun is resting high in the middle of the sky, as you will be carried through the market without even knowing you were moving. But come, we must make our way in and visit this certain meat dealer as this is where we are to cross the path of the nurse. She will not be there for long and will most definitely not give us her ear in the middle of her business. We must catch her the moment she finishes her purchase."

"I am with you, good sir. Lead the way." I will look to stay with the friar as tight as I can. If I lose him, then I will be lost and prevent the proper execution of this mission. He knows where it is that we need to end up, and even as others will try and get in my way, I will need to be as cunning as a man my age can be. Though, if I happen to rudely hit someone in the name of accident, my age may allow me to bow my head in apology and continue without meeting my end by their sword.

Though, as aware as I try and remain, to the path of the friar, I cannot ignore what I see around me. The vibrant colors of the fruits are much brighter in Verona. Where do they grow these pieces of decadent pleasure that make them as colorful and large as this? Even more brilliant are the fish that hang from the hooks. From what ocean are such fish bred that they are each a meal for a family or two? Amazement and wonders such as these continue to show me that I have not lived as full a life as I should have. I have been fortunate, but I have clearly lived my private life as enclosed in a dungeon as a criminal locked away for the most violent of crimes. To be known for my work, I sacrificed all else. Now, my window of life begins to close and this final breeze of Verona air awakens my senses to renew my eyes of what this life could have held.

"It is just there. Keep your eyes open for the nurse. We must not miss her," the friar says, as we stand to the left of the plaza, facing a table covered in meats. Even these meats look as if the mighty animal that gave its life were as massive as two I have known.

Nevertheless, I watch for the nurse and instantly notice her as she walks away from us, as if to leave the market.

"Good friar, she is there, leaving. We must hurry," I say, as I point to her and allow him to go ahead, as his speed is far greater than mine, and even if I were to start ahead of him, he would pass me in very few strides.

"Good nurse! Good nurse, please stop!" he yells, seeing that the noise will not alarm anyone, as it combines with all the other noises from the great mass of people gathered. She turns, as I notice, and sees the friar approaching her. It is good that he is a friar, as for any other, a person may not wait for someone who screams out to them as we do. Her stance is unyielding, and she does not show any concern or fear that we arrive at her feet, slightly out of breath, but with urgency that she herself does not express.

"Good nurse, a word with you, please," the friar says. She nods her head and stands still. "Let us move to a more private place, if you please." As he says this, another man walks up from behind her and stands tall and strong. His appearance makes me believe that he is her protection, or personal servant who carries the market items back to the house.

"Peter, make your way back to our residence; the meats need to be brought to the cook. I will follow you shortly. The friar would like a word with me," she says, as she looks at him and then turns back to us in one swing of her body.

"Are you sure you will be safe? I am as good as any man with a sword and can protect you as good as an officer of Verona," Peter says, as he places a hand on his sword but does not remove it from its sheath.

"Yes, yes, go to. This is the friar of our church that wishes to speak with me. I need no protection from a man of God, unless it be my ears that need it. Farewell. I will call upon you when I am home," she says, as she waves at him to leave. Making no word or expression, he turns and walks away.

"Now, good friar, what is it that you would like to speak with me about? I am listening, and can offer you time, but my day has many more chores ahead of it that will soon take importance over words."

"Yes, good nurse, I will not keep you. I am unsure on how to begin this, but you must make yourself present to the church as soon as your ability and time allow," the friar says, and I nod to support his statement to her as it is most dearly important that she come to the church.

"Good friar, I am not prepared to offer my prayer at the church as of yet. My heart still grieves, and the church does not at this moment have the healing powers to take away the pain that may very well live there for the remaining days of my life. God is great and mighty, but so is the depth of my sorrow."

"Good nurse, by the heavens, it is not prayer that calls for you to come to the church. I know you are a goodly child of God and follow his word no matter where you are. There are other matters there that are in need of you to come. They are the most important in nature and desire, of both topic and person for you," he says, as his request becomes more urgent and she senses this about him through the motions of his arms and eyes, and the way his body hangs in the air.

"There are no matters of subject concerning the church, nor person either, that would need me to come to the place of worship so urgently." She is strong in her stance and I feel we may lose her if we do not give her the speed of our message. I cannot hold back and allow us to lose another person.

"It is the fair Juliet," I say, as I interrupt them and make our cause known.

"I am not sure who it is that you are, old man, but do not ever speak that name in my presence again. If you knew the weight of such a name to my life, you will use your judgments wisely and leave before my fury matches that of Lord Capulet. His rage, I know, still hangs in the air, as you discovered yourself."

"Good nurse, as I am a man of God, I cannot lie. All my words are of truth and nothing more. The apothecary may have spoken too harshly, and for that I apologize, but he speaks the truth. Calm your rage and give us an open ear and open mind. There are matters beyond your understanding and by the hand of God himself that will much amaze you." As he takes a breath, I can see the slight fear in his eyes as he prepares to say what many would never speak and have other believe they are sane. "Juliet's spirit walks the church, and as spirits walk the earth for a reason, there is a message we look to deliver. If you come to the church, you will with any luck witness what it is that we have ourselves experienced."

"Juliet's spirit walks the church? In my many years, I have never heard a friar speak such words that would make me question his position in the church. I will report this to the prince when he returns," she says. I feel that I may have brought the end sooner than it should have come. Why did I act so foolishly and open my mouth?

"Good nurse, as Juliet herself knew you would be like a stone atop a mountain, impossible to move, I can prove to you she sent us," the friar says. "Did you not claim to her that you were out of breath when returning to her with the news of Romeo's desire to marry her some weeks ago? Did you not complain of aches and pains from your body, both head and back, from 'jauncing up and down' to fulfill her wishes? And even as you spoke to her to, henceforward, carry her messages herself and finally report that a husband waits for her at my cell? Then, did you not also speak with her of marrying the good Paris, after hearing of Romeo's banishment? Did you not call Romeo a dishclout, to compare him to Paris, as he lacks so green, so quick, so fair an eye as Paris? Do these words not bring such a private conversation fresh to your mind? Do you not recall such words spoken by you just weeks ago?" She stands in complete surprise from his spoken words.

"My good God above, how is it that you know such words shared only between she and I?" she says, as her amazement now has her seeking more.

"From her mouth itself, as I have spoken to you. I do not deceive you, good nurse. Come to the church, tomorrow morning, after the sun is freshly in the sky. Say to your lord that you are prepared to pray and seek leave to speak with God, and I warrant you, you will speak of much more than Him after you enter my doors."

Her eyes are wide and her expressions are of fear and worry. I believe we have given her such words that there is not other reason needed. Even if she does not confirm her belief,

I can tell that she has more wonder about her, that not appearing at the church will empty her soul faster than the proof of any false statements.

"O' me, my dear Juliet. Her spirit returns to the church? What matter so great forces her pure soul to return to this world? Is she well? Does her soul have marks that torture her mind? I must speak with her. Answer me!"

"Good nurse, please, hold yourself strong and come to the church tomorrow. Speaking with her directly, I cannot guarantee you may be achieved of doing, as none other than myself and the apothecary here, have seen her or spoken with her," he says, as he gestures to me.

"It is true, gentle nurse. I have spoken with her as well," I say, to agree upon the friar's statements. "She asks for you and no other. But even as I have seen her ghostly image, with the friar here, I have seen others walk into the room, as we stood in conversation with her, and not even know that she was there. It did much amaze me." After sharing my experience, she has a look in her eye that is so alive I doubt she will sleep tonight.

"My poor soul, how I have grieved for her. I will come tomorrow, but please be aware, that if this is any sort of trick, both your souls will report my manner to God himself and offer my apology to Him for taking your souls as justified as I will be. I will walk with the devil himself to keep her goodly name as dear as I hold it." She finishes her warning to us and then turns and leaves in complete distraction. I do not doubt she has the power to send our souls anywhere and anytime she sees fit. I am most happy that I can speak of Juliet's existence, being that I have seen and spoken with her myself. I would be much afraid if these were just the words of the friar and not my own as well.

"Well, good apothecary, it looks as if luck has found its way to our side. Finally there is a glimpse of light that will bring us one step closer to our desired resolution. But now to the other. Benvolio will not be as easy to persuade. Yet, like the history of conversation I was able to offer to show the nurse that Juliet sent for her, so do I have words from Romeo to do the same."

"Now I see where you went this morning after waking me. Very wise, friar. Very wise indeed." He smiles and nods to me, which is his humble thank you that I have grown to understand. With this turn of events, as the nurse will now appear tomorrow, I feel even more sure that we will be able to speak with Romeo's man, Benvolio, and bring him to do the same.

"Shall we walk, for even as we have sparing time, we might as well make our way there and speak with him. But first, let us visit this fruit stand here. You will love what amazement they offer," the friar says.

I am prepared for such a meal, as energy will be needed to make it on and try to speak with another who will surely show the same such emotion for the matter we will talk of. But also, I cannot wait to try some of these fruits.

As I bite into an apple that must have come from a tree in the Garden of Eden, I realize that I have no idea where it is that we go next. The wonder alone is exciting, yet there is only so much wonder I can withstand in my heart and nerves at any one time.

"Goodly friar, this is the most amazing of fruit I have ever had. Where does such fruit grow? Mantua has never seen such growth and beauty as this."

"Yes, these are fruits that are more rare than one would know. I have traveled much in my years as a friar on my early spiritual endeavors and through all of the regions of this land; Verona has some of the sweetest fruit that has ever been tasted. Outside the city walls, there is a valley that protects the trees that grow such fruits. The rains are most abundant, offering nourishment for growth. It has been intricately designed by God himself I would imagine."

"This does sound like a place I would desire to travel to one day. In that notion of travel, where is it that we go next?" I ask, as I would prefer to stay here and eat all day, but such a wish cannot happen.

"You are the most appropriate time keeper, my friend. Shall we go, as the walk there will be brief, but it is not a place where I would prefer to go."

Taking in the market one last time, in all the glorious bounty that it provides, I turn and follow the friar out of the square and we head back to the narrow streets that hide this small heaven on earth.

"Friar, we have been many places since I have been in Verona, and I greatly feel that you have been many places before I arrived here, so where is it that you would prefer not to go?" I ask, as such a place, which brings the thought of the house of Capulet to my mind, must have a special reason to keep the friar away.

"This is a thing that you must keep under your breath from this point on. You must not utter a word of it after it is all done. If you knew of the history you would understand as well, but since this is new for you, please trust me."

"My good friar, without another word spoken about it, you can trust me to never repeat what we are about to see and do. My mind, as much as it has been a vault of memory, loses most memories just as quickly in my age."

"I understand that well, but make sure that you do not forget to remember to not say a word of this. We go to a house where Benvolio spends much of his time grieving for the loss of Romeo and now two other deceased friends since then, I would sadly assume. Benvolio and Romeo were cousins, but they were even closer than most brothers. They shared all things, but this is not one I thought I could imagine. And with that, not even Romeo knows where we go and must never know."

"I promise you, good friar. He, nor anyone else, shall ever know we go where it is that we walk now, by way of my lips. Then thus, where is it that we go?"

"We go to Rosaline's."

Chapter Eight

"Rosaline? Who is this Rosaline? I have not heard a word of her spoken to any as of yet," I ask the friar, as there are more names than I can remember, but this is not one that I can summon up into my memory.

"Rosaline was a great love of Romeo's, but a love that never returned a strike of affection to him. He loved her most dearly; well, it may not have been love, more of a lust, yet their union never occurred. Even still, he yearned for her for many a days. It was only until he met Juliet that the strings of his heart were truly played and the word of love appropriately settled into the chamber of the mighty organ. The name of Rosaline was soon forgot."

"I see, I see. Two men cannot love one woman within their lifetime if they are connected in any way," I say, in recognition of stories I have heard in my years. "Jealousy is a true emotion that trifles with love and makes such moments more painful and lost. I have seen this and watched as men fought in Mantua for this same jealousy. It is sad to see men fall so low."

"I follow you in your words, and agree to the depth of the meaning. Yet, even as Romeo has found his love, as short and brief as it was in life, but continuing in death, such experiences now may tarnish the pure friendship and kinship in memory these men have for each other. Heaven knows if they will meet in this afterlife, but let it not be by our words that cause their love to fall apart." The friar is wise to keep a watchful eye on the feelings and souls of all that tread within his world.

"Ever so true and wise, friar." Even as I do not grasp a full understanding of the friar's mind and can only hope to know how it works, he has much knowledge in the ways of people and love. His many years as a friar must have taught him thus. The more I spend time with him, the more I understand and trust him. I know I will learn much from him, even with the little time I have remaining on this world. There is always something to learn that one can carry with them in this life and quite possibly the next.

"We are almost at her family's house. Just as before, we will entreat him to come to the church tomorrow morning, same as the nurse, and together we will bring them to our cause and mark them as the soldiers of our battle. Romeo has armed me, as Juliet did with the nurse, with words so touching to his heart that if he does not mark us upon initial request, these words will bend him to be the peacekeeper we desire him to be."

"Once again, friar, you show your years of knowledge that ten men would be envious for. I trust in your plan and support you to the edge of all reason." Showing him this support, I hope, will further the trust between us and open him to being more comfortable with my companionship. There cannot be doubt, whether in my mind or his, for what we are attempting to do. Strength of resolve is most important. I may be weak in ability but strong enough in mind that these old workings of joints shall find energy anew.

The friar walks up to a house, on a street like every other, where the houses are side by side with no space in between to show much semblance that they are separate estates. There is more space of land in Mantua and, with such a gift as that, the houses have breath between them. Yet, as Verona is much more beautiful and offers more desire to reside within, it is here that people choose to live and thus, the houses are one upon the other, with not much space across from them as well in these narrow streets. It is only the rich, that of the prince, the Capulets, and Montagues, that live as they do in this city.

Standing before the door, he looks at me, grins, offering the customary nod, and turns to knock. I am thankful there are no guards or gates here, as the more we came upon them, the more were they that disliked our presence and likely had thoughts to end our lives for sport. This visit upon an unguarded door, where someone of the house will answer, will be most welcoming.

As the door opens, an attending maid to the house answers, a similar age to Juliet's nurse, but a softer face that does not look to grab my soul in hand and maneuver it to verify my truth. She could move me with her breath alone.

"Good madam, greatest of apologies to disturb you on this fine day, but I am looking for Benvolio." The friar is soft and honest in his request, with no trickery of words or desires. These are not people who look to deceive others for personal gain. These are the citizens of Verona, those that live to be happy. I may assume much in this, but through the brief appearance of the inner workings and the demeanor of this maid, it is all too easy to understand.

"Good friar, as it is you that calls upon him, I am not going to turn you away, as I have others. He does not wish to be seen in these doors, as his grieving has been much still, for the loss of his cousin."

"Good woman, I understand his loss to the center of my core and would be happy to offer words of support and passion." The friar keeps his firm and welcoming tone, allowing him to be greeted by a smile.

"Please you, come this way. I will call for him and my mistress. They have spent much time together and meeting with you may be a welcome reprieve."

The maid walks us in and directs us to the room on the right as soon as we enter. This must be how houses in Verona are designed so that when guests arrive, they are escorted into comfort in the same direction each time. This marks another difference between Verona and Mantua. In Mantua, one escorts their guests to the room that looks its best at that moment in time.

Walking into this room, their study and resting place, I feel more at home with the comfortable appearance of this space. There are two very welcoming couches spaced apart from each other, with a small table separating them in the middle of the room. To the corners are a couple of small tables with various decorative vases upon them that look to have been family pieces handed down from many generations of their elders. We seat ourselves on the couch to the left, as I still move my head around, taking in the portraits of people that are likely former residents of the house. There are maybe four or five paintings but I do not place much attention to them, as I desire to hear the friar's plans well before we meet our man.

"Goodly friar, you said to me you have words to speak with Benvolio that will awaken his mind and allow for him to join in our mission of ending the war. My concern rests with the fair mistress, Rosaline, in that she may join him as he meets with us. Will you still speak of Romeo's ghost with her in the same room? Will she be allowed to know our secret?"

"You are wise to ask but even more wise to think of such a situation. I did not think of it myself until we entered this room. I believe I have a way of saying what is needed without informing her of who is at the church. If she were to find out, I am not sure there would be much to concern us, other than that she may believe that I am mad."

"We, my good friar. She may believe that 'we' are mad. I will not leave you to speak of our truth and not offer you full support. I guess that we shall be even more strict in our words and hope to speak our minds without using the words from our hearts."

At the same moment I finish my words, in walk Benvolio and Rosaline, hand in hand, and in the same manner as those customary in Verona, where he holds the door open with his free hand, allowing her entrance into the room first. They gently seat themselves across from us on the other couch.

Side by side they sit, bodies next to each other as if connected, and hands still joining each other's, intertwined like vines wrapped around a tree, as their union of fingers rest upon his knee. They seem very content to be together, as their warmth appears very natural. Their bodies seem very much at rest. They glance into each other's eyes and a smile erupts from their mouths, as if they held a secret that the world now knows. It is a warm smile, one that looks to recapture images of the recent past that affirm a moment of love, whether it be physical or emotional, that they shared.

"Benvolio, I am thankful for you taking time from your day to meet with us. We will not waste too much of your time from this early afternoon with our presence," the friar says, in full smile, with a warm heart.

"Good friar, I am always happy to see you. I am sorry that I have not attended Sunday mass these last several weeks. Even as my soul speaks to God on a regular schedule, I cannot attend his house at this moment of my life. My soul is just not prepared. But may I ask," bringing his attention to me, "who are you, gentle sir?"

"Oh, yes, my apologies. I am Paul," I say, now playing the part without waiting for the friar to speak on my behalf.

"Yes, this is Paul. My apologies as well. I have allowed his company to be so common in my day that I had forgot that you might not have met him as of yet. He is assisting me and learning from my teachings in hopes that one day he will learn the ways of a friar."

"Pleasure to meet you, Paul," Benvolio says. "Learning the ways of a friar at such an old age does not offer you much time to practice the art, once you have achieved it. I do not mean any disrespect with this; it is just an observation."

"I am not offended. It is, well, my calling, shall I say, to know of their purpose and reasoning." I say this and then look to the friar, as the attention toward me has made me very uneasy. I should be stronger with my words but my nerves are so worn, that the once clever terms I believe I once possessed may still be in the dungeon of my mind.

"Mistress Rosaline, pleasure to see you as well," the friar says, to not offend her by not addressing her directly up to this moment within her family home.

"Good friar, it is nice to see you as well. You are always welcome to my family house. And as you, gentle sir, are assisting and learning the ways of a friar, you are also always welcome."

"I thank you," I say, to keep my words brief so that we may get to the matter.

I know that my mind is hungry for this to be over and to get this lad and the nurse to the church tomorrow. The sooner this issue comes to a close, the sooner peace will fall instead of bodies, and the souls of Romeo and Juliet shall be free to move on from this world, and maybe even comfortably still, my own.

"Benvolio, as you have stated that you have not been to the church for some while, which I will admit has come of notice, I would like to invite you to come tomorrow, early as the sun does rise, to meet with me and discuss some things."

"Good friar, what things need to be discussed? I have found a new start to life and much comfort in the arms of this house," he says, as he looks back at Rosaline and shares an intimate stare, eye to eye, that shows she agrees with this statement. "Rosaline has been my savior from eternal grief and comforted my soul greater than any force of nature could have predestined. She has welcomed me with much respect and opened her arms and her heart to mine, healing my weakened state."

He says all these words while holding a steady gaze into her eyes. She smiles and appears to want to kiss him, but that the friar is in their presence, this prevents their lips embrace. They are much more committed to each other than I would have imagined. When two people are joined together in such times of grief, there is an instant flicker that brings their emotions to the edge of their skin. Yet, after a very short while, the flicker no longer shows as the candle burns out and the reason of their union finds no more purpose than the apple fields after the picking season has ended. In this union, it seems they have found more to focus on and continue their love.

"I am happy to see that love has fallen into your arms and greets you well," the friar states, reassuring them that they are joined with right. "All my children deserve to have love be within their lives and hearts. Yet, even as you have found such reprieve from your grief, I would still desire to have you come to visit me." The friar is more direct, and it appears that

Benvolio is continuing to put up a wall toward visiting the church. His body is drawn to Rosaline, and the attraction holds his attention the same. Why is it that people fear a calling to church when the friars themselves ask? Do they think God will be there, waiting to judge their souls?

"I thank you, good friar," Benvolio says, glancing back at him. "I will find time and love to do so, but I am not in the place of mind or heart to do so this soon. As I go to my father's this evening for dinner to discuss other family matters, there will be good cause and reason for me to not use more words than what will be shared with him after such an event. I require days of solace to rejuvenate my soul."

"My goodly son, I do not look to add words that would cause infection within your eye, where the rank poison of old things would die," he says, as he makes facial gestures with the raising of his eyebrows to Benvolio. Rosaline focuses all attention at Benvolio with an eye that will not leave his face. This is most in tune with his desires, as I can feel that he speaks the words given by Romeo. "Come to me for a goodly feast; I shall compare one face with others that I will show you where I can make a swan appear as a crow," he says, and again, using facial gestures toward Benvolio that seem to confuse Benvolio, to make his own awkward shows of confusion.

But then it happens, and the words used by the friar bring recognition that makes Benvolio's eyes open wide, as does the full moon at the peak of its cycle. Rosaline, lowering her glance, focusing on their joined hands, does not see this show of amazement. He looks to her and then back to the friar, eyes filled with urgency.

"Friar, these words seem…familiar," he says, as his demeanor has much changed.

"I shall have him there that bears the light and carries the torch, who can back my words. Come tomorrow, as the sun rises, and I will give you words more clear and direct that shall much amaze you, more than you appear within this moment." The friar has baited the man with his well-constructed words, and it looks, by the fear in his eye, that he has tempted him well enough that there can be no other answer. Benvolio recalls these words, where amazement in the eye speaks them as clear as the friar stated and the moment Romeo pronounced them himself.

"I will come, as these words, that have only ever been shared by one, have not been spoken of since that day. Nor are there any alive that can speak of these same words." He looks to Rosaline and holds back a force of emotion that he desires to release. "Prepare you, as the sun rises. Be thou the bearer of reason on how you know of these words, lest my imagination play its games, and I shall honor thy will forever. If any truth bring me to believe this is trickery whilst we speak, I shall never look upon the church again," Benvolio says, as he makes his words clear in meaning.

"My good son, I will much amaze you, and teach you things that will open your eyes to more than just the love and beauty you have here with you." As the friar says this, Rosaline returns her gaze to the conversation by smiling at the friar and then locks her gaze unto Benvolio. She does not seem to be of the mind as we, as her awareness was staying within her mind and affixed on her love.

"I will leave you both, till tomorrow," Benvolio says, as he stands. Rosaline stands with him, and we follow suit and stand with them.

"My son, I will see you tomorrow. May your day be as present in love as it started before we arrived, and may your dinner with your father this very evening prove loving as well."

"I very much thank you. Until tomorrow," he says, as he looks to Rosaline to say her farewell.

"Being that I will not be there tomorrow, good friar, it was pleasant to see you again. Our family doors are always open to you. And to you, good Paul."

I nod, as does the friar, and they leave the room, hand in hand, as they entered. His amazement has not left his eye, whilst he leaves, as he looks back to us in the moment the door closes.

"Good friar, that was very strong in approach. You said words that did not startle the fair Rosaline, but that put much amazement in the lad's eye. I myself did not much understand what it was that you were saying at first, as your words confused me. Though, I believe that it would not have changed his expression in the least even if Romeo's ghost did appear in the room with us, as your words had placed him in a realm of amazement. He is much in wonder over the thought of where the spoken words came from. You have baited him well."

"I thank you, good apothecary. These words of Romeo's were shared between them intimately, and from what Romeo said, could not have been repeated by any other. Benvolio took much praise in himself for speaking them to Romeo, as Romeo stated that Benvolio has never been one strong with such persuasion of words. The event proved one to remember, for them both."

"I would agree that it did. Where is it that we go now?" I ask, as our duty for the day, to get the nurse and Benvolio to the church tomorrow, has been achieved.

"We can very well do whatever it is that our hearts desire. I could see by your desire that the market would be a place you would very much like to visit again. With time in our hands, we can walk back through, on the way to the church, or wherever we settle our feet."

"Good friar, you speak well-crafted music to my ears. I would very much like to visit the market again and learn more of the astonishment that is housed within its realm."

We walk from the room and the maid waits for us in the hall. She smiles and lifts her arm to show us the way to the door. We both bow our heads and leave the house very proud men. My fear did ride strongly in my blood, as talking to these two, Juliet's nurse and Benvolio, to come to the church to visit with the ghosts of their loved ones seemed very unlikely. But that the friar carried such deep and intimate words with him, it did not prove as hard as I would have thought. Now, with this duty done, I am gifted with a return to the market, and if God allows it, I will enjoy some foods I did not even know existed.

Chapter Nine

Let it be a result of my old age, or let it be the result of some of the finest foods I have ever tasted, but the events of attending festivities at the market started and ended so quickly that time has been lost within me and all that is left is the sweet flavors in my mouth and the pleased stomach that calmly rests within me.

"Friar, that was most excellent, I thank you for the pleasures of everything you introduced me to. I only wish I had known of such pleasures these many years ago, as I would have traveled to Verona just for this. No matter now, as even this one visitation has been pleasure enough."

"It is a wonder how so many stay in the happy health that they do, as the offerings are plentiful and enjoyable enough that I ponder how it is that they find a moment to not dine in such luxuries."

"Very true. May I ask a question, please?" I say, as I know the door will be open for it, but I choose to be polite to my host.

"By all means my good man, do not hold anything within you. My ears are yours."

"I thank you for your continued kindness. Where is it that Romeo and Juliet are buried? I have been wondering greatly why it is that they remain trapped in the church. Though, even more deeply and fearfully have I questioned to myself; are these the only souls of people that are trapped here, and if not within the church, within their own homes, or some other place?" My question brings much wonder to me, and my mind begins to contemplate the thoughts of how ghosts have more than likely existed since the creation of man, but that I, or many others, have never seen of them before this.

"They are buried behind the church, in separate plots of land, where each family buries their dead. I know what it is that you think, but as many have been buried within the grounds of the church and I have never seen a sight of ghosts such as this before, I am not sure why it is that they still walk the earth, trapped within the walls of this cathedral. Yet, I equally wonder, how many other ghosts do walk around us, even now, that either do not make their presence known and we are unable to decipher or that we cannot see with our eyes but stand next to us even now."

"It is a wondrous thought, and if I were to place so much time and effort into it, I doubt I could outlive the process. I recall, when first coming to the church, I did see freshly laid dirt, which I later realized were those men recently lost to this foolish war." My images recall the newly dug land and the darkness that surrounded the graves.

"There are many on these holy grounds buried due to this foolish war. Their lives taken well before they had the chance to openly live them. The young, so full of life and energy, should be better taught to channel the passions they have toward love and work, than toward the hatred they have been born into. Yet, as the old men of the families lose the vision of humble nature, they only reflect the bitter souls that mold the young to lift their swords before using their words." These are wise words, deeper than the graves themselves.

As we near the church, returning from our efforts of the day, the sun is still in the sky and a beautiful light is glowing on the face of the front wall. It illuminates the stained glass so beautifully, making the church more of an object of art than a sacred house for prayer. Looking to either side of the church, I do not see Christian, the unfortunate, resting as he has each time I exit. Though, he does not ever seem to be here when I return. But, as my mind comes back to itself, clearly I would not be here either if I knew the market had been only streets away from these walls of holiness.

We enter into the church, through the first room, where we stop to bless ourselves with holy water, and walk into the main part of the church. I would have thought Romeo and Juliet would be anxiously awaiting our return to learn of our efforts, but they are not to be seen. Being such an important day for us all, the result would seem so significant that, like a dog to its master at feeding time, I would have thought they would be at the door. Then, in the distance to the left, my ears are drawn toward the confessional, as I hear voices coming from behind the small, curtain-covered box. The friar acknowledges the same, as he gestures that I remain silent so as not to disturb them, as he allows them much private time whenever they are together. Their voices carry and echo within this grand hall, filling the empty space. And again, I hear Romeo speak of nothing but love to Juliet.

"If you recall, my love, I ascended a wall as high as a mountain to first pronounce my love for you. That love, as strong and embedded within each artery that pushes and pulls my blood, still holds the shadow of that flow in my ghostly state. If there is a wall in this afterlife you speak of that will block our spirits from being together, then another wall shall I climb and conquer, as nothing can stop my love for you, in this world or the next. If I would live a thousand deaths, then I would choose each to end with my love for you."

"O', Romeo. Your strength of will could carry ten thousand souls over the wall; I would never doubt your love. And it was my love that I sent through my mind's thoughts to your abilities, to scale such a wall to make it to me. Never were two souls destined to be together, as ours are sewn within a fabric that is only complete when our embrace holds us together. What brings such concern to my words is something far greater than what we can control. What if God himself asks to keep us apart, separated if not within two realms of heaven, but that one of us flies to heaven and the other falls into the fires of the deep? What then?"

"My love, my Juliet, let each angel fight my flight, as I follow you to your cloud in the heavens. Let every spirit that walks in heaven that I call kin tempt me to a glorious retreat upon their dream. Let the gripping hands of the devil reach from the circles of hell and attempt to drag me down to his personal chamber of torture and flames. And let God himself meet me at the gate and refuse my entrance. There will not be a power able to stop my love, as the force of affection in me would strike a blow to reshape heaven, that Gabriel himself would be unable to be the deliverer of messages."

"If I could kiss you now, all the power in my lips would prove the worth of my love, that you in the same breath speak from your own mouth."

"I would refuse my invitation to heaven for one kiss from your lips, even if it meant hell would be my bed of fire."

As these passions increase, the friar and I question our listening upon their conversation, and turn ourselves to walk toward the door near us that will lead us to the bedchambers. My foolish balance leaves me lacking grace as I turn into a small table, which houses several Bibles on top of it. My interaction with the table sends the Bibles falling to the ground, making a noise so loud that all voices and movement stop after the last page finds its resting place on the floor. Looking back I see the heads of both Romeo and Juliet come out from the confessional, without the curtain moving, and look upon us. I have disturbed their verbal loving embrace, as they exit and come to us faster than the wind.

"How now, what news?" Romeo asks, as his anticipation makes his alertness like a sparrow warning other birds of an approaching predator.

"Did you both think to retire to your bedchambers without announcing your arrival and speaking to the duty of your days?" Juliet asks, as she, in the same alertness, comes even closer to us looking for an answer that will calm her anxiousness.

"As we entered, we did hear you both in conversation that we felt did not warrant an interruption. There was no disrespect, but more, a greater respect for your privacy." The friar, well spoken as ever, gathers their attention to calm them.

"That the words of God has startled and alerted us to your arrival, there was no choice," Romeo says. "But come, as we stand here now, let us hear. What is the outcome of your meetings? Did the nurse consent to come? Did you speak my own words to my cousin, Benvolio, that he will also wake with the rising of the sun and join the nurse to be much amazed? Leave us not in wonder, for nothing can be so cruel as to have such knowledge within you and that you hold it in your grasp, teasing us by showing us the glimpse of its tail."

"O' how news brews in the mind of our elders that they hold off and allow the unsteady current of our youth to travel like ravenous winds across the land. The nurse did such evils to me in my life, especially upon the word of Romeo's desire to marry me. She held off, bringing me newly formed requests, over and over, that she will sooner inform me of your answer. Will you both hold off and once again release an answer to this steady flowing stream of questions?"

"Juliet, I will speak, and inform you of all it is that we know," the friar states, to begin to calm them, as their desires overwhelm every cavern of their beings. "I used your words to the nurse, Juliet, after requesting her presence to the church when she initially denied me of her attendance in the visitation. Upon the private history of you both that we spoke, she in amazement agreed to appear tomorrow as requested. And for your cousin, my dear boy, Benvolio, even he in the same manner, refused my request due to grieving for your loss. Yet, as we spoke of your history as well, he proved intrigued to appear so that he may witness for himself the marvel of our invitation. Thus, our duty has been done, and they will both appear."

"Friar, well done. Apothecary, in that this affair would not have had such welcoming resolve without your support and knowledge, I thank you as well. This is very good news," Romeo says, as he looks up to the heavens in the joy that we have taken a step toward the peace they so desperately desire.

"It was our pleasure to be of any help toward the outcome of peace," I say, to show that this is of my desire as well. Little does he know of my grief that still pools in the caverns of my heart. Even as he stated his desire to end his world with whatever tool that would have allowed him such an exit, it was still by my hand that his last breath found its end. I cannot shake these feelings of regret that I wear like that of a hat on my head, as the feelings rest heavily on my mind and soul.

"They will both appear tomorrow, at the rise of the sun. This task is not yet joyfully achieved, shall I remind you all. It is the fearful mind that rests for only moments at a time at night. They may have agreed to appear and will very likely come tomorrow, but their minds will not allow them to lessen their strength and be deceived. They will doubt and question themselves even more than if you appeared to them in full image yourselves. They will have a night to process their thoughts and gain doubt. We will need to be prepared, work on the execution of the introduction, and guide them in the comfort of knowing that you are here, in your spirit forms. Apothecary, your eyes seem heavy from the day. If it pleases you, retreat to your room and I will call upon you for supper. Until then, I will work out the forming of this meeting tomorrow with these two."

"Friar, I thank you, and as you are a man who knows the depth of our souls, you have picked me as ripe as fruit from a tree that was soon to fall. I will take my leave of you all. Do not hesitate but to call upon me if I am needed for anything further."

"We most certainly will, good friend," the friar says, as he pats my shoulder to thank me for the day.

"We are both in much thanks for your service to us and only desire to one day repay you for your efforts. Until the day calls upon you again, we wish you a happy rest," Juliet says, in the sweetest of words. There is no doubt to me how it is that Romeo loves her so deep and took the actions that he did. She could ask of me to walk from here to the moon, and without a question as to how I would do it, I would sooner leave and climb the air.

I acknowledge them all and retreat to my room. I am very tired; there is no question to this. The tensions of the day, with the conversations we had, and the overwhelming visitation to the market, which has left me full unto my grave, have removed all hope of action, beyond the walk to my bedchamber. If I were to rest my head and not awake till the sun called out my name, it would not upset me one second. I cannot imagine one more meal entering through my lips. Yet, if the friar is to place the effort into it, I will not deny him this.

The sooner I walk into the room, my head falls upon the pillow of the bed, and I am off to the dream world that has longed to come.

Chapter Ten

A knocking at my door wakes me, and my heart still shakes at every shock of sound that I am not prepared for.

"Yes, hello. Come in, please," I say, in my dazed state of awareness. The friar enters and smiles widely at me, with the soft eyes of a parent. He does have a way about him that greets your soul softly, ever so welcoming, which allows for my soul to rest from my reaction to being awoken. "Is it time for dinner?" I ask, as I hope that I have not kept him waiting long.

"My good friend, it is morning already. I called upon you last evening and knocked on your door as I did just now, but no sounds were heard. You looked as tired as I've seen a man when you retired for some rest, and thus, I thought a night's sleep held you tight and would be best for you."

"Morning has come? My heavens, as refreshed as my body reports, it does not feel as if I have slept a moment. Time passes in a way that I cannot sense it, where in Mantua, every day is a heavy burden, as if I watched each grain of sand fall. It does amaze me how the great use of emotions can empty my levels of liveliness and still seem as if time has not passed when it soars with the watchful hawk."

"I took the peace that whispered from your room as a message that sleep was of more value than another meal. Worry you nonetheless, there is a meal waiting for you now. If you will be happy to join the nun in the kitchen, she has it prepared. I will be in the church hall, waiting for our dear friends' arrival. I do not want them to appear without a pleasant greeting to welcome them. If you do not mind, I will leave you now and meet with you when you are done."

"My desire agrees, good friar, that meeting the nurse and Benvolio at the entrance would be of utter importance for when they arrive. Your warmth will allow them to keep their minds as open as the doors they enter through. I will consume this quick meal and meet you in the church as well."

The friar smiles, nods and walks from the room. I, in my customary manner, rise from the bed and arrange my clothes to look respectable. My heart still races. Not from the shock of being awoken, but from the thought of what is about to come. Never, in my years of living, did I think I would come upon a ghost, but not only to have seen one and now preach to the world that they exist, how unlikely a thought but how true to the situation. Though now, I speak with them as if speaking with an ailing soul needing an elixir to heal a foot mold. To make this even more interesting, I will soon attempt to convince two people, with the full leadership and guidance of the friar, that their loved ones are here dwelling among the living, in the form of walking ghosts upon the planet. How impossible it seems, but that we have resolve in us that direct the truth in no other direction, we shall not fail.

My heart calls to me and releases a true feeling that I know I cannot fight; I cannot eat any morsels of food. God, forgive me for not joining the nun for my meal, but my nerves are too tied into this fate, that they burst from my skin and call me to the main part of the church.

Walking from my door, I stride down the hallway and make it to the front of the church, believing this is where the friar, Romeo and Juliet all wait. As I walk through the door, my assumption is correct. They wait at the front of the church, in complete silence, all standing and looking within every direction in the church except for directly at each other.

Walking up to them, I nod to announce my arrival. I am met with the same gesture from the friar, light smiles from Romeo and Juliet, and stand attentively next to the friar to join in the motion of the scene.

"If you did eat your morning meal, this shall be the fastest I have ever seen a man eat," the friar says, as he speaks his words with his eyes remaining on the front doors.

"I did not go to the nun; please forgive me. I could not imagine eating when we have such importance ahead of us."

"It is well, my good man. The nun will likely save it for whenever you are ready. Our hearts and minds are just as focused. The sun has risen and, with that, their arrival should be very soon. Apothecary, remember, they will not be able to see Romeo and Juliet as we see them. It will be our task, if not mine own, to translate what is said and convince them that these two loving souls are here with us. I believe their minds are open, which should allow us to bend our words so they will see the image in their minds. I have already asked God to grant them the same vision we both possess, as the nurse and Benvolio were even closer to these loving children than us. Thus, we shall see."

"I will be prepared to speak when needed, but my presence to this matter is of support for whatever you will need of me," I say, showing my support to this mission and my willingness to do what is needed.

"For that and all other things to this end, we thank you," the friar says, as he smiles and looks upon the doors' eager opening.

I do not believe that I have seen him as prepared as now, with his energy higher than the church bell that rings in the steeple. I wonder, when I know that I should not, whether

Christian, the unfortunate, rests outside the door, as he has each morning that I have walked from the church. He has been there, speaking mysterious words that I shall never comprehend. When we leave, whenever that may be on this day, I will make sure the friar follows me closely, so that if Christian does once again speak, the friar will hear what I have heard. It will much amaze him. Even if we must play the part and set Christian to the scene so that he may just observe me, prepared with the friar being within an earshot of the words. This may also be the moment that I may understand what it is that he says, hoping the friar may solve the puzzle of his mysterious words.

But soft, the church door opens. The pleasant creaking sound of the old wood agrees that the friar was good with his words and convinced these loving people to come. I doubted him not. As the door opens in full motion to greet our guest, in walks the nurse, slowly, with a cautious pace. She turns her face back to the street, seemingly to address someone that follows her, and speaks some words to prove someone is there.

"Peter, you may wait out here. I will return to you shortly," she says, as she walks the rest of the way into the first room. Juliet stands, her eyes melting with love from the voice of this woman, who has yet to even enter the main church hall. After what appears to be the nurse blessing herself with holy water, she walks in and sees the friar and I standing to her right, leaning against the last row of pews, just steps away from her. She welcomes our view with the softness of her eyes and greets us pleasantly.

"Friar, good morning to you. Good morning to you as well, sir," she says to me with an anxious face. She has excitement in her eyes, but she also appears afraid. I very much understand this and would carry the same obvious fears in me, if I had a taste of what it was that I was about to experience.

Juliet walks up to her, standing directly next to her, with emotion that must overwhelm her. To be here, as she is, unable to leave the church, unable to touch her one and only love, and now to see the nurse, a woman as dear as a mother to her, must be so difficult for her young and inexperienced emotions to handle. I do wonder if her heart and brain, as sharp and witty as she has been, still experiences the same pulse of emotional depth as she had upon her existing days. Do ghosts continue to authentically feel as they once did when they were living? This 'other' world leaves me at such a loss.

"Nurse, we are grateful for your coming. It is a marvelous thing to hear what we had spoken to you and you continue to be as strong as you are to believe in my word and come this morning," the friar says with his warm heart and words.

"Yes, I had very much considered not coming. As I have said, I am not ready to speak with God and pray for my soul. But as you have spoken of my sweet Juliet, no matter how foolish this may appear to be, I am here," she says as the hesitancy flows from her body like waves of heat from rooftops in the summer afternoon.

"Again, we thank you. Please do not be startled upon the arrival, but we also wait upon one more, from the house of Montague. Benvolio is to meet us here as well, as they have requested for you both to assist us," the friar says, looking over at the door, wondering if anyone else has walked in. Romeo himself stands closer to the door, awaiting the arrival of his cousin. Like Juliet, he is excited to see of him again, as any in their state who cannot communicate with the world would.

"Did you say, Benvolio?" the nurse asks, as her eyes gain more sadness than wonder. I did not think how uncomfortable it might be to have one of each household together like this. As open as these two individuals are to loving their fellow citizen of Verona, it may appear to others of their own households that their meeting may not be as accidental. It is dangerous to be thought that one would conspire with the enemy.

"Why, yes, I did speak of Benvolio. Nurse, do not be concerned. Even as he is of the house of Montague, he will not harm you nor show any ill will to you. He is a kind lad, who cares for the meaning of being here as much as you. He will join us straight." The friar feels calm and steady in his words, and I agree that these two should have no issue with being here within the same hour.

"Friar, he may join you straight, yet his visitation will not be upon his own choice, as you would hope." She says this and holds back emotion that looks to clearly surface from within her. Why is it that many speak in riddles within Verona? I wonder if she did come across his path in the street before entering and assisted him in changing his mind to come within these walls? Even if he were to come later, it shall not prove to change our course. We are set, as no force can stop us now.

"Did you encounter him on the way here, as he has made some choice to arrive later, or changed his mind and is being forced by another?" the friar asks, within the same thought as I.

"My dear friar, you are the receiver of news last it would seem, as only when his body arrives, will you know of his will." She bites her lip and steps back one step from us. I turn my head to look at the friar, as he looks back at me, and within moments of understanding, we look to Romeo, who has already left the doors and walked up to the nurse.

"Friar, have her speak more. Words have been shared by her, which offer much misunderstanding. She must not know what it is that she has said. Prithee, have her speak again," Romeo says, as his emotion begins to rise at the meaning of words the nurse has offered.

"My good nurse, please say again. My ears are old in their age and do sometimes miss the understanding in the spoken words of others," I say, to use my age as I have the ability to do.

"This boy, of the house of Montague, he shall come, but not by his own power. In the night, upon the streets near the market, this man Benvolio, and one of my house, Sampson being he, were both found dead. It was most grave of a sight, from what the messenger this very morning did report to Lord Capulet. They were found dead, together, as if they were in a quarrel upon each other's head. You shall see them both upon this day, as I know that Sampson's body will be brought here soon for the prayers for his soul."

There is much shock and wonder in our own souls, as the friar and I are lost in thought, as not a full day has passed that we sat across from this boy. Though now, his spirit has been released from his body and makes his way to the heavens. Will he search for Romeo as he ascends to his paradise? But soft, where is my mind? Quickly I look to Romeo, who, down in his knees, folded over onto the ground, rests unmoving. Juliet stands over him, not saying a word, but in full understanding of what he is feeling within him.

"Nurse, I thank you for this report, as we have yet to be informed of this horrible news," the friar sadly states. "This is most heartbreaking to hear. Two more lives, of the young and virtuous, lost upon a pointless war between two families that cannot find peace. This tragedy will most certainly be followed by even more blood if rule and order cannot be restored. There must be a truce, to allow time to bring such authorities to the head of the matter." The friar feels the loss of these two boys, but even more, feels the pain releasing from Romeo as he still rests, face forward on the ground.

However, in a storm of ferocity that would overshadow the fury of a volcano, Romeo lifts his body to the sky, still on his knees, and screams like I have never heard one scream before.

"No! Benvolio! Noooo!" And as his voice ends the shriek toward heaven, his power vacates his frame as he slumps down with his head hung low, releasing grief as a cloud releases rain.

"My sweet heavens, Romeo, my love. And poor Sampson, a dear boy of my house, who followed his friends with a heart that would openly do anything they would ask for them. Though, foolishly, he was always ready to defend friends and strangers alike in a quarrel. This honor, as great as it was for the family, was not supportive in the desire to out-live his kinsmen." Juliet, standing over him, wishing she could embrace him now more than ever, looks helpless to her desires. Even as the other deaths have been most upsetting, the knowledge that two have fallen at once, more than likely upon their own argument and quarrel with each other, does affect the grief twice as greatly.

"I see that peace and silence grabs your tongues," the nurse calmly speaks. "This news did silence me the same. Sampson was a dear boy, though not very smart to his own desire to be a man independent and free, but nonetheless, a kind heart. If it please you, I can return later in the day if you need this time to grieve," the nurse says, as she begins to feel uncomfortable in our silence.

"No, good nurse, it would please me more if you stayed now with us," the friar says. "You see, we spoke with the lad yester-morning, as we spoke with you, as he was to come and know of his kinsman here, Romeo, and the ghost-like state that he is in. Yet, as you are here, and time now seems more at a constant and ever-increasing speed, if we do not act now we will lose the grip of any chance to bring peace and spare the remaining lives of each family." The friar, in constant and strong thought, holds his emotion within to keep focus on the reason that we are all gathered here together.

"Is she here? My dear, sweet Juliet, is she with us now, within this very room?" the nurse asks, as she looks around, hoping to catch a sight of her that would send her heart through joy and sadness at the same moment. Juliet, standing over Romeo still, looks down at him, and then slowly walks back to us, just a few steps away. She once again stands next to the nurse, reaching out to touch her, but failing in her desire, as her hand passes through the nurse's shoulder

"Yes, she stands next to you now. To your left is your Juliet." The friar says this and regains his peace, allowing for the nurse to turn to her left and let her mind's eye form the image she most desires.

"O', my sweet Juliet," the nurse begins. "My love, my little princess, how I do miss you so. The grandness of my love, of your marriage and then of your loss, has sent me to places of joy and sadness that I have never felt in such waves. I have lost one such as you once that was my heart's keeper, but to now, have lost another that filled that vacant space...O' my soul cannot bear one more loss if it not be my own soul that travels to join yours."

"O' goodly and loving nurse, I miss you as sweetly. Even as my Romeo completed my life's will, I am ever so empty from the love that I no longer receive from you or can share. I should be the happiest girl in Verona to have one such as yourself care and raise me as you did." Juliet looks over to us, after speaking her love, knowing that her words do not touch upon the nurse's ears.

"Shall I say that Juliet has spoken to you and says she misses you as much, and is thankful for the many years you cared for her as you had, allowing her to feel the most fortunate and loved girl in Verona." The friar, using some, but not all of Juliet's words, speaks enough that the understanding is the same. The nurse, after hearing what the friar said, begins to allow tears to fall down her cheeks, even with a small smile cresting on her lips.

"O', my sweetest and loving little one. That I could hold you now, I would have you in my arms, kiss your cheek, and then show you the back of my hand for not coming to me for more support of your heart, than to have your life's end my only thought." The nurse, now allowing the love to flow within her, feels the disappointment a mother would, that Juliet did not trust in her more to help her through the emotions that brought her to her end.

"Come, good nurse, to my chamber where we shall share more words and purpose," the friar says, entering into the dialogue. "Juliet, if it please you, come along with us as well." The friar says this, lifting an arm to show the nurse the way. She offers him a look that makes me believe she is still not in full belief of Juliet's presence, even after she has spoken to the air.

The friar then shifts his head quickly, eyes locked with mine, informing me in sight that Romeo still rests on the ground in need of attention. This is to be my duty? How will I comfort the boy in this time of grief? I do not possess the skills, as the friar does, to warm his heart and show him understanding as a father would.

They walk away, down the aisle, as the friar speaks with both the nurse and Juliet. The nurse, reacting to the friar's conversation with Juliet, looks around in the air hoping to see her, as the friar supposedly speaks with Juliet. This could be a comical exchange on any other occasion, but as love and death are the theme, it does not settle well to laugh.

I turn my awareness toward Romeo, walking slowly in his direction until I stand above him. I would place my hand upon his shoulder, but it is not an offering I have the option to give. There is no physical comfort that people usually share that will allow me to give him the support he needs, that might also prevent me from having to use my words. Nevertheless, I must speak with him to soothe him and continue to give him hope and purpose to walk these halls and desire to end his family war.

"My boy, I am deeply sorry for the news you just discovered. I did not know this friend of yours very well, but by the man that you are, I would think that he had as much honor and love for family as you show." He does not move after my shared words, as his head is still hung low and eyes closed. No motion from him informs me that he either acknowledges my words or did not hear one word of them. Has his grief affected him so deeply that I may not see him again, the inner boy that held passions like many hold their wealth? I will speak to him again. He needs to fight this grief, as there are greater matters at hand. Many times, we must sacrifice our deepest desires to move another outcome in the direction that it must go. I must find my words.

"Romeo, in my earlier years, as young as yourself, I had a friend that I would say was more of a brother to me, such as your cousin appears to be for you. There were many adventures that he and I braved, through many travels just outside of Mantua. I recall all those years deeply, as I do not brave such travels at my age any longer.

"I had lost him, as you have lost your cousin. Circumstances different, as his death was somewhat my fault. We were at the great rock, which overhung an immense lake, just north of Mantua. Each year we would travel to the highest edge and look upon the greatness of the lake. But more, we would look down and wonder if it would be possible to jump down into the lake from such heights. He always seemed superior compared to others, at so many things, that I am not sure why it was that I said he could never achieve the dive into the lake without hitting the rocks at the bottom near the shore. I was jealous of his abilities. I was jealous at the way he was always so helpful toward others. I did but whisper the dare to him, and it was within moments that he leapt from the cliff. I myself ran to its edge to watch the outcome." Holding emotion back that erupts inside of me from those days, I stop to breathe. I can feel the weight of the moment when he jumped once again. My heart jumped along with him. I had never felt fear so strongly. I must continue.

"He did not make it to the water, as the cliffs had many lower levels of jagged rock that stuck out far enough to interfere with his path, but not far enough for us to ever see. He landed a distance down, breaking his neck on the collision with the jagged plateau. We could not see this protruding edge from where we stood. I had killed him. I had placed the dare within him, within his mind, taking away his common sense that such things should not be done. Alejandro will always be locked in my memory. Those events will never see rest in my soul, as I revisit the tragic incident at different times in my life, allowing my soul to feel the pain I had felt that day. It was shortly after, through all my regret at what I had done, that I chose to become an apothecary and help those that he himself had the gift and ability of doing. I did not have his words to soothe or move those with one speech, but I did enjoy the sciences and had an understanding of the body."

As I finished what was to be an encouraging speech, I feel the regret resurface back into my soul that had been locked away for some time due to the forgetfulness that accompanies my age. That foolishness that struck from the deepest and most pitiful part of me changed so many lives for the worse. It shall be he, in heaven, if I should make it there, that I would search out and plead for forgiveness. If it be not heaven that I am destined to go, then my punishment will be serving in many ways. I will burn for what I had done to Alejandro and I will burn for what I have done to Romeo.

After gathering my senses back to my eyes and pushing down the regret once again, hoping that it will stay locked within me for as long as I can prevent it from showing itself, I see that Romeo has lifted his head to me and looks at me with great focus and begins to speak.

"He was very much like a brother, just as your friend was to you. In our family, at all events we were forced to attend, he and I would be by each other's side throughout the occasion. Granted, I was close with Mercutio as well, one that I myself had a hand in his death. I feel and understand your pain, good apothecary. And I know you feel such pain for me, in believing you had much to do with my death. I assure you, my death would have come with or without your poison.

"Benvolio…dead. I cannot believe it, even as I know what my loving Juliet's nurse spoke is true. Sampson, discovered just as dead right by his side, is even more puzzling to me, unless they had died by each other's sword. You and the friar must go to discover what happened. We must know of the circumstance. If need be, I will break down these walls and search for reason and enact revenge never seen in Verona."

"Romeo, your heart is in the right place, but it is without question that the friar and I will go to this place where both men fell. I know that he will want to speak with those who found them and discover the situation of their life's end. I will make sure of it as well," I say, offering as much support and reason as I can, showing him he is not alone.

Romeo stands and looks at me as one I would assume would look at their father after receiving such words. I very much hope that what I have spoken may inspire him to keep within the mind and action of our task. This boy has gone through much grief these several weeks passed, more than a person should suffer in a lifetime. But now, he continues to suffer such misery in his afterlife. Maybe this is his purgatory. He that took his own life, and by that, bound to suffer the pains as God has spoken. I have seen death, as being in my chosen field of work death came upon many that I could not save. I grieved that I could not spare their lives. This boy has seen life after life leave this world and each time, it is one that has deep involvement with his soul. It is as if he is being punished for loving too deeply and living too passionately toward the enjoyment of his life. It only makes me wonder if the sins of his fathers and grandfathers have all passed down to him, as he was the sole heir of the family, and he suffers all the pain that has accumulated since the first soul had been lost. If this be the case, then his spirit will forever receive torture and pain. My heart drops to its lowest point in the sadness I feel for him.

The voice of the friar comes from the far end of the church, as when I look back, I see the nurse, Juliet and he walking our way, the friar positioned in between them. He speaks directly to the nurse, and then turns to his opposite side, where Juliet walks, and speaks with her. The nurse still looks around him, as if looking for something she has lost. Her eyes are focused on the hopeful belief of Juliet's ghost. She has been convinced of the situation, as her face seals her soul's content.

"Good nurse," the friar says, as they meet me back at the front of the church. "We will call upon you again once we know more and can advise you on what it is that will need to be done. For this moment, go you home, and act as if nothing has changed. If anyone should ask you where you have been, or even why it is that you came here, just inform them that you and I spoke and you confessed your sins as well as prayed for Juliet's soul. This is not so far off of reality and thus is not false words that God does not want us to share."

"Yes, yes. That will be my word. Juliet, my love," she loudly speaks now addressing Juliet, as she looks around the room, moving her head in several different directions. "I have prayed for you every day since you left me. I miss your smile in the morning when I come to call upon you," she says, looking to her left, beyond the friar. Little does she know that Juliet stands directly in front of her. This is once again comical in nature, but not one breath will I show toward it affecting me. That would show utter disrespect for the emotionally intense situation we are in.

Juliet speaks words that I do not hear, as being in my own mind, I have lost focus to stay within the moment.

"Nurse. Juliet says she misses the way you would join her in her bed to rouse her in the morning, many of the days you shared together, and wake her by tickling her feet," the friar says, as he continues to repeat Juliet's words.

The nurse sheds another tear. She has had an experience that moves her deeply to every word spoken. There is much love between them. Juliet seems to pour her love into those she cares for, and they in the same act of gesture, offer more love than the seeds of a pomegranate.

"Goodbye, Juliet, my love. I will come back soon so we can speak again. I will inform you on how your family fares each time I come and notify on the health and safety of your parents. Be well. I will see you soon." She kisses the air in several directions, hoping that any one of them will come into contact with Juliet. After the nurse walks out the front door, rejoining her attendant, the friar lets out a sigh that removes much weight from him.

"That was one of the most complicated conversations I have ever had. God love the nurse, but as many times as I instructed her as to where Juliet was standing, she would move her face and eyes as if spirits are ever-moving, floating both up and down. Juliet, I cannot imagine what she was like as your nurse. The large number of questions was greater than the quantity of questions I receive on the existence of God and heaven."

"Yes, good friar, as you know her from our family's attendance in mass, she is one to question what she does not understand. Even as such things are overwhelming at times, it comes from a deep love within her." Juliet, looking back at the door, takes a moment, before returning her gaze to Romeo and walking up to him.

"How are things here, men?" the friar asks, looking to receive a report on how things between us went. As Romeo stands and looks well put together in his mind, there is not much urgency to respond to the question. Our calmness allows for a brief pause that is welcome in the states of urgency we have been experiencing.

"We are well. Romeo has asked that we go to find out more information on the tragic situation discovered this morning." I say this, but clearly know that the friar must also be thinking the same thing as I. What else would have importance over such a matter as this?

"You well advise us, Romeo, and that is the only thing we have within this day to do. Juliet and I have decided to send the nurse back to her house, until we can devise a plan on the best ways to use her. With the situation of last night's deaths, we need to act upon these events before we lose the heat from the scene." I can tell that the friar regrets his choice of words, but it is reality of the moment. Deaths have occurred and will continue to occur unless we find a way to calm the families and end this foolish war.

Romeo turns and faces Juliet so that they are eye to eye. I see the deepness of their love and they stand as raw as newly wounded animals. He still does not have much power to speak, and she senses this and remains just as quiet, yet engaged. I have seen this with those in love, where their souls are so tied together that words are not needed in the understanding of their minds. They are one mind, one union of their deepest desires. I wonder if, being in this ghost-like state, that they have attained an even higher awareness of their emotions with each other and have united into one conjoined intellect?

"Good apothecary, shall we be off?" the friar says, as he desires not only to leave to find out more about the deaths but also to give these two more time alone.

"Yes, I am prepared when you are, good sir. I will follow as you see fit." Knowing that all will be well here, I am prepared to seek out more information on the events from last evening. I am much intrigued by this, as there are two more now dead found together. It is clear that they have killed each other, where the fatal strike ended both their lives at the same time. Did they realize their encounter would be their last moments living? Do any ever realize such things when they engage in a fight?

Lost in thought, the friar stands at the door, looking back at me. I see his glance and rush to him, following out the door quickly. When in the depths of my mind, there is much I miss that most would be aware of. Is it my age? Is it my brain? Lord knows, but I can only assume that the older I get, the more this may happen.

Chapter Eleven

"Good sir, I knew, as you are an apothecary, the great conjurer of soul-saving elixirs, that you would have the ability to find some calm corner to place his great sadness. Nevertheless, very well done on soul saving with Romeo. We were not apart from you for long, as I felt the need to rush back and assist you with framing his mind back to a more stable place. I did not think I would return to see him so settled. Please know, I mean you no disrespect. Romeo is a boy captured by his emotions and, when they get the best of him, it is far easier to dig a hole to the other end of the earth, than to find him and bring his emotions back to a calm state. What is it that you did?"

"Friar, I was so in fear once you left. I normally do not have the words to craft comfort as you do. Yet, once you were gone and all was quiet, seeing Romeo as deeply affected by his loss of his friend, I was drawn to a situation from my youth that was of so similar a fate, that as I told him the story, he found his centered self once again. Call it what you will, being luck, being that of choice words, but my life spoken to his and the similarity of the happenings in youth, awoke his senses and brought him back."

"Whatever it is you did, good apothecary, you did well. It took much to convince the nurse, but she related well once hearing many more stories that she and Juliet shared. What proved impossible, was trying to guide her to where Juliet stood. Even as I directed her to look directly in front of her, she would browse around the room to the open air, looking for Juliet to appear. More of her power rests in her heart than in her mind.

"This way. The nurse instructed me to where we shall find the grounds that the bodies were found on. It was right off of the market. They will have closed the street from any person walking across the site. I am hoping that the same officers will be there, for as you know, they attend my church and my relations with them and their families are strong."

The more we walk, the more I imagine how they were found and how they ended up dead. I envision a mighty duel, using many of the streets around them, turning away from the blade as it flies by their heads just grazing a cheek or slicing strands of hair. They must have dueled on for hours, slicing away at each other until they each finally succumbed to the wounds incurred by both. There will be much blood on the stones, as blood spilled works its way into each crack and crevice and leaves behind a remembrance of what took place. I do wonder that if these families kill themselves off as steadily as they plan, there will not be any left to write further history, and the violence will finally come to an end. If this mighty globe be a dream, then this is how I would assume the heavens would envision it.

"It is here," the friar says, as looking up in the distance to our right, two officers stand at the entrance to a street holding a powerful stance toward none passing them. They clearly look to be blocking anyone from entering with faces as solid as stone and hands placed on their undrawn swords. This most definitely will be the place.

"Follow me close, good apothecary, but please allow me to do most, if not all, of the talking. I know these men, different from the last but equal in love, and they will hopefully inform us of what happened." I enjoy that he knows all these men, to allow us such private information that others would not be allowed to know, by just walking up to them and questioning the scene.

"Officers, good day to you both. I am glad you each attended mass last weekend. God watches you and protects you against all harms, I am sure." The friar is wise to relate with them so closely.

"Hello, good friar, how does your day?" one of the officers asks. He seems kind, which suits us well. These kind men make such news sharing as easy as breathing.

"I am well, I thank you. God granted me another day and I serve my purpose as best I can. If I may ask of you, as I have been informed that I shall be receiving two lost souls, is this where last evening's tragic event occurred? And if so, what did you find? You see, as I look to greet their spirits and show them the path to heaven, it is helpful to know how they died so that I may use choice words when in deep prayer." I could not imagine if the friar had chosen another profession, what power he may hold from the wise choosing of his words. Could he not have been a government official, or a great philosopher, or even the most cunning of thieves?

The officers look at each other in their confused state, wondering what should sharing such knowledge cause harm to, and the officer who has been in silence shrugs his shoulders, and smirks, as he does not see any reason why it would not be approved information to share with the friar.

"Well, good friar, as you may already know, two men were found dead here. One was Benvolio, of the house of Montague. The other was Sampson, of the house of Capulet. Each man was found dead, within steps of each other, slain by the sword. Yet, the puzzling piece that we are not to share with anyone, is that each of them were dead within steps of each other, both had their swords drawn and at their sides with hands still grasping as if to never let go, but neither of them had one drop of blood upon either of their swords blades. This is the same as all the other bodies found, but that they were found dead together, it is most strange. How can two men, found dead with their swords drawn, killed by the sword itself, but each of their swords show no sign of blood on them? In my training, even if their swords would have been wiped from the blood, there would still be shows and traces within the deep channels of the steel, discoloring the metal. It is most baffling and strange."

"Tis' very strange. These two men were found dead, together, swords drawn, like all the rest found recently of each household. Each sword not found to have blood on it, yet each man is dead by a sword. That only concludes to confusion, but more, whose sword did take their lives? Were they the fallen men in a larger quarrel, who did not strike but one man, yet received blows that caused their deaths?"

"There has not been a conclusion on our side, as even the previous murders do not have a witness nor a hint as to who may have killed them. This war between the families is bringing much work to your door, friar, as there is no other thought or reason as to why their particular bodies fall", one of the officers states.

"Yes, yes. This sad season of death has made my prayers as constant as the rain during the wettest spell. I should hope that it does end soon, for the sake of the lives of those who still breathe. I thank you both and pray you to be safe. I will see you at mass on Sunday."

"Thank you, friar. May God be with you and to you as well, sir." They are kind officers, who keep the peace and have a good understanding of laws and respect.

I nod to thank him for his remark, as we walk away and stand several yards in distance from the officers at the edge of another street that shortly leads to the market, so that they cannot hear us discuss our affairs. The friar begins his thoughts out loud for both God and myself to hear.

"My heavens, they have died the same as all the rest. What is this puzzling situation that we do hear of? How can two men, with swords drawn, within an arms reach of each other, not look to have one drop of blood on their swords, yet both are slain with their own blood soaked through? How is this possible?" The friar ends his words, and looks up to God as if an answer may float down to him from the heavens above.

I wish I could find a conclusion or reason, but I am not a man that knows much of sword fighting and cannot imagine a situation such as he questions. There were days within my work where wounds needed to be healed, but the cause of them did not enter my desire to know.

"Friar, I wish it were so that I could offer you an explanation, but I do not well understand this, the same as it confuses even you. I can only imagine a larger quarrel between many men, and their deaths are the result, but can it be possible that they did not achieve one strike on any other man?"

"I cannot see how it is likely," he says in this wondrous state. "One man would have had their back turned to the other at some point in the duel or offered a weakness in fighting style, that would have opened the opportunity for them to strike. Even just one strike. Blood on a sword does not wipe away as easily as one would think, as stated by the officer. The metal of a sword, even as it appears as smooth as the image offers, is not what it seems. There are many grooves and unseen marks that would hold the blood in its cavern and leave behind the proof. These are not just pieces of information that I alone know, as they are proven."

We are lost in our minds, as we stand and wonder how these events can occur. It will have to be through the officers and even the prince, when he returns, that a solution and answer will be offered. Verona is a marvelous and mysterious place. Even I, a man that has seen most of what life should offer it, still find amazement in these newly traveled streets. Suddenly, a voice speaks out from near us, interrupting our dialogue.

"Good friar, you can wonder all you like, but not even your God will give you an answer to what is happening in the streets of Verona. Even I, as brilliant a man as any, have not found my timing to be exact, to fall upon the killings and their killer. Let my staff be my guide and round me to every hole that welcomes it, I shall rouse the spirits to give me an answer well before your divinity shall allow it."

"Who speaks to a friar in such a tone and harsh word as this?" Friar Laurence asks, as even I am in wonder as to who would address a man of God so rudely.

"What, ho! You heard my voice? Goodly friar, did you hear what I just said?" a man from behind us asks, as I myself can hear his loud and wild voice approach us. We turn and see this man, excited that we have heard his voice, walk to us quickly with eyes as open as a window in the spring season.

"Yes, I did hear you…" the friar begins to say, as he turns to the man, but then stops speaking and stands in awe.

"Friar, are you all right?" I ask, as his amazement leaves him lost in speech. This strange man stands before him, excited to be here within our presence, and the friar seems much amazed by him as well. "Friar, will you not speak to him any further? Should I call the officers to come and join this conversation for our safety?"

"There are no officers that will have a hold of me, nor man on this earth that can affect my desires," the unexpected visitor says. "Old man, you shall eat of my knowledge and allow your age-weakened soul to nourish from my sight and mind. Even upon your eyes and ears, my image appears it seems and voice can be heard. Well, gentlemen, shall we dance in joy, for by the power of God, who rests with you nightly in your bed good friar, my spirit has found its voice!"

This man speaks quite rudely to us, as he takes hold of his arrogant attitude to capture his listener in most unprepared surprise. That the friar still stands in shock and does not speak to this man to quiet his mouth puzzles me even more than the harshness of his words.

"Mercutio! It cannot be. How is it that you are here? Where did you come from? You had passed many a day and your body has been gone, placed within the soil of the earth, and yet your soul still walks the grounds of Verona?" The friar addresses this man finally, named Mercutio, and wonders why this man is here, in Verona. He seems like a man of the Verona style, as his mouth places him among the wealthy that feel as if they can speak as they want to anyone, even a friar. In that the friar has spoken of his body in the earth, it seems he has also found his life's end, and I wonder if he has been banned from heaven, similar to the way Romeo has been, as the friar has said his body has been buried several weeks already but he still roams the streets. "Apothecary, as my heart does ache in wonder at this man's sight to my eyes, am I to believe you can see him as well?"

"Yes, good friar, I can see him as clearly as you. He stands before us. He even called out to you, which I heard as rudely as you have. He should know better than to speak to a friar as inappropriately as he has," I say, as I stand firm that this man is not a man we should address due to his rudeness, unless an apology were to shortly follow.

"Good apothecary, this is another spirit. This man, Mercutio, died just days before Romeo. I prayed on his body and buried him behind the church. This is not a man of flesh anymore. Watch." He swings his hand across Mercutio and it passes through him, no different than with Romeo. As my thoughts had already begun their belief, my mind is now assured at this spirit's form.

"Good friar, this is Mercutio? Romeo spoke of him when I looked to calm him and told him the story from my youth." The name now hangs in my thoughts from Romeo's words.

"Romeo! What do you mean you spoke with Romeo? I have heard of his death by his own hand and even that of Juliet. One hears many things when only his ears can interact with others. How is it that you speak of Romeo? Does he walk the streets as I, lost in this endless maze of the afterlife? Speak, old man, do not let your last breath be left in the air as you die before you answer me. Where is Romeo?" Mercutio asks, even more excited than before.

"Does he speak with everyone in this manner, friar? I have never been so offended by a person in my life." I am left with a weakened tongue and a pause of heart that the friar has not spoken to him about his manners, but that only assures me that this man has been this way even while he was alive. I hold my opinions back, as I know I must address him as a gentleman would. "Yes, I have spoken with Romeo, as the friar has done the same. He is within the church, locked inside its walls as if trapped in a prison. Juliet is there as well."

"They are both within the church! Well, does God do a deed that offers peace to those who have hate in their blood? They must move the crucifix from its wall with the hatred their families do share. Let Romeo finally have an adversary that can match his power and skill with the sword. If he be likely to strike upon her, his disposition of love shall trick her into his arms as he strikes her down with his ghostly blade." Mercutio laughs as he finishes his words, as some amusement to their fate pleases him.

"Why would he strike down the woman he loves and even died for? You are a much-confused spirit, Mercutio. You should direct your spirit's awareness to more reliable whispers, before you speak of such horrible acts upon two destined lovers," I say, holding back much emotion I know I could share. I have never been so affected by someone, but of the way he speaks and whom he speaks of, I cannot sit back and allow such knavery to sit in the air unattended.

"Apothecary, there is much that is not known by this man. Mercutio, let me inform you of what brought your life's end. Through the hot blood of Tybalt, unable to allow forgiveness and understanding within his soul, a quarrel ensued, taking your life from you well before God needed your soul. This much you know. After your fall, Romeo did slay Tybalt to avenge your murder within the brief moments that followed. However, unbeknownst to everyone, it was that very same day, before this foolish quarrel began, that I married Romeo to Juliet in my church. The slaying of Tybalt satisfied Romeo's revenge for your death, but also brought banishment upon Romeo, away from the woman he married not hours before. And this killing was also from the house of Capulet, direct cousin to Juliet. Romeo had killed her cousin and received banishment for the ill-thought slaying." The friar, enlightening Mercutio with this heretofore unknown information, creates looks of amazement upon Mercutio's face that are easier to read than a child's nightly story.

"Why, how foolish, old rivalries such as this do make those not even directly involved pay for acts not even handed to them to control. Romeo, that fool, stood in my way and held me from quarrelling with Tybalt, hoping to prevent me from sending his soul to heaven. Though, this left me unable to defend my life, allowing Tybalt the upper hand to strike his blade well within me. Nevertheless, he got his, the knave, as Romeo took every life this Prince of Cats had and skinned the fur from him to place him in his rightful place. But what of this marriage you speak of? To Juliet? How man, when his heart was for Rosaline?"

"As I am a friar, I cannot alter the truth to appeal to your ears. On the evening of the grand party at the house of Capulet, they met, fell in love and requested of me to marry them as soon as they had time and place. Their love, so deep and authentic, as Romeo had never spoken so authentically as he did of love in my eye, brought me to marry them for their love and in the hopes it would teach the families themselves to love. But in no time did fate wield its unwelcomed hammer upon what could offer a future of peace and bring us to this day that we now live."

"Ha! Romeo in love. This is not new for me, as he falls in love with all that walk upon his eye and offer him a smile. The white of her teeth that smiles at him, is the potion that induces love's magic and gives him reason and purpose to walk among us. Signor Love does rouse his spirit at the sight of a returned eye!" Mercutio speaks what would be ill of his friend, but that they are friends helps me to understand the angle he speaks from. Even still, his words are more than I would want from any friend of mine.

"They have a love that I myself have never seen," I say quickly, in defense of the boy I much respect. "Upon their love did the word itself find its meaning. You speak harshly upon one you yourself say that you love, but that Romeo's mouth spoke of love for you I am offended for him." I had to speak these words, as I could not allow such horrible things be said about two souls who love each other more deeply than the sum of all those on this world.

"You read me wrong, good sir. I have love for Romeo that none would know, even deeper than any woman could show. For our friendship since our youth has bonded our souls, so that in each life we return, he and I shall rouse the cities we live and burn down all those that get in our way or oppose." Mercutio, in what appears to be his first serious emotion he has shown, takes his stance as Romeo's man.

Silence falls upon us. I cannot speak, as my anger may come through me and bring this to a place where we may not recover. The friar looks at me and is now content that I have silenced myself as well, though I can see he understands my passion to defend Romeo. He seems to know this Mercutio, and in the depth of such knowledge, must know that this is the way this man is. I do not understand how any man could befriend this person.

"Friar, I had attempted to come to you at the church, as I have been on these streets since I myself lost my life. For some unknown reason, every time I approach the church and hope to enter, I am suddenly back here, at the market. I have entered other places as well, such as the prince's house, house of Montague, and even returned to the house of Capulet, but the church will not allow me in. My thoughts make me believe that God is punishing me for my sins and that I will walk Verona for eternity. Yet to hear that Romeo is within the church, I can see that he punishes me even more, as he will not allow me to see my friend." He looks to the sky, raising his fists as to strike the clouds. "God, I am here! You want to come for my soul and show me the way to purgatory? I stand awaiting your wrath! My hands will be here, held behind my back; come, show me your might! Are you not brave enough to challenge me now that as a spirit, I may strike upon you?"

"Mercutio, upon mine ears, I ask of you to stop this. You offend God and me, by using such words. Give me time, and I will help you find the reason you are not allowed in the church and still walk these streets. Yet, to use such harsh words will not permit you to get any closer to God's kingdom." The friar takes his stance against the crude nature of this man and looks to correct his misguided path.

"Friar, I will hold my peace, for now. I will do as you instruct, but know that my will is stronger than any man you have ever met. A lifetime in Verona would please me, for the food and the women are plentiful and grand, but that I cannot enjoy either in this form I am trapped, I shall burn Verona to the ground by tempting the devil to come for me and show him all the sin that he can feed upon. Do you hear that?" he yells to the clouds, once again, but then looks to the friar and places his hand over his mouth. He is a wild spirit, and one I would not like to have met whilst he was alive. I see much of Romeo's passion in him, but that Romeo has enough awareness to know when to show his rage, makes him the wiser man.

"Apothecary, shall we return to the church and speak more of our findings in concerns to Benvolio and Sampson, as well as inform Romeo and Juliet of these same findings? We may even grant Romeo the knowledge that Mercutio is outside the walls of the church in the same ghostly state that he also resides in. I feel more has befallen on us than we were prepared for, and now, we will need even more thought and time to figure how it will be that we end this war between the families."

"You look to end the war between these families?" Mercutio once again yells. "Good gracious! God, you are as insane as any that has walked in Verona and thought they had come to paradise. Good friar, the only ending of this war between the Capulets and Montagues will be once the last drop of blood from the last heir to their names has fallen and washed away in the rains that carry the filth from the streets. Peace is not a word that either of these households will ever understand. Even before my mouth opened its lips some weeks ago and pronounced my fate to each damned member, they have been cursed. A plague a' both their houses!"

I hope what Mercutio speaks is incorrect, as a curse as deep as what seems to lie between these families may just end the way he has foreseen it. If that is the case, then all this effort the friar and I place into this 'talk of peace' will be all for naught.

"Mercutio, wait you upon the market. We will call upon you when the time is in need, and by the calling of this affair, that will be upon the fall of the first leaf within the fall season. There is some reason as to why we now speak with you, as fate does not bring you to me for any other reason. We will soon learn of it and place it into effect. Until then, be well."

"O', good friar, I will be nothing but well, for who can move Mercutio but Mercutio, when not one, other than yourselves, can hear nor touch Mercutio. I will wait for your call, since waiting is all I have."

As we walk away, Mercutio speaks toward many who walk by him, continuing the rude demeanor he did express to us. If he knows that they cannot hear him, why is it that he still speaks? Is it to hear his own voice? Or does he hope that he will fall upon the path of two more that may hear him and allow for this voice to once again be heard? The friar may be accustomed to his words, so harsh and uncalled for, but my ears do not experience such words as common, and I find it rude that he addresses a man of God as so.

"Good apothecary, we will return to the church and convey our information as we have received it. I fear that as motion has furthered itself toward the war, more lives will fall in the same such numbers, if not greater. I have some thoughts in mind on how we entreat the lords of each household to our place of worship. In the church, no man dare strike down upon another. If sin is as feared for a life in purgatory, then never will one murder another within the grounds of the church. That would be damnation twice the worth."

"My thought centers my brain around one solitary idea I cannot find an answer to, but that Romeo may know. However these men have fallen, there must be some that have the skill with the sword to defend themselves to not be struck by their opponent, but that can themselves strike a deadly blow quickly. This is the man, or men, that we must speak with. Granted, when I speak of "we", I mean with officers, or some sort of protection for our lives."

"You are wise, good apothecary. If we cannot find these men in the action of the murders, then we shall speak with them well before they commit the murders themselves. The church is straight ahead, but soft, look. Officers stand at the doors of the church. What is it that brings them to stand guard at the house of God, where angels themselves have been granted this duty of protection? Let us go to them and quickly too."

Looking ahead, I see that there are three officers standing there, watching the area around the front of the church. We rush to the doors and speak with the first officer that connects eyes with us.

"Officer, what ho! Why is it that you come to the church and stand watch? Is there something that you require of me?"

"Good friar, we are glad you are returned. A nurse from the house of Capulet is within. Something unfortunate has happened, and she rests inside to gather her soul before we bring her back to her house."

"I thank you for your service, good men. I will speak with her of this concerning matter, and send her out to you very soon, so that you may escort her home and bring yourselves to rest as well."

As we walk in the door, we hear the nurse speaking, and we hear Juliet responding to her. There is not a complete conversation, as the replies of Juliet do not match the words the nurse speaks out to her. As we enter and are seen by the nurse, she comes running to us, tears in her eyes, frightened it seems to a point where her expression shows that she is not of sound mind.

"Good friar! Good friar! He is dead, he is dead. I saw the blow and his fall. He is dead and I could not help him. He told me to run and I did; I did as he said. O' the poor man, he is dead." She runs into the arms of the friar and weeps on him, as he embraces her to support her body and mind. She is well shaken up from what it seems to be another death. Juliet comes to us, with the same intense look of fear and sadness.

"Friar, she came running in, yelling and crying," Juliet says, looking to inform us of what she knows. "The soldiers came shortly after her, as her screams were loud enough to wake the dead themselves. She did yell out for you as she first entered, but as you were not here, she yelled out for me. I heard her calls and came upon her cry, but as she cannot see nor hear me, I have not had the ability to soothe her soul. Peter is dead. She yelled it several times, head moving in all directions, as she could not see where I was. She did not say anything more. She just yelled, Peter is dead."

"Thank you for this information about Peter," the friar said to Juliet, as she stands close by, waiting to see how the nurse was.

"I did not tell you it was Peter. How did you know? Is it being spoken on the streets, that Peter is dead? O', what a horrible and rash deed. I did not see where he came from. It all happened so fast, that not even Peter could respond well."

"Calm yourself, good nurse. Breathe, slowly and easily. We need to hear your clear mind and know of what happened. Once you are calm, please inform us as to what happened," the friar speaks, in a slow and soft voice, hoping to soothe the mind of the nurse and calm her demeanor.

She moved herself out of her embrace with the friar and stood, wiping her eyes, and looking up at the ceiling as if waiting for God to grant her the power to speak. She is very shaken, and her mind looks as busy as tending to her household at its worst times. My heart does ache for her. She has seen much sadness these past several weeks. She lowers her eyes to us and shows that she is prepared to speak.

"As we left the church, Peter and I sorted our affairs and were making our way back to our house." She pauses to collect herself as she speaks. "Then, from out of a shadow, a man steps out, sword already drawn, and attacks us, swinging the sword at me. Peter, in quick defense, draws and raises his rapier and blocks the attacker's sword from connecting with my body. Peter yells at me to run, run, and holds the man off, placing his body in the path of the attacker. I heard each strike of their swords as I ran, but as I quickly looked back, I paused for just a moment as I thought Peter might run as well and join me. Even as I achieved a good distance, I could still see them moving in their defense of each other. Each swing Peter made missed the man, as this stranger's speed was more cunning than I had seen in other quarrels I have been present for." She again gathers her breath. "But then the man struck Peter, and as it appeared he slid his sword across his arm, relieving Peter of his sword.

In the next strike, his sword pierced Peter's chest, straight through so that the sword came through his back. At this, I ran once more with much speed, as much as my legs would allow. My screams were loud, and as I turned a street, hoping to make my way back to the church, I did come across these officers, who granted me immediate protection. Two of them ran in the direction I pointed, to attend to Peter and catch the murderer before he did take flight. But they returned with no sight of the man who looked to have done in the good Peter." She begins to cry and lowers her head to hide her tears.

"Did you not see him or get a look at his face? Is there anything you remember about him that may assist us in finding him?" The friar asks questions that may help us in approaching the families and know who ordered this attack. In that the nurse is of the house of Capulet, I am to assume that the Montagues ordered this attack, but I cannot make such an assumption without proof. As Romeo nears, I myself think of an idea that may assist in this.

"Romeo is here now, good nurse. If you have any image in your mind that may direct us to knowing this man, describe it now. If he be of the house of Montague, then Romeo may know of him by your description." As I say this, I look to Romeo, to acknowledge the thought I have shared.

"I have checked the church, and I do not see any doors that have been opened, where this man may have entered, if he followed the nurse here," Romeo says. "I believe you are all safe. But as I heard what the apothecary has just said, please tell her to look into her mind and describe what she can to me which may inform whether this is a man from my house and who it is."

I repeat what he has said to the nurse, allowing her to think and then speak when she is ready. Romeo prepares himself to hear of what member of his family has just killed another man. These deaths have been too frequent and affect those that are closer to the blood of any others.

"Good sir, I cannot describe the man. I am sorry. I had run so quickly, and my frantic blood cloaked my eyes at the initial sight of him but also from the distance I had made, and his quick movements, it was hard to make out a specific feature. He had a sword, he was a man; that is all I can recall for you. It is as though I had seen him before, yet equally it was as if I had seen him for the first time. If Romeo is here and can use any of my words to float within his memory, then God be with him. I am so affrighted that I am not sure I shall ever feel the day where the images and this pain will not haunt me. If the officers are still at the door, I will leave you now and return home to inform the Lord Capulet with what has happened. Peter may not have been a blood member of the house, but that he was of the house, it shall not rest well on the lord."

"Good nurse, I will be here if you need me for anything," the friar says, in his loving nature. "Yet, if the image of this man does come back to your mind, please inform us so that we may place his likeness in the minds of others and position an end to this foolish bloodshed that stains the stones on these streets so that red is all we will ever see. If but one man can be caught in the act of these killings, then that shall be more than enough to stop the foolish bloodshed."

The nurse bows and walks to the door with the friar, who opens it to greet the officers who will take the nurse home. This is even worse than the moments we had just witnessed before this most recent of events occurred. Two Capulets, dead within one day. This is happening faster than we can find its cure. Men are dying closer to a pace of day and day, where the first few had several more passing days between them. The lords of each house look to grasp the upper hand and send men to kill the others before the dust settles back on the ground from each fallen man. Is there anything that can be done to stop this war before every head has fallen? It is all happening so fast that I am not confident we can wrap the ends around this desired outcome.

"This is horrible," the friar says, as he comes back into the church. "Peter was a good man. His abilities in his mind may have been limited, but his soul was as honest as any other. All he looked to do was protect the nurse. May his soul know that he died doing his duty and he did save her from sure death. I will pray for him when his body is brought within these walls. There is so much death, that I am not sure the mortuary below can hold all these bodies. We have come across one or two and maybe even three, but these numbers are greater than any have seen. I will have to speak with the nuns and find a way to make it work."

"If there is anything that I can do, good friar, please let me know." As I say this, I take a look at Romeo and Juliet, who stand away from us in conversation. I wonder if they themselves are trying to find the answer in their minds and help us figure out whom it is that has such powers from their households to kill like this.

"I have asked the nurse to speak to Lord Capulet and ask of him to come tomorrow morning so that I can speak with him but on these holy grounds. Perhaps the images of God and Jesus on these walls may correct his soul from the anger he does possess. Yet, the ability to remove him from Lady Capulet may additionally offer me more capability to find his mind and speak more precise rational words to the parts of him that will listen."

"Do you think he will come?" I ask, as my fear of seeing him again still rides on my nerves from our last encounter. "He did not appear to want to entertain more conversation with us. His mind is set on blood."

"Good apothecary, there are more in my vault of words and their groupings than I have informed you of. You see, I have told her that I need him for prayer on the lost men of his house, and to verify how and where their bodies will be buried. She will not mention the truth of why I have asked for him to come. With this in mind, he will appear, as such duties must be attended to. Even if he were to think anything more, the lord of the house must keep his affairs in order. In the same, we must also find someone to go to the house of Montague and entreat him as well."

"Would sending a nun for the call to the house of Montague be appropriate? I would not assume any other reason for a nun to request my presence at the church, but that of the same you spoke for Lord Capulet, to get his affairs in order."

"Signor apothecary, you are a wise man, well beyond the understanding of your knowledge that you allow yourself. This thought of yours shall do finely. I will send a nun tomorrow morning, after speaking with Lord Capulet, and have Lord Montague meet me here in the afternoon. This shall work well." As the friar pauses, I see his mind still hard at work, gathering his collection of words.

"I am not as wise a man as yourself, good friar, who can see such paths of things, but if I were a man requested to come to the church by a nun, this would be the reason I would expect."

"Excellent well. Shall we retreat? For as the day moves on, my hunger grows and my legs do require rest. Time has flown from the world, and the sun has moved his course faster than I would have thought he could go."

"If it please you, I would like to rest here a moment," I ask of the friar, as the peace within the church is calming me so well that I would prefer to remain within it for just a moment longer. Seeing that Romeo and Juliet have also walked away without informing us, this offers me the solitude that I crave well enough and even more than food from the market. Though, I pray such a thought against the splendid realm of heavenly foods does not prevent me from ever experiencing the pure joys of the market again.

"Yes, by all means rest yourself here, and meet me in my chamber when you are finished. Maybe it is so that you are likely on the path to become a man of God like myself." The friar nods his head, smiles his traditional smile, and walks away to the back of the church, to the door behind the altar.

I walk myself down the aisle and seat myself in the middle of the pews. O' my heart is worn from the events of this day. I have seen more sadness in such a short period of time, than in all of my days as a functioning apothecary. My heart does beat hard within me, and my soul cries out to me to find more peace in my life and in my soul before its own end comes. Even if I choose to take my life here, within this church, at the end of this affair, my soul is not yet prepared. I am fortunate I had not taken my life before these moments, or my impact into the next realm may have been even more painful. It may take me days to cleanse my body of all the pain from current situations and the past that has worked its way into my mind and refreshed their stained memory. Verona has not completely placed itself into the image that I had always thought. The beauty and amazement is here, but to maintain its bounty beyond all this conflict and death would be hard to achieve.

I hear a noise, voices in the distance, coming from the door to the left near the altar. This is the same door the nun surprised me through when I first arrived. Does she come again to call upon me? Running in comes Juliet, through the door without a touch. This would be most shocking to one that may be standing here, if they could see spirits and did not know these two occupied the church. Within a moment of breath following comes Romeo. I lower myself in the pew, almost out of sight and keep myself silent. If I attempted to move any lower I would be on the ground. At my age, I know I would not be able to achieve standing very easily from this grounded position.

"Romeo, if I were to plead to God now, here within his church, then maybe it may work. Would it not be fair, as we have left this world from our living existence, that we sacrifice ourselves once again to offer peace to our loved ones that still live and carry on our name?"

"Who is to say it will work? How will we verify that this agreement we will offer will give its result to our families? Thus, I leave my soul to chance that such an agreement may send us to the pits of hell, taking me from you forever, and not know whether it has given our families the peace we pray they find? Fie upon it, I cannot blindly give you up."

"Romeo, think of it. Our love is more than God can control. If you and I are bound together for the rest of our days, both living and dead, then anything we offer cannot prevent us from being together. But can we not at least try and give our families the peace they deserve and allow them to live, even if chance play a hand in the outcome? Shall we be selfish and not allow them happiness? Think of it...peace with no more blood on the streets.

Your family will grow and prosper. My family will do the same and find their ends in heaven when God has called upon them at the age that is right. We, under a most brave vow, will end the war without using the friar and the apothecary, who also brave their lives for us. I do not see any other way around this solution. What say you?"

"Juliet, I have lived many a day. The sun did rise and I took delight. Flowers bloomed and their scent awoke a desire to breathe. I may not have lived very long, but I lived very well. But in all that I did and all that I looked to do, none of it was worth another moment without you. I would trade every flower and every breath to be with you. Having you here with me is all I will ever need to survive the fires below. The devil can hold me down in the flames and direct waves of liquid fire on my soul, but it will affect me none if you are there to love me when his torture is complete. So if you ask me to vow to end our love, to sacrifice all that is within me to let chance take a hold of our fate and never be with you again, then I say nay to that and let our families find their own peace."

"Love, you shall always have me. I am in your heart. I am in your mind. When you walk, I am there, whether you see me or not. When you breathe the scent of a flower, it is me that you breathe in. When the sun does rise and shine down on you, it is my loving grace that touches and warms you. If you find a way to the fires of hell, then know that when each fury of pain hits you, it is with my love that they use you. I have that same thought within me, that no matter where it is that my soul ends up, whether I see you there or not, you will be there with me, protecting me and loving me like you have since we met. Now come, let us go to the bodies below and pray for them. Maybe we will see their spirits rise and speak with them when they do. Either way, our respects should be paid to them, as they are in this conflict fallen and we the immediate meaning behind the swords that took their lives."

As they walk from the altar and leave the church hall, I am in a moment of shock once again, but with a love that surprises me more every time I happen upon its words. These two are the creation of love and have it in them where no other person has felt something as pure and sweet as what they do possess. I am honored to see such love in my life, whether it be in my heart or theirs. Looking around the church, I view each holy image and thank it for my life. This has been a gift, regardless that pain has been at the head of this horrible situation. I rise from the pew and walk slowly to the door in the back. The friar waits upon me, and I have the peace I so desired.

Chapter Twelve

Walking into his chamber, the friar greets me warmly with his smile that would make a sinner a saint by its effect alone. He is a goodly man, one I would have gladly befriended regardless of this situation. His church would be one that I would have attended, if I chose to attend mass and worship God within His home. My words seem to speak of me in a way that I no longer have choice or that I cannot do these things once the peace has fallen. I am not sure that speaking with the friar of my intentions toward myself will be wise, as I cannot see him allowing me a day of rest where he would not advise me to stay within this world. I would be a flower to a nest of bees.

"Good man, I see the peace in your eyes that you so sought for, as you took your moment in the church when I left you. Do you see how God can work his magic upon us and clear our souls and minds to bring us peace everlasting?"

"Dear friar, I will not disagree with you upon the power of God and his loving hands upon our souls. Though, I am sorry to inform, that it was His creations of love and not His words that brought this peace to me. Praying in the church, Romeo and Juliet happened upon me and were speaking of their love. The feelings they possess, the way they express their devotion to one another, it is more than I have seen even between those who have spent more years than twice both their ages together."

"Yes, dear sir, they have a love that I myself have not seen prior to their union. I married them upon a very short passing of time, following the moment they met, immediately leading to the exchange of their vows. Many others that would enter my church speaking such occasion to hurry into marriage receive a pause from me to allow them to gather their wits in their hearts, to verify this is what their souls truly desire. Yet, these two were different in that. Romeo, who I have seen in and out of love, was under a distinctive potion with Juliet. His mind was of no other thought, but also captured the focus of a man that has all his wits in hand. It amazed me as it does you."

"Shall I ever look upon love like this again, good friar; I am not sure my eyes will have the ability. But that Romeo and Juliet are also no longer of this world terrifies me; who will show others what love is and how to hold it as strongly as they? Who will set the example to those in Verona, holding the truth to the moment of love? I have learned my craft as an apothecary from those that did it before me and he that did it before them. Is not love learned the same?"

"Shall we hope that love comes from within us, born into our souls at birth. That you have seen their love, you are much rewarded, as am I, but would you believe that such love came from those that have as much showing of hatred than love? Look at their families and this ancient strife between them. Would you think love could breed from such hate? I would have thought that they would sooner learn the art of the sword than the heart, but it was not so."

"You are correct in thought. I would never have imagined that love would be stronger than fallen blood between such old foes."

A knock at the friar's door brings our conversation to a stop. Do Romeo and Juliet stand outside the door, now that they have learned how to use their ghostly frames, and look to inform us that they hear our words?

"This must be the nun, as we are late for supper," the friar says as he prepares to speak to the inquirer. "Please enter," he says, as he stands and readies himself to leave his chamber under the preparedness of the moment.

"Good friar, I am sorry to bother you," the nun says, as she enters the room slowly, but stays at the door.

"No bother at all; it is our forgetfulness that brings you here. We are late for supper, and we do apologize for this," he says, as he walks from around his desk and stands with me.

"Well, then you will be even more late." As she says this, I look at the friar and roll my lips, as this woman's wit is pleasurable to witness in the clothes of a nun. "There is a messenger here to speak with you. Pray you, he is right down the hall. Shall I call him over?"

"Why yes, please invite him in. May I ask, a messenger from whom? Did he state where he is coming from?" I can see his brow rise, as this visitation invites wonder as to who would send their attendant this late in the evening.

"From the prince. I will call him down," she says, as she walks away, leaving the door open.

"From the prince? Good apothecary, be at your best. This man will report every sight seen and word spoken. This is very like speaking with Saint Peter, the angel who will greet you at heaven's gate. What he sees and is told goes to the ear of God directly."

Footsteps approach and my heart races, as I have never been in the presence of someone who would report my mind and actions to a prince. But what in faith brings him to us this late in the evening? And from the prince? As he walks into the room, my muscles tighten my stance.

"My good friar, good evening to you, sir. And good evening to you, sir. I am sent by the prince to request that you accompany me to His Majesty's home to speak with him this very night. I will wait upon you in the church, if it please you, but I pray, as he awaits our return, I beg you make haste and follow me presently."

"Good man, you bring awareness that shall not be misused. We shall be with you shortly," the friar says, as he looks and nods at me to verify that I am with him in thought. The attendant bows his head and walks out of the room.

"He will wait for us in the church, but we must not keep him waiting for very long. Are there any effects that you need or shall we go now?" the friar asks, as I can sense the nervous strings as his voice trembles with his words.

"Do you know the cause of this calling from the prince?" I say, hoping to hide my nervousness. "There is an urgency that I feel in the attendant's voice, as well as a calling this late in the evening, that brings me to believe that this is of an important nature."

"Good man, I did not even know the prince had returned. This is most shocking to me as well. Yet, that he calls for me this late in the day, there is much urgency to it. Let us go, for I do not want to keep his man waiting nor the prince himself. Even as he has called upon me alone, I know that the matter he will speak of will be more rewarding to his mind if you come as well and speak of the same actions that I have seen. Your voice, in the same words as mine, will allow his mind to make decisions that are right and just. His return can only be due to the matter of the war of the families. He has grown weary of their struggles and will want to strike down on them harshly for the deaths that have recently occurred. He has warned them of further violence following the deaths of Romeo and Juliet. Clearly, they have not listened, and thus, clearly, he will strike with a mighty sword upon them for these events. Come, let us away."

The friar walks out of the room, and I follow him at the same speed as his pace brings me. He does not seem to fear many a man, but when the prince calls, as I would have to also assume for myself, he goes with a vigorous urgency, as if God has asked to council with him as well.

As we make our way into the church, we meet the attendant in the main church hall and begin to walk to the doors without saying another word of greeting. The attendant bowed his head to us when we arrived and turned immediately to leave. He did not show dissatisfaction with my presence with the friar, which can only mean that he is in full understanding and agrees upon the action that it is welcoming for me to come. I was quite worried that there may be a concern for my appearance as well, as I am not a citizen of Verona, but the question was not raised, so I go to it with them.

There are parts of me that are excited, as I have never met a prince. Yet, that we are being called to the prince, there is not much that speaks to comfort in the concerns of our calling. It is not a visitation that welcomes us for dancing or for a feast. We are called for due to the murders within the city, I am as sure of it as the spring flowers now only bring beauty, but that there will come a day when their seeds of growth will bring humans to their knees.

The prince must seek the friar's opinions and also the blessing from the church as to what he will want to do to the families. If death is a commission they must meet, then the friar will be asked to bless their souls before their lives are ended.

It is not long before we make our way through the streets and come upon the residence of the prince. Similar to the houses of Capulet and Montague, there are high walls here, and many more guards at the gate. We are instantly allowed in, as the guards witnessed the attendant coming toward the gate from a distance, walking past many alleys and houses.

Cold, hard eyes gaze at us as we enter. The closer I look, the more I notice that they gaze upon me. They seem to know the friar, as all within Verona should, for the holy man that he is, but they have never seen me before, and that brings awareness to their forefront. These men are trained to die for the protection of the prince, and their demeanor justifies the claim. I would not choose to cross any one of them.

"As we enter, we will be greeted by several people," the friar says, in a strong whisper of a voice, to prepare me for what we are about to experience. "Bow your head each time. Do not speak unless you are spoken to. Try and keep eye contact far from your choice, as engaging in such things will call question as to why you are looking at them. It is better to leave some conversations unengaged."

I nod my head to verify my agreement to his contract. The friar informs me well, and I will do all I can to follow his words and follow his path every step within this realm. I care for the respect that he has within these walls, and I do not want to change the way he appears in these citizens' eyes, especially that of the prince.

Entering the door, I am once again astonished by the sight of the decorations. The homes of the other families were well decorated. They have amenities that I had one day wished for and even some I knew I could never achieve. Yet this castle, shall I call it, where the prince resides, is even more astonishing. The gold that covers the furniture, that trims the paintings, and that hangs from the chandelier, is outstanding. Accents that would welcome many through the gates of heaven welcome those that visit the prince.

Another difference that calls to my immediate awareness is that we do not enter the palace and find our place of meeting in the first room to the right. As this is the fashion of most homes, this is not how one visits the prince. We walk deeper into the estate, through grand rooms, where history shows its face in the paintings of the former kings, queens and princes of these lands. Down this long hall we walk, by each face that once sat in the royal chair.

Within a long feeling and yet short distance are two grand doors with furnishing of gold in ancient scenes of war. These doors look quite important, as something or someone great and powerful must be behind them. As they open, our first image is of the prince sitting on a throne, guarded by several men on each side. As we enter, the doors behind us close, and we walk closer to the prince, but are stopped several steps away. The friar bows and I follow suit quickly. As the friar stands, watching through the corner of my eye, I stand, and remain at full peace. I leave the focus and aim of my eyes resting on the floor, admiring the marble and its patterns, waiting for a moment when I am allowed to return my eyes to gazing level of all others in the room.

"Good friar, welcome. I thank you for coming so late in the day. I would not have summoned you if it were not of the utmost importance. And who is this that arrives with you? I have not seen his aged face in my city before, as men of his age would bring memory back to me quite quickly."

"My lord, this is Paul. He is learning the duties of a friar and understanding what it is like to live a friar's life. I am showing him the responsibilities of the calling, and he has been by my side these last several days. I thought it would be well received if he joined me, if it so please you, my lord."

"Yes, it is welcomed, as more than one set of eyes upon situations such as these, offers me a better look at what I hope to gather. Welcome, Paul."

"Thank you, my gracious lord," I say, with a bow, and stop there. To this point, he is a kind ruler it seems. Though, in the back of my mind, informing him that my name is Paul is also frightening. If the day did come that he were to find out my real name and know that he has been tricked early on, my name and my head may roll on the floor of this mighty palace.

"Now, to the matter for which I called you here. Friar, I will be placing my hand at the throat of both the Montagues and the Capulets, as my returning to our fair city hours ago was harshly welcomed with stories of defiance and blood. Some three weeks ago or more I called upon the families to find peace between them from the foolish deaths of their children, Romeo and Juliet. Two such young children, killed by their own hands, from their history of hate and violence, is a shameful mark on them and our city. Each man of the house shook hands, agreeing upon peace between them. But now, as I return from other stately matters, to protect Verona from unwelcomed foreign interests, I find that the peace has ended and even more blood than I could have imagined myself has spilled." The prince pauses and looks around the room. He holds himself well for a man that clearly is upset and disappointed. I hear the friar clear his throat lightly, as if he were preparing to say something.

"My lord, these events you speak of are true. I can verify all the names of those that have fallen, as they rest within the church." The friar keeps his words short and detailed. He is smart to not carry on, as the prince himself looks ready to say more.

"That information I will gladly accept after we are finished here. It is my understanding that those who have died are youths within the families as well?" the prince asks.

"Yes, my gracious lord, they are all children of the two families." The friar seems to bow his head with every piece of information he offers the prince. I should be aware of this, for each time I address the prince as well. I did not do so initially. I hope that does not bring a sour look upon me.

"I will require a list of the names of each that have died. Their names shall be placed on a plaque that will hang within the house of each family to remind them of their horrible nature and the evil deeds that have been done. Jasontonio," he says as he calls to a man resting to the far side of him, "after the conclusion of this meeting, speak with these men and gather the names of those that have fallen. Include those that have died within this very month, following the deaths of Romeo and Juliet." The prince demands this of his man, and his man nods and bows to verify he heard him well and will do his asking. One would not be wise to refuse to do the asking of this prince. The more he speaks, the stronger his rule appears. Yet, even in his present state of anger and clear frustration, he holds himself calmly. This is a quality that someone of the royal family must have to maintain the essence of power.

"We will stay upon the end of our meeting to do our service," the friar says, bowing his head and smiling. He then looks over at the prince's attendant, Jasontonio, nods his head and offers his smile to verify he will meet with him.

"Friar, what has happened to my fair city?" the prince says, as he looks up at the ceiling and ponders the words, more than poses them as a question. "There is much beauty within these walls, where flowers bloom the bond between nature and our world unite them as if they are lovers. Many travel to our grand market, as it offers everything one would ever need. Our citizens are hard workers, who want to live a happy life and enjoy their families and friends. I grew up here, playing in the streets without a concern upon my head. Now, wherever it is I go, I am reminded of the bloodshed, either by the words of the scared citizens who witnessed the actions, or by the stones where blood still freshly marks them like battle stripes upon a warrior's face. I cannot find the peace I have so desired. I have been a fair ruler, kind, with much compassion that would allow the honest of heart to be forgiven for small and foolish acts. Yet now, that fair and loving side of me has found its end, and my rage shall gather its fury-stricken arms and assemble each one of these cursed Montagues and Capulets. Once together, they will learn of their punishment that will either end their lives or end their history within these blessed walls of Verona. Any that speak one word of objection will lose their tongue, any that wave their hand to plead otherwise will have their arm removed, and any that run from my verdict will no longer have the ability to move, as in their state of death they will become one with dirt. This is my decree. Come the rising sun, my men shall gather and receive orders to embark on my command. If any come to your church whilst my men gather their households together, send them to me here by my direct order. Do you receive my word, good friar?" the prince asks, as his rage increases word by word, in the desire to finally end what has scarred his great city for years.

"My lord, without question, I have heard your will and shall inform any who walk in the doors of my church of your desires. This much I know, that Lord Capulet will be within the church at the start of the day to instruct me on the burial desires of those of his house that have died. At the end of our meeting, I will inform him of what you have said and that he must come to your majesty's estate." The friar is a wise man to inform the prince that Lord Capulet may attend his church, as he told the nurse to speak to him. The prince is of sound mind, but his anger shoots from his eyes like light from the sun, as his rage reddens his complexion from the fiery blood that flows like lava within in his veins.

"Friar, you have always served me well. This will not be forgotten. If the Lord Capulet does meet with you, inform him of my wishes and make the urgency in your voice show him the immediacy of my command. You have cared for this city for many years and it shows with many of the citizens I meet and speak with. We shall speak again soon to discuss plans of improvements to the church, as the years have not been kind to some of its features. I would like for our church to be the symbol of God, as the market has been spoken to be a symbol of life and commerce. I will leave you both, as I need to prepare myself for this day to come. Jasontonio will gather the needed information and show you out. I thank you again for coming."

At the end of his words, he stands, and his guards gather themselves with more attentiveness. The friar and I bow to him, as others in the room do the same. Walking from the throne, he leaves out a door to our left side. The friar looks at me with a moment of great relief but then with much worry mixed together, and as the seconds pass, the weight of our calling rolls from his mind and he becomes more focused and clear in his attention.

"This matter is well ended for us. I cannot imagine the scene of what we will see tomorrow. Pardon me a moment, good apothecary, whilst I speak with the prince's man." The friar pats my shoulder and walks to the prince's attendant, Jasontonio, to offer the requested information.

I am much relieved as well. I was not sure whether more involvement would be requested of us, or if the prince himself was going to show his disappointment upon the friar's handling of the events and take out punishment on his head, which would be equal to mine. Even as I look to end my own life, the torture the prince would put us through would have been far more than my body would desire to endure. Exactly as he said, this has ended well for us. I cannot think of the confusion that will ensue tomorrow. I hope that we will head back to the church after this so that the friar and I can speak of our story and how all of our information will be disclosed and shared when the officers gather the families. I fear more blood will fall, as each family will fight to be taken. If there is any sense left in their minds, they will do the prince's bidding.

The friar calls over to me, as it appears we are ready to go. I walk to him as the attendant and the friar begin to lead us out of the hall immediately and back upon the path where we entered. I do not look at any others within these walls directly in their eyes, nor do I say a word to anyone. It is best that I leave this place without causing an incident or bringing attention to myself.

Leaving the gates, the friar grabs my arm lightly and leads me slowly down the street, away from the prince's estate, and toward the direction of the church.

"O', good apothecary, this does not suit these families well. The prince has stated his intention and will follow through with it like Noah and the great flood. He will drown the voices of the families with his authority and send their souls away from his graced city. In my years as a friar I have never seen such actions. I would plead for him to offer forgiveness, but I am sure that day has come and gone."

"If there were ever a time in my life where I was happy to not be a part of one of these families with much wealth and power, that time is now. It proves to me that all the money in the world cannot keep one from the swift hand of justice. They are doomed," I state, thanking the powers that be that I was born under the grace that I had been.

"They may be doomed tonight, but if there is one thing I know of good Verona, it is that a royal command tonight may be altered to a state where their death will come whenever God has originally stated. I have been through such matters before with these families, and have saved them without their even knowing. Even as this command by the prince seems like the end of the families, I know of a way we shall save them. Let us get back to the church. I will inform you of my plan that will begin with Lord Capulet at the church tomorrow morning and then sweep through the family like a refreshing breeze."

"That sounds most well," I say, with the air of relief that we may have a hand in saving the useless bloodshed. "These families will need to build your new church with their bare hands, stone by stone, for what you have already done and will continue to do for them. I wonder if they will ever know what hand God plays in their lives to help them as such. You are too kind, good sir." As I speak my words of praise, another voice calls out to us from a place unseen.

"O' help, please help me," the soft voice from the alley to our right calls out. We look and see a man on the ground, reaching up to us from the alleyway stone ground. The friar walks quickly to him and I follow. I pray this is not another murder, as this man may breathe his final breath in our presence. If it be so, and as near to the prince's estate as this is, the prince may take his actions this very night with his own sword.

"Good man, are you all right?" the friar asks, as he stands over him, grabbing his arm and holding it looking to help the unfortunate man to his feet.

"Good gentlemen, I am but a poor man, with no ability to live. Can you please help me?" he asks, as he stays on his knees and struggles to get to his feet.

"Dear son, let your faith fill your body and we shall carry you to the church to offer you shelter and food for the night," the friar says warmly. The friar is a good man, as every person he comes across that is in need of help receives his assistance and endless fountains of love. His heart is as big as the whole of the church itself, which God will need to offer him such a large paradise, or greater, in heaven when he arrives.

"To the church?" the poor man states, as if he realizes his blessing has come. "To the church?"

It is as if he uses questions, more than he blesses himself, with speaking the word of the church. He must be far gone in mind, as his appearance makes him look to be old and one who has been on these streets for some time. He looks up at me, and his bearded face hides his age well, but his motions speak to him being close to my age. His eyes are almost closed, as the long days and nights, sleeping on these stone streets, have left him no rest with which to heal himself.

He looks to the friar, which I know will warm his heart and flush the thankful words that he will feel from this saving grace. He struggles to rise, and the friar holds his left arm strong with both of his blessed hands, to offer as much support as he can. Once he has taken to his feet, I will assist as well. In my own fortune, I would hope God will look down on me and thank me for helping the friar like I have.

As if the power of the heavens blesses him with speed, the poor, powerless man rises to his feet surprisingly quickly, but faster than I can believe I see him raise his right arm, hand clutching a dagger, and thrusts the dagger into the friar's chest, near his heart. As he stands straight up, he now supports the weight of the friar, as he looks at me and then back at the friar. His voice growls as words begin to be spoken.

"I am not in need of going to the church, you holy fool. I am in need of all the valuables you have within your possession. But even now, I am fooled, as a friar and an ungodly old man like you do not usually carry such wealth on your persons. I was hoping you were family to the house of Capulet or Montague, as these rich people always carry hundreds of ducats on them just for the sake of carrying them around in their high esteem. Yet, I have chosen wrong. And for my ignorance, this is what you will both receive as a gift from me," he says as he twists his hand that holds the blade in the friar's chest, causing the friar to be lost in his pain. "And the best of it, is that blame will fall on the foolish, wealthy and greedy families that cover this city in filth, as these quarrelling families do still fight in these streets, and leave bodies dead many an evening. This may be my first soul I take," he says looking at the friar, "But it will not be my last," he finishes saying, looking over to me.

He forces the blade deeper still into the friar to make sure he does the job well. The friar looks at him, in astonishment and amazement, gasping for breath, unable to say anything. The friar then turns his eyes toward mine, as speechless as I am, being that we looked to help a man in need and find death within our path. I cannot let this be. I must act, to try and save his life and spare my own.

"O', help. Help!" I yell, as I still stand in the street, within view of the prince's gates. As I look toward the gates, the officers look at me and begin running in my direction.

"You fool, you have called the prince's guards! When the time is right, I will find you and send you to heaven with the good friar." He pulls the dagger from the friar, wipes it on the friar's clothes, and runs in the opposite direction. The friar falls to the ground hard, as I am not able to catch him from the thief's release. Within moments, the guards are here, see the fallen friar, and look down the alley and see the thief running. They immediately take to foot after him, leaving us alone. I rush to the friar's side and hold his head up as he gasps for air.

"My good friar, I am sorry. I did not see the blade rise within his hand quickly enough where I could make a motion to stop the attack. There was nothing I could do. I wish that there were, but there was nothing I could do." I begin to feel tears fall from my eyes. My heart aches and pounds as I hold him. An increasing hollowness fills me and chokes the air that would smoothly pass. How can this be? How can the friar, on a mission from God, receive an attack that may take his life?

"Apothecary...good sir," he whispers, but softly, and with much forced and painful effort.

"Do not use your energy for words, my good friar. As the guards are come to save us, they will call for one who may mend as well. I am only learned in the arts of medicines, but not one that could stop this blood from exiting the wound." As I hold him, I see blood on the ground begin to gather into small pools. Once again, the stone is stained by the blood of the innocent. "You will be back within the church reciting your mass sooner than you can expect." His eyes look at me as I talk with him, but they close more quickly than they can stay open. "Stay awake, good friend."

"I do not...believe...I will have...time. I will under...stand, if you...choose to leave, and not...complete...our...mission. God will...forgive you." He coughs loud and hard, as blood begins to erupt from his mouth with each exit of breath. His robe is now drenched with moisture, as his blood escapes his body with the force of an over-flooded river. His eyes are locked with mine. His breaths are fewer and fewer. Then, even as his eyes stay gazing into mine own, his life leaves his body and the stare becomes vacant and hollow. And within this moment, his body no longer holds the spirit of the man that looked to do everything he could to encompass love and peace.

I have seen a spirit leave one's body many times. There was hope in me that the friar could be saved, but God did not send a savior to his side. On my knees, I hold him, and support his body in case the spirit may return by God's good graces.

"Please, God, do not take this man. Bring his spirit back; I cannot do this alone. As he is a man you have chosen to represent you on this world, you cannot take him yet. There is much still to do," I say, but as the night still carries the sounds of peace, and no wings of angels come to grant a holy touch to revive him, all looks to be lost.

"Goodly friar, you were a man as wise and blessed as any I have met. Your heart cared more for the citizens than for the pain and suffering you yourself have taken on. May God carry you to your place in heaven and welcome you into paradise. I will do what I can to follow your good graces in this world and do what I must to stop this war," I say, hoping that if his spirit still floats in the air, he hears my devotion. "But wait! What is the information that you knew would save them once again? Good friar, speak once more! What is the knowledge you were to bestow on me when we arrived back at the church? Good friar!" No response is granted.

All is lost. He was to tell me of his guaranteed plan to save the families and stop the war. If I am to brave this storm of hate and save them, I will need this information. How will I know what to do?

Noises from behind me sound into my ears, but I care not to look. If this is another thief or some other cruel soul, let them have at me. I do not have the will to go on.

"Old man, we have captured the dirty thief. We will send help for the friar as soon as we reach the prince's grounds," the guard says as they pass me, but looking back at the reality of the scene, they realize that they need not send anyone to save him, as he is already lost. "I see. We will send someone to help you. Come, filthy peasant. Watch what the prince does to those who murder in Verona. You have reached him at his most ripe of moods."

I look at the thief, this man that has taken the friar's life. He shows no thoughts or feelings for his actions. His face is like a newborn baby, looking at the world. He must be mad. How does one take such a life as this and feel nothing? If I were a man of war, I would act upon this moment now to strike him down. Though, I do not have such power within me. The prince will deal with him justly, I am sure.

Holding the friar, time is floating around me and not moving. The wind no longer crosses the air around us. The stars are covered by passing clouds and their light does not shine down on us. Sounds come from around the corner, as two men arrive to help with the friar's body. Looking at me gently, they step into our union and pick up the friar's body with much care and attention.

"We will bring the friar's body to the church, once the prince has seen him and ruled on the man that has done this evil deed," one of the men says to me. "You need not appear to the prince to speak of your story of what has transpired, as the guards have said enough. You may return to the church, if that is where you were heading with the friar." I nod to inform him that I have heard him well. They leave and I remain on my knees, within this spot. Looking up to the sky, the clouds have moved, allowing the stars to shine. The wind returns, brushing across my face.

What am I to do? I am lost in the panic of all these actions that need to be taken upon the families, all falling in my hands. How can I do this alone, without the good guidance and support of the friar? Looking at my hands, I see his blood upon me. The life source that ran through his body now rests in my palms. Will the knowledge he possessed now feed into me through this blood left behind?

A noise sounds in the distance, bringing awareness that I am now alone. I must get back to the church. The evening passes quickly and the more the stars shine, the more light that shows my image to those around me.

Moving quickly, I hope to recall the way the friar brought us here. I have looked to gather more familiarity within the city, as the friar and I traveled around. He knew every path and well enough that his eyes did not need to lead him or place markings in his mind for remembrance. Though, he is now dead.

My eyes again shed more tears for him. He was a man that I could call friend, as I have not had one of those in many a year. I have not trusted another man with my mind and soul, and thus, never called another my true friend, not since Alejandro. The friar, the kindest and warmest of men, was the only person I have ever spoken with where I did not hide my words. He was a kind man. Nevertheless, he is gone. And now I, returning to the church, his house, must inform not only the nuns who will surely grieve at his loss, but Romeo and Juliet. He loved them dearly, and this must have been the reason why they are stuck within the church. They will not take to this information well, as grief rests on their spirits like a hat on one's head. Now I must inform them of his loss, the messenger of news most despised, who will then be trusted to carry on with his mission. Is this your calling for me, God? Is this why you have introduced the friar into my life and brought me to Verona? So shall I try, as I will honor the memories of the friar, by carrying his duty and saving these families.

The streets all appear to be the same to me, but as if God himself means to offer me a small semblance of assistance, I see that I am close to the church, as the moon shines on the steeple, showing me the way. There is meaning in my steps. The church comes quickly upon my path and I walk to the door and pause. I have strength within me that the friar himself has seen. He brought me on this mission with him, as he knew I could walk hand in hand with him to bring peace to this city. Empowered with his will, I shall do exactly so.

As I open the door, there is screaming coming from within the church. I hear a girl's voice yelling, and it can be no other than the fair Juliet. The closer I approach the main part of the church, I see Juliet in the distance, standing at the altar, looking up to the heavens. She appears to be crying heavily, as great sadness seems to have fallen on her. Does she know that the friar has been murdered? The guards could not have brought the body this quickly. It is only moments into my thought, that I realize the true meaning to her sadness.

"Romeo! Romeo! Where are you, my love? Where have you gone?" Her screams are powerful and passionate. She seems to have lost Romeo, but as they are trapped within the church, I am unsure how they can lose track of each other that it brings such emotion about. I move quickly down the aisle and make my way to the altar, standing there, allowing her to finish her thoughts and look down to me and approach me when ready. Her quick glance in my direction allows her sight of me, as she immediately runs down and stands before me.

"Good apothecary, he is gone. Romeo is gone. We stood before each other, here at the altar. I cannot remember what it is we were speaking of, but as a fog does sometimes fade when the sun appears and is gone, so did Romeo. His image faded away, as we were locked in conversation, eye to eye. He was here, and then he was gone. He is gone." She begins to cry harder once again. I wish I could comfort her more, with an embrace that would allow her to feel my support. When I would support someone who would lose their loved one due to illness, a simple embrace would settle them and calm their rage of sadness. That such thing, I cannot do with Juliet.

"When was it, Juliet? When did he fade away, from spirit form to nothing at all?" Concern falls upon me, as there may be a connection to the disappearance of Romeo.

"It was perhaps one hour ago. I cannot be certain. Time is not something I willingly track, as each day and moment blend into one locked within these walls. I cannot tell when the last time I saw the sun from the previous taste of its warmth. Only the beams from its glow enter the church through the colored glass. Only God knows how long I have been here and which day this is."

"My dear, there may be reason for his disappearance." I say this and she looks at me with much concentration. She knows that I am hiding something and can see into my soul. It could be that her spirit power allows her easier access into the deeper parts of the living.

"Good apothecary. Where is the friar?" she asks, as her eyes look to the door, waiting for him to walk in behind me within steps of my own.

"My girl, he too is gone. The good friar has been taken from us." I pause, as my inner well of emotion begins to surface from the deep cavern. "As we left the prince's house and made our way here, a man called out to us from an alley, crying for help. You know, as well as I, that the goodly friar could not ignore such a call from one in need. He acted quickly to assist this man, but within moments of understanding what was in his intentions, he stabbed the good friar in his most precious of organs. In the anger that overwhelmed this most evil man, he chose to take the life of the friar for not having the wealth he had hoped he would carry, coming from the prince's home. As he prepared to attack my person, the guards from the prince's gate came upon the scene. He has been seized by the prince's guards and will with all knowledge of such an offence suffer by the punishment of death for what he has done."

"O', what have these times become? All of those I care for are being taken from this world. What curse is this that removes every person who I have loved in my life, whether it be the living or the dead?" Her sadness mounts on top of other sadness, placing her pain on her as if grief were stacked upon her shoulders in the form of mountains.

"Juliet, I do not mean to bring more concern to your mind, but it is only going to get worse as the sun rises tomorrow. You know that your father is due to come here and speak with the friar once the sun has risen. That duty now falls upon me, to speak with him and hope to alter his mind from war to love. Yet, the prince has written in mine ears that tomorrow, he will gather all of the houses of Montague and Capulet to his domain, and either banish them from Verona or else end their lives from this world. I would not think he would take such harsh actions as this, but his hatred for the violence has come to a place where ridding the city of this same violence is the only way he seems to believe it will end. The friar did inform me that he had a plan for this, that he was still able to stop it all from happening. There were words in his mind that he knew could transform the minds of the families and the prince to stop it all. Though, before he could enlighten me of his knowledge, he was struck down and his life taken, well ahead of his calling."

"The prince does not show mercy in these orders. My dear father and mother and the nurse! O', what rashness against life and peace do men of power have when they cannot use time and mercy to heal. That I could fly to them now and warn them to leave the city before the choice is not in their hands to make."

"Your father does come tomorrow. I shall speak words to him that I would hope the friar would have used, and if this does not settle his blood, I may warn him of this order by the prince. Juliet, I am not a man that can end wars such as the friar had the power and the will to do, but I will hope to help all that I can to prevent further blood from shedding."

"Good apothecary, you are a just and honest man. I thank you for all that you have done." As she says this, she gazes back at the altar area, once again looking for Romeo.

"My dear, what I meant to say as well, was that is it not strange that as the friar lost his life, Romeo would seem to have disappeared as well? Do you think these events may have some affect upon each other? Could one life leaving this world end one spirit's life as well? Was there a connection between their souls that each needed to be out of their bodies to leave this world?"

"I did not think on this reflection either. Does it not seem odd that two such situations, happening in the same hour, be not tied together in this mystic world? Does this mean that Romeo is truly gone? Will he not come back for me, to carry me into the heavens he spoke so well of? Am I alone in this church forever? Good apothecary, I will take my leave of you. There is much sadness in my heart that I cannot bear to show, nor can I speak any further, as my words will be drowned by tears that will now forever run as my existence here will forever entrap me to my bed of misery."

"Juliet, please do not think so. If Romeo has found his way beyond, then you will follow, I am sure of it. There cannot be room for more spirits on this earth than in heaven. Your undertaking is almost done, and you will also find reprieve in the heavens soon. I swear upon it. However, if it be not the hand of God that will free you from this captured state, then Romeo himself will likely crash down from the region beyond this one, and come for you as you know he will."

"Thank you, apothecary. You are as sweet as the friar has always been to me. Maybe if this world allows it to be so, you will be the next friar of this church. Good night, good sir." She turns and walks away, toward the back of the church, toward the door where I first saw her beauteous form.

"I should only wish to be as great as the friar. Good night, dear girl," I say in a whisper, not needing for her to hear, but willing the intention of the peace it allows me to feel for her.

As she is gone, I look to the cross and know that the goodly graces of God are needed more than ever for all that is at this instant expected of me. I cannot think that such a duty would ever have been placed on me in this life. Nevertheless, it has, and I must live up to what is desired of me. If not for me, if not for the remembrance of the friar, but for Juliet, whose soul I must try and free from the church. I will find a way. Though, for now, I must go to the nuns, and prepare them for the friar who will be brought here soon. They have greeted many a citizen, but they do not know of his fate and should be well warned and prepared before he arrives. O', God, your power and grace is needed now more than ever.

Chapter Thirteen

Morning has arrived, waking my mind and my bones from another night of restless sleep. Friar, you did haunt my dreams with the visions of your untimely murder. Your fall was even more grand in my mind, as the earth shook to the heavens when each part of you compounded with the dust. I reached for you, but could not come to your side. My tears flowed more than a waterfall feeding from icy mountains. Dreams are the reality of our days brought to us in a way where there is no hold of the active moment. Never has a dream been within my control, where the outcome has favored my soul. However, the days that I now live are within my hand, and each finger shall play the part of the sculptor to form the image of my mind's eye.

Moving myself to sit up within my bed, this day shall stir me to be the man that I have never expected I would progress to be. I knew that through my work I would heal those afflicted by illness and help any who would fall within my means of knowledge. Then this, a heroic calling, one that the friar would look to perform without even realizing his dutiful outcome.

Prepare you, my soul, for what is to come about will move you more than the devil chasing you himself. That I will save these families from certain death, I am not convinced, but every effort within me will gather its strength and challenge the boundaries of all that I know to strive for the result.

Rising from my bed, I arrange myself from the shifting of the night. The friar had awoken me upon each of my days here, but this day is new and yet lacking of the warm greeting I would normally have received. His tender smile and nod of the head will not be forgotten.

Leaving my room, I walk to the main of the church and enter through the door behind the altar. The church is quiet, as there is no sound or movement as I cross the threshold into the vast and spiritual realm. This is relaxing for greeting my soul into this space but worries me. I am alone within these walls. The mission within itself rests on me.

Walking up to the altar, I stand behind it, looking out at the pews down the aisle. Empty seats will once again be filled, but those who come to grieve will not only do so for the lost ones of their families but now for the friar as well. How will these citizens react to the killing of the friar? He has been here for many dedicated years, serving these people of Verona as well as he was able. The burden of all he took upon himself must have been great.

Alone, without considering any other family within these walls, these two, the Montagues and Capulets, caused more grief and suffering in the city and in this church than a thousand families. What is it that caused such an ancient strife between them? Was there a fight for land, for authority, or for love, that created such hate between each other? This is what I feel would help with these families accepting their differences and living here in peace. If it could be discovered how it was that the first sword swung in anger against the other, then this war could be ended and peace could settle into their souls. Imagine what a petty situation could have been the start of it. One look, one word, misunderstood, even on this very day, shedding blood, years upon years later.

But soft, near the front door in the distance, there is movement. It is Juliet, standing in her longing desire, awaiting the arrival of her father. The sun has risen, as the ancient art within the windows shines the historic images upon these walls. To be the friar, to have lived as him and worshipped within this church, is something that even as I stand here, I admire and find pause for.

Walking down from the altar, I move to the front of the church, to where Juliet stands, so that I can speak with her and know of her mind. She must be filled with emotion she does not yet understand by the newness of her youth. To lose those you love, to have such blood fall for actions that you took whilst you were alive, must be hard to bear on her green soul. The fruit of her being is yet ripe but has been plucked from the tree of life.

"Juliet, I am here. Have you seen anyone enter the church as of yet?" I ask, even as I am clear to the answer regardless of my asking. I will do whatever I can to keep her mind keen and comfort it when I can.

"Goodly apothecary, good morning to you. Not a soul has entered this church, alive or no, but my watch will remain here as my father should be here soon. Knowing his mind, he will want to come to arrange the burial of his men and then leave to return home quickly. Time wasted upon matters that have no importance or that take longer than they should send a signal to his soul to summon his too-well-known rage." She informs me well, and in her eyes, there is a weight she bears that I can easily see, but yet she holds it well enough so that it does not spill into her outer image.

"So shall we wait here, and when he enters I will first inform him of the fate of the friar and that I am standing in for him. Then, with you here with me, we shall turn his mind to know that you are present within these walls and what your purpose is of being here. I shall speak of your entrapment and that the only way for you to leave this world and enter the afterlife of peace is through the same peace between the two families. If this does not move his soul, where I believe such words should move mountains within him, then all shall be lost. Yet, from the anger he did possess, in the one time I came across him, I am sure his love for you would move the sun."

"You are wise, good apothecary. Whether it is that you and the friar are the same soul, or you have learned much from him and carry on his will is still open to be seen. Even with the sadness that I feel for his loss, there is a place in my heart for the man who carries forth his memory."

"These are kind words and most appreciated my dear." My heart now feels even more for this child, though she be not of this living world any longer. If it be that I am here to help her, then bring on this day so that I may succeed within the task.

I care not ask of whether she has seen Romeo this day, that his disappearance may have been as brief as a passing breeze. She still seems empty without him here, as if a piece of her has been lost. I have been present for those who have lost their loved one, the man or woman whom they married that they had spent most of their life with. They grieved long but found peace one day. That Juliet has lost her love, I am worried that as the love was deeper than any I have ever seen, her healing, even as a spirit, may never see an end. Though, for that, I will myself pray.

We are alerted as the door opens. To each other's eyes we glance, as her partially calm state now vibrates with anxious awareness. He must have finally arrived, and it is now time for me to become the man I am meant to be. We stand back, waiting for him to walk through the entranceway into the church. As I stand to the side, whoever enters will not see me at first, but once they enter into the main of the church, they will see me to this side and prompt me to begin my task.

"Juliet!" the woman's voice strongly whispers. "Juliet, my flower, where are you?" she says again. If I am not mistaken, this is not the voice of her father, or even that of her mother, but as my thought gathers its shape, the nurse walks in, and sees me standing to her right. She immediately walks over and with the urgent expression, smiles at me, and looks around for what I feel is the search for Juliet.

"Hello, gentle nurse. What brings you to the church today? Was it not Lord Capulet that the friar asked of you to call upon to the church? He did inform me of this, but I may very well be mistaken."

"No, you are not mistaken. The good lord of the house is on his way, and should be here straight. I have come, as I always have in my years, to be here for my dearest Juliet. Whenever her parents would speak to her, I would be there as her protector. Her emotions are soft, yet like a storm that comes from the sea, they can be wild and come without warning to change design on the sea and land."

"Good nurse, you exaggerate the show I did put on for my dear parents. I was never of that wind," Juliet says. As she looks at me, I see that she would like for me to express this to the nurse.

"Juliet is here, good nurse, and says that you do speak more of what she enacted than the show of emotion within her. Most of her passion was like that of a play, only for the show of those who watched, but not truthful for what rested deep in her." I now see what the friar had done within the previous meeting between them. He was a patient and honorable man.

"He should be here soon," the nurse speaks with sudden urgency. "I will hide myself, for whatever it is you will speak to him of, and when he is gone, I will stay and comfort Juliet however she needs. Do you hear me, sweet girl? I am here, my love. Your gentle nurse as ever. Sir, I will hide in the confessional, as it is in the middle of the church and will allow me to hear all through the curtain. Juliet, I will be in the confessional if you need me, dear! You can join me as well, if it please you. Romeo, you are also welcome to come to me as well, if you need, as my love for Juliet extends to you." She walks away, looking around, still hoping for a sight of them. She does not know of Romeo's fate, and as I look at Juliet, she remains silent, with her head down, holding in the raw emotion that would force waves of tears she wishes to cry.

I can see the pain in her expression. The name of Romeo spoken touches her deeply. I did not wish for it to be spoken so that she may keep focus, but the nurse, without the knowledge we possess, has uttered it in a loving gesture. I need to hold her mind together, as the knowledge she possesses, that I will need to speak with her father of, is more valuable than all the riches of the earth.

"Juliet, prepare yourself my dear, for your father will be here shortly. Recall the words spoken between you both that will assist him in believing that you are here. Search for stories of events you two shared alone, search for words that he spoke to you that no one else should know, and gather all these intimate meetings in one thought as we cannot be sure that he will stay once he realizes why it is that he has truly been summoned here." She nods to me, as her words are not yet ready. She still gathers herself from her thoughts of Romeo.

As her reaction to my words was quick, I do not fear that she will be ready for his arrival. She is a strong girl, the strongest I have ever come across. I hope that before these events find their end I may speak with her one last time and reflect on my thoughts of how proud I am of her and how strong a woman she is. If she were my daughter, I would do nothing but speak of her amazing efforts, her strong will and the woman she has grown to become. My history with her may not be as deep as all these other people, but my feeling of what I know can lay the foundation for my words.

As soon as the curtain is drawn and the nurse finds her place, the door once again opens. Our moment has come. My blood courses through my veins at a speed I have never felt. This may either be a normal reaction to such a moment or else my heart may have found its time to give up its beating and send me to heaven to rest from all that has taxed its weary beat. As I still stand and breathe, it seems I shall live on. There is a clear part of me that wishes it were my last moments, as this freshly developed task is here and fear covers over my skin with each drop of sweat that releases.

Upon the desired hour, in walks Lord Capulet, with two men. Each attending man is a guard that protects him from harm, and each one is large, like framed stones of persons that could support the base of a mountain. They have size and mass greater than any men I have seen. They could defend not only Lord Capulet, but also God himself if he visited this world and were in need of a show of force.

"Wait you both outside", Lord Capulet commands to them. "I shall be fine within the church. Inform me if any situation from without that brings concern. I shall be brief, as the burial of our men will not need much conversation. Go." The men look around, at all the curves of the church and eventually at myself. I do not look like much of a threat in my old years, and they agree as they leave out the doors without offering me a second glance.

As the door closes, Lord Capulet walks to me, glancing at my appearance. I can tell he does not approve of my clothes, as they have not been cleaned in some time and are not of fancy form. An apothecary does not dress much more than this, but Lord Capulet would not be one to know such things. A family such as his would send an attendant to fetch medicines needed for their family. He has likely never stepped foot within the doors of an apothecary or many other tradesmen's shops.

"Sir, if you could summon the friar, I would like to get through this matter of the burial arrangements." He says this and looks away, eyeing the church and his surroundings. As the late hour kept information locked in the night, he does not know of the friar's death. What should I do? If I inform him without care, he may leave directly and not offer me the time I need to speak with him. I must begin with information on Juliet if I am to offer reason on why he should stay, listen, and question. I motion my eyes to Juliet, as Lord Capulet looks elsewhere. I hope that she understands the meaning in my eyes' expressions.

"O', yes. Apologies, good apothecary. I could not help but see my father here before me and the way he has spoken to you. It has been weeks since I have seen him, and such time away does offer a different image of him I am not used to seeing, even with the memories that call upon my immediate emotion," Juliet says, as she stands firm, looking at him in wonder.

"Are you going to fetch the friar, or shall I call for him myself? I do not have time to wait for your old bones and mind to work my words into the depths of your brain," Lord Capulet says, as we stand there, and I begin to show panic in my features.

"Tell him that I am here, holding you from fetching the friar. Tell him that I have come to the friar many times in the recent past before I died, and that it has locked me here now." Clearing my throat and gathering my courage, I repeat her words to Lord Capulet, and he within moments of their understanding looks at me as if I am mad.

"Is this the workings of some joke, old man? Do you think I offer a jest with you upon my desire to leave here, that you speak of my daughter and her visitations to the friar? I shall have you beaten for your rude intentions. Now fetch me the friar!" he yells, as his patience has come close to ending. Juliet screams as well, reacting to his outburst, but as he cannot hear her, it does nothing more than shock myself. She looks at me and begins to speak again.

"Tell him this: Juliet did not want to marry Paris, because Paris was not the love she had hoped for in her life. Juliet loved you dearly, good sir. Even as you said that this one child was too much from what God had given you, even as you said that she should get herself to the church on that Thursday to marry Paris or never to look you in the face again, and even as you said, *"An you be mine, I'll give you to my friend- an you be not, hang! Beg! Starve! Die in the streets! For, by my soul, I'll ne'er acknowledge thee, nor what is mine shall never do thee good. Trust to't,"* and then you left the room in much rage."

After repeating Juliet's words, his eyes open to a full gaze, in amazement of the words I have uttered, which now come alive in his mind as his memory calls them a-front. He knows that these such words did arrive from his mouth to Juliet's ears, and that there were likely no others outside his house, especially myself, that should know such knowledge of things.

"Are you a devil within the church of God? How know'st you these words? I shall, with the friar, conjure such a fury from God that you shall pray to return to hell and its fires for your sins against me and all men. Good friar! Come! A devil rests upon your grounds that must meet his end." Lord Capulet begins to walk down the aisle toward the altar, but only gets halfway down, as I decide to offer him more information that he does not know nor understand.

"Good sir, the friar is dead," I say in a calm voice. He turns and looks back to me as I walk to the beginning of the aisle and slowly walk toward him. His look of horror covers his face, as if it were painted on. "I did not kill him, as he and I were friends, even in the brief time of our meeting. Late last evening, as we left the palace of the prince, we were attacked by a thief who deceivingly thrust a dagger into the body of the friar. I myself was spared as the officers of the prince's estate came to capture the fiend. He is within the dungeons of the prince's estate, if not dead by now. So call the friar all you will, but it is Juliet's spirit that is within the church, not his."

He is still surrounded by a questioning of horror and doubt. There is no more hiding of any truth around me.

"You have gone mad. There can be no other reason for your wild words, old man," he says, as he looks around for the friar still.

"Lord Capulet, Juliet's spirit stands beside me, even now, and has spoken the words I have said to you, to make you aware that she is here. She and I are bound by the deal that I had struck with Romeo when he did live and suffer much since my weak will. It was my poison Romeo drank that took his life. And it was by the action of his life's ending, which brought forth the scythed hand of death to Juliet's hand as well. I am to blame and for that, I am here to help them free their souls from this imprisonment upon our world and within these church walls and move them on to the afterlife. Believe me or not, but she is here. I could not have known anything that I have said to you. If you do not believe me, question me once again. Ask a question that only she will know. There are no other persons here to offer me advice. Think of her youth or of a matter that most affected you both. She will hear it, and I shall inform you of her answer. If it please you, speak when you are ready."

"Excellent well, my good apothecary." Juliet says. "You have spoken wisely. If there is a challenge such as this placed upon my father's mind, he will not run from the test. He feels himself as wise as a philosopher from ancient times. Watch as he searches his mind, as his eyes look within him for an question." Juliet comforts me in my challenge to him, allowing me to feel more confident in this interaction. She was right, that I could very well be holding the essence of the friar within me to carry on his legacy.

She could not be more correct in her words, as he positions his eyes within his head, searching for history that only he and Juliet will know. This shall prove to be the deciding piece that will bring him to my level of thought and allow me to plead for him to press for peace upon the Montagues along with the prince.

Good friar, if you can hear me now, wherever it is that your soul rests, I may bring forth your soul's delight in the aspiration that you wished for. Watch as I use such words that you yourself did invent. May your soul know that you have inspired me to be a man of your own words and act out the will you so desired.

"If this be a trick, you shall pay the price, not by my hand or my guards, but by God himself who cares for such spirits as my daughter and those that dwell in heaven. But, if what you claim is true, then I speak to Juliet, and ask of her this question: what was the name of your sister?"

"O', good apothecary. Follow me in my word as if each that I speak came from your own soul to your mouth. This matter shall be touching to his heart that he may weep at my answer, so be gentle in delivery and soft in speech. He may be a man of fury and rage, but it is only because he does love me and all of our family so. Thus, speak this and watch as this man will change before you…"

I take a breath as she speaks and I absorb the words in my mind and my soul to make them my own. Holding her instruction in mind, I speak.

Chapter Fourteen

"Lord Capulet," I say, preparing my breath, "her name was Olivia. She died at birth and would have been Juliet's younger sister. You had told Juliet that a sister had been born and that she had been given the name. You said that God had needed Olivia for his kingdom and He had taken her there just as she was born, as her importance was of the utmost. Juliet believes that she was of the age of three when you informed her of this and states that you have never spoken of it again since that day." As I spoke each word, I walked closer to him, but still offered a distance of six or seven rows of pews so that I did not add pressure to him with my presence. Juliet had walked up to him as she spoke her words to me and stood beside him as she finished, gazing at him allowing the intense moment she recalls to consume her.

Looking at him now, he is in another world, even as he stands unmoved where he did. Tears begin to fall, as Juliet had said they would, and his body loses its energy and rage, with each breath he takes.

"How could you...? How is it, that you know this? I have never spoken a word of it to anyone. Not one solitary person, not the nurse, not one person within our family, or member of the extended house, knew of her name. It was only shared with Lady Capulet and Juliet alone." He begins to look around the church, in wonder, hoping that what I have said about Juliet is true. "If she be here, Juliet, where is she?"

"She stands next to you, good sir. As she did speak these words that I did repeat, she walked to you and stood with you. I can tell there is pain in her eyes, as she remembers the name as well. I am sorry to bring such sorrow to you, but this is what she believed would allow you to open your heart and see that she is here, next to you, within the church." I point to his right shoulder, and he moves his head in that direction. He looks up and down, but that he cannot connect with her image, even more sadness falls upon his soul and spreads to each outer sensory.

"Juliet? Are you here, love? My love, my dearest, I am sorry. I did not know that the depth of your soul was as deep as the levels of the earth beneath us. I took you for a child, one with visions that I could not understand nor accept. I should have opened my eyes to you and seen the woman you had grown to be and were becoming. I am deeply sorry. My ignorance did force your love away from me, as I pushed you to your fate." He allows more tears to fall, as his pain releases from his heart. He feels the wrong he has done that now rests heavily on his shoulders, forcing out all other lost emotion from him in his deepest regret. I know this feeling, as I have had it myself.

"Lord Capulet, she says that you should not speak any ill to your actions. You are a loving father that cared for her like a father should. She does not blame you for her fate, and asks that you remove such sadness from your soul and look to fill it with love." He lifts his head up to the ceiling, as his eyes look to connect with God. I feel as if his inner desire brings him to now pray for her, as any prayers from her passing weeks ago may have carried other thoughts, words and feelings with them, of not such pure, loving intentions.

"She instructs me well, but the pain…I feel, shall go to the grave with me. Never will a happy brow appear on my face, as my only child ended her life due to my ignorance of tradition and my blind eye to love. She deserved better than a father that brought such sadness to her soul. I shall repent until my last day and hope to free her soul from this prison, as you have informed me. What else, good sir? What else can be done to free her from this place? I shall not rest one night until her soul joins God in heaven and leaves this forsaken city that our family blood has stained."

"Lord Capulet, that is why you were brought here today. The goodly friar, God be with him now, sacrificed his life to try and bring peace to your families. Upon his death, Romeo, who was here with Juliet since their passing weeks ago, has faded and for all we know and can understand, travels to his spirit's resting place. It is my understanding and belief that if we can bring peace between you and the Montagues, Juliet's soul will also be free from this place and ascend to God in heaven."

"Then, good man, speak of what I must do. Inform me to your knowledge of the steps I must take to free her from here. She will not one moment longer be imprisoned on this earth, when her soul should be by God's side, resting on the clouds above. Speak!" He has much passion in him to resolve her imprisonment within the church, which may carry a motion to force him to end this family war. We have found the inspiration that I am sure will end the blood from falling and bring peace to this beautiful city.

"The prince does this day call upon all members of each household to his estate. There, he will strike down a punishment for all the fallen members of each family. I heard it myself. It will either be banishment or death. Whichever way his graces sway him at the instant of the gathering, he will choose. If you were to go there now before any have been summoned to him, speak of the desire you have to end this war, plead for your lives while informing him that it will be peace from this point until the end of time, then there is no doubt in my mind that Juliet will be released from these walls."

"Good man, as I walk to the estate of the prince, I will have all those that serve under me either swear their loyalty to peace, be banished from our bloodline, or killed otherwise.

My will shall be struck down, that all will know of my desires, especially those of the house of Montague. There will be a new Verona that will prosper long after I am gone. I will send my men to each house, that of the prince and of Montague, to know that I come in peace to both, speaking of the same such peace, or I will give my life to them." The passion in his eyes releases flames as like the sun upon our world, and will warm or burn all those that cross his gaze.

"This will do well, Lord Capulet," I say to show my support. "I shall accompany you, if it please you sir, so that the intentions you speak of will have more weight. And I shall offer my life the same, as offered blood for such requests show the truth behind all intention."

Lord Capulet smiles at me, showing his gratitude for my joining on this mission with him. This interaction has ended just as the friar would have wished. My heart soars to the sky, as I am as light as an angel granted his wings. The friar shall rest his soul in heaven and look upon Verona as he always had, with love and admiration. He built this fair city to be the loving place that it is, and shall see it return to such a state as this, even from heaven.

The door opens behind me, as the wind rushes in and the noise of its closing sounds through the church. As I do not face that direction, I know that the guards are likely come to escort the good lord home and then to his bidding. It is better I do not engage them in sight, so I am not shown the weight of their might.

"Good sir, welcome to the church. I know you, do I not?" Lord Capulet says as he addresses whoever has just entered the church behind me. With these words he speaks, I realize I am wrong in thinking that the guards have entered. If this be one of the citizens of Verona that worship with the friar in this church, I best speak with them to inform of his passing. This shall be a difficult service, but one I am prepared to grasp the responsibility of, for his memory.

As I begin to turn, I am struck on the back of the head harshly, sending me to the ground instantly. The pain is overwhelming and passes through my entire upper body, as my fall has not spared my bones below either. Facing forward down, I am able to lift my upper body with my arms to look up at the passing person. Why would they strike upon me, an old man as I am, but also within a church?

"I know this man's face as well, but I cannot recall from where. The features are familiar," Juliet says, hearing her speak her words with my haze of confusion slowly lifting, as I can now focus more on this man and his approach to Lord Capulet. As he nears him, he begins to speak.

"Good day, Capulet, lord of shame. How dost though, pig? Do you come to the church to repent for your many sins? Please, do not let me interrupt you. This man you speak with, that now lies on the floor, shall not interrupt you either. Kneel down and repent for your sins," he speaks with slight anger, but sure of his words. As I look up, I see this stranger grab Lord Capulet and place him into the first pew to their side and force him to kneel. As Lord Capulet fights against the wishes of this man, the stranger takes his sword from its sheath, and holds it to his throat.

"What, are you mad?" Lord Capulet says, shocked in disposition, with a hint of fear in his voice. "My guards are outside and any sound of a struggle will alert them to enter and take your life from you. Choose your actions wisely, dear friend, for once you select upon your path there is no going back." Lord Capulet looks up to him from his kneeling position, and I can see his anger building once again, losing the softness he had achieved. This man should not want to engage in his fury, as I am witness to its power.

"I have chosen my actions with the utmost wisdom. Your men are dead. I have already introduced them to my sword, and they lie on the street bleeding, for following such a man as you that is valued less than the worth of trash. Look you, here, upon my blade. This is their blood. All those that follow you shall have the same result as this. Now, let's have it, dog Capulet. Speak to God and repent for your sins. If I do not hear the sin which I desire from you to ask for God's forgiveness, then I shall strike you down and send you to him to ask Him most personally and have Him bring you to light of what you have done." The stranger removes the sword from Lord Capulet's throat to allow him to speak uninterrupted.

"Good God, strike this man down!" Juliet screams to the heavens above, but to unheard ears around her, except mine own. "Stop this devil from harming my father. My life has already been given to your kingdom; do not let another come. Nurse, good nurse, help! Come from your curtain and help your lord and master, my father," Juliet cries, as she is desperate to save her father's life but is powerless to affect the situation. She strikes at the stranger with her arms, but her arms pass through his person, as if the image that only I see were not there. She cries and looks to every corner of the church to find some way to stop this man.

As I am still stricken with haze upon my head, I cannot lift myself to create an action to help him. Let it be the strike to my head, let it be my age, but I am without ability to assist him. If only the friar were here, he would have the words and the strength to act.

"Good sir, you know not what you do," I say, with weakened voice. It is the most I can conjure, but I hope to remove his awareness and delay whatever actions he chooses to take. The bodies of Lord Capulet's guards will likely be found soon, and with that, officers will come upon their duty to make this man pay for his slayings.

"Old man, I know, to the very point of my sword, what it is that I do," he says looking at me intensely. "I have come, following this fool from his home, to have him repent for such murders that rest on his hands. Never will such a fiend walk among the honest citizens of Verona and appear as a man as worthy as they. This false image will not be placed in the eyes of innocent and worthy people, who look to enjoy a happy life. I will make sure of that." His intense stare returns to Lord Capulet.

This stranger, within the age of Romeo, if not a year or two older, challenges a man that can be his own father's age for murders that he has supposedly committed. Yet, what murders has Lord Capulet committed, as a man of his late year's can barely lift, if not swing, a sword with the power and intent to kill? That is the reason his guards are always within his voice's call.

"Sir, in all this time I have been here since arriving from Mantua and spoken with those that have shared history, Lord Capulet cannot have murdered any man. He did not have the time or ability to take a life." This is still the most of what I can say, as my head carries pain as one would carry a child that tortures them, for the service in the duty of raising them.

"Old, intruding fool, I bid you hold your tongue, as your service shall come soon enough. I have seen what you have been doing with the friar and even watched as the friar lost his life. You have been through much, but it will not compare to what I will do to you when I am finished with this villain of false hope. Now you vile and despicable Capulet ass, repent for your sins. Allow me to hear what I long to hear, and I shall consider sparing your life. No others have spoken the name I have been waiting on the wind to hear them repent and thus they have met their end. Your men, Gregory and Sampson, spoke not one word of him, and thus, as you have seen, they died in the streets. I asked each of them to pray, and all they could muster for words was prayer upon their own lives. None did they pray for you or any other of your household. And not one word was spoken that I myself was waiting to hear. Thus, I had them draw their swords, but little did they know how to use them. I welcomed them to greet my brother in heaven and placed my sword into their hearts before they knew how to swing theirs. The only man that showed knowledge of the sword was that man of yours, Peter I believe his name was, your nurse's servant. He did swing well, but connecting his blade with the air was as good as he could perform when attempting to strike upon me. His arm had power, but lacked speed. I could hear it with his swing, as it connected with the air."

"You? You are the one who killed my men? You villain. Who are you, that kills for the house of Montague?" Lord Capulet is much angered, but knows there is no action he can take against this man. Even he realizes that such a man that can kill his family, especially his personal guards, is far too great for him to physically challenge.

"I spit upon you for speaking that name, as despicable as your own, to be the holder of my personal heritage. The house of Montague has felt my sword as justly as yours. Each one of them fell as quickly as your men, the fat and lazy knaves. Abram and Balthasar died quite fast, as their spirits were desiring to be freed from their prison within their bodies. Each of them, like your first two, prayed for their own souls. Pitiful fools. The only man that showed any honor was Benvolio. Of all the men, he was the only man to pray for someone else's soul but his own. He cried out that God protect his fair Rosaline. She shall be one that I will likely conquer before my duty is done. Yet, what has pleased me even more than this thought of taking his woman is that each man that I have killed has had the action and death blamed upon each other's families. For each death, the other household has taken the unknown responsibility. I have heard the talk in the streets. I cannot say I have ever had a more pleasing time of killing as this, as each life I take has the charge brought to another man. Now, to you sir, let's have it. Pray, and let me hear the one that you have wronged, or by heaven, you will join all these other men, whether it be heaven or hell that you go."

This man's anger rides on his skin and his emotion is strong. Whatever reason he has, to have killed men from both houses and allow for the claims of responsibility to stay upon the households, must be of vengeance as strong as a storm full of sound and fury, that makes up his purpose of living. Yet, this is the man, not one from the house of Montague and not one from the house of Capulet, who has started the war and killed all these men that have fallen. He is the one that broke the peace Verona has longed for, for his mission to have all those that he has killed repent for someone he has not named. Who is it that he swings his sword for? He has spoken of a brother in heaven. What has happened to that man that he dedicates his life to killing so many men from each house?

Looking back to Juliet, she kneels next to her father, as if supporting him in this deadly moment. I can see her whispering in his ear, but I cannot make out what it is that she says. Her tears fall and her ghostly energy is bright. I feel even more pain for her, not just from the loss of Romeo, but that her father has a man standing before him that looks to take his life. What a world is this that we live in?

"Speak now, Capulet. I cannot hear words coming from your tongue," he says, as he pokes Lord Capulet's shoulder with his sword.

"I pray for my life," Lord Capulet says.

"This has not started well for you; my sword wants to taste your blood," the stranger interrupts with saying.

"I pray for my wife, the Lady Capulet; may she forgive me for my years of rudeness to her and any hand I may have unjustly laid upon her. I pray for my Juliet, that her soul be happy within heaven and travel there now, or whenever God sees fit. I pray for my family, each member who has loved me as I have loved them. I pray for Verona, my fair city, which I have cherished all these years and, regardless of my disagreements with the Montagues, could not leave her beauteous face." He stops there and begins to cry harder. His will is broken from such devastating situations, as to know of Juliet's existence here, and the errors of his past that now come to the forefront of this mind. My heart feels for him.

I move my legs, slightly, hoping to gather the strength to stand. If I can rise, there is a chance that I may distract him, allowing Lord Capulet to attack him from behind and allow us to have the upper hand.

"Old man, if your legs move any farther, I shall introduce them to my blade, which will stop them from stirring ever again." He says this as he holds a strong stare at Lord Capulet, yet pointing the sword in my direction. His vision is vast, seeing the small movements from my legs that are resting behind me. He must be one that has trained for war, as his expertise with the sword has bested every man he has challenged and that he has sight beyond sight, to see things that cannot be seen. As my own vision returns to full clarity, my mind gathers the pain from his strike, but also the pain of recognizing this man. Do I not know him as well? Have I not seen him before? There is familiarity in his look. This city is large, and I have met many a person and seen many a face, but there is more here than a passing remembrance from a glance. I feel as if I have been in the presence of this man before.

"Capulet devil, you have one more chance to pray for the name I am waiting to hear, and if you do not, I will send you to your grave so that you may speak with those in heaven and hell who have suffered the same fate and have now discovered the answer they lost their lives for. Speak!"

The sword has risen to Lord Capulet's face, one movement away from them becoming one union. I can see him slightly shake, as he appears to clearly understand that his life is coming to an end. What name does this man want to hear that will allow Lord Capulet to live?

"Sir, I have prayed for all those that I love and for all those that I have wronged. There are no other names within me that I can speak to. Whoever it is that brings you here to force my soul to repent for, you must inform me of. If you refuse to do so, then use your sword as your desire wills it, for I will not arrive to your pleasing." Lord Capulet finishes his words and melts into showing images of a calming nature about his air. A man that dresses the appearance of his face as such has prepared himself for death, as he knows there is no way around this man striking him down to end his all.

"Father, do not give up. Look for the name within your mind. Who is it that he speaks of? Father please; I do love thee but not so much so that you shall join me as a spirit." Juliet cries and tries to hug her father, hoping that the colored hint of air that are the shapes of her arms, leaves within him a hint of the large quantity of love that makes up her being. I gather my might to try and delay this situation.

"Good and kind sir, of whom you have not shared your…"

"Peace old fool, I shall be with you shortly. I am attending to matters far greater than you. If you wish to die first, I can make it so. Though, as I doubt this is the reason of your rude interruption, I bid you to keep your peace!" His rage is in his grasp, as the sword in his hand shines from the light that comes from the windows of the church. The handle appears to have so much metal that each of his fingers looks wrapped in its design. It is as if his sword protrudes from a fist of steel.

"One name more, petty dog. One name more." He is incensed. No power of God or the devil will alter his path now. Even if Lord Capulet spoke the name, I feel this man will swing his sword. I must look to rise, whether it takes my life before his or no.

"I have no other names for you, villain," Lord Capulet says. The stranger, smiling at the response, shifts his wrist ever so slightly, and even the most gentle of a turn slices across and through the throat of Lord Capulet. Lord Capulet's hands raise to his neck, but the strike, of such a lethal art, forces the blood to leave his body at a speed where he will be dead within moments.

"Father! No! No!" Juliet screams, as she tries to catch him. Though, her air cannot stop his falling to the ground. As his body connects with the floor, its final resting place before each man's burial, Juliet bows down to him and cries for him. As all the stranger sees is Lord Capulet dying on the floor, being that Juliet remains unseen to all but me, he stands satisfied and achieved. His stare is of a pleasing nature, as his work here is now done. However, if his goal is to kill every member of each family, then there are still more who live that will meet their end.

"Old man, have you prepared your soul for God? This man here, this leader of treachery, now joins his men in heaven, or hell, wherever it is that he goes. His wife will be next, then the nurse, who shall be within the same home, and all the other of their house that stand in my way. This is the matter of my resolve, to make those pay who are responsible for the death of my brother." He speaks, but his eyes have not come off of the body of Lord Capulet. He has great fulfillment in this death, but this satisfaction looks to not be his first of its kind. His glorified eyes show the pleasing nature of the kill, but I can sense there is more within him.

"Sir, who is it that you kill for, this brother of yours? I have not heard any speak of him, as far as I can tell, since no man I know has fallen without having the name of a Montague or Capulet. If you can inform me of his name, as I have been much around these families since I have been here, I can enlighten you if he has been spoken of and prayed for." He now turns and looks to me, his intense eyes focusing on mine own. He shifts his body, to direct it at me, but does not move to approach me.

There are several rows of distance from where he stands to where I rest on the ground, held up by only my arms. I will not be as fast as he, if situations come about that I would need to defend myself against his charge. His youth and knowledge of the sword couple together to place me at a disadvantage. He raises the sword and points it at me, eyes locked into mine.

"Old man, I will not speak his name, being that such a name should be spoken by only God himself, as he was foolishly called to heaven well before his season. He was a man greater than all these men combined. As we were brothers, we did much love each other in our cores, but one would never see us upon the city together, as our differences of demeanor did not allow us to make the waking hour ours together. My life, after my service for the prince of Verona, has been focused on education and learning. My brother chose to ignore our father's request to educate himself in his early years, and had spent much time and effort in the middle of these family battles between these headless chickens. He has lost his life for this. He was a friend to a Montague and killed by a Capulet. Thus, all of them deserve to die. All of them!"

"No man deserves to die, my lad. No man." As I say this, he lowers his sword to his side and stands in confusion of my statement. He does not seem to agree. I must be choice with my words, as his blade looks to want more blood to spill by its edge.

"What do you know about death, you old fool? By your clothing, you do not look to be a man of any skill in taking lives. Your old bones do not look as if they have seen battle or else you hid behind others who fought, you coward."

"I know quite well of life and death, dear boy. I am an apothecary. I have saved more lives than most can speak to. God may have called many to heaven that I could not save, but that was by his desire to have them, not my inability to save them. There was one, the poor boy that I was not able to honorably help. I more sent him to his death than I can account for preserving his end. But now Romeo walks in the spirit world and looks for his way to join God in heaven. How I do wish I had that moment back within my grasp to stop my hand."

"Hold your voice, old man. You say that you are the man who did off with Romeo? How in this world did you, such an old and broken man, kill the youth? I should be thankful, as it would have been my duty if he were not dead already." He smiles at hearing of Romeo's death. I cannot place this man or why he does this unkind act upon these families. He is happy to hear of death, and such a manner as this is not proper for a man of honor as he claims to be.

"Son, your joy upon hearing of death is not suitable and less so in the church. I will not share with you the boy's sad demise, as you are not worthy of such information. You kill for your brother's memory, which you tarnish more than you honor. How can you know if he would ask of you to kill those who had a hand in his death? You say you never spent time with your brother but that you can speak to his wishes and desires? That is most unnatural. I knew this friar for only a number of days that I could place within my hand. Yet, I feel a bond with him that could be spoken of like a brother. He was killed, in the streets, for all the wealth on his person, yet as he was a friar, he had none. His life was lost for no purpose otherwise. I could travel to the man who took such a God-given life and strike down upon him. And if I could not get to him, I could murder those who hold him captive, saying that they are scum of the earth for not killing such a vile man. Do you see this placement of events, in the trail of blood that would be left behind? Where is the honor in it for the sake of the blood of one man?"

"Old, foolish, ignorant man. You know nothing of a brother's love. When blood runs through the veins of two men that come from the same mother, there is no end to what one would do for the other. Ask yourself what would you do if that man were placed before you, on his knees? Would you not strike down on him for his evil act? Do you not see that his action not only took the life of your dear friar, but that he would have done more evil upon others, and if I were to guess, he already has?"

"I am not God. I do not judge a man and lay punishment upon his soul for his actions. It is the duty of the heavens and of our own leaders, such as the prince, who will decide upon life or death for this man and his actions." He does not change his expression. He still has satisfaction in his eyes from murdering Lord Capulet and all those that lay within the morgue below. This is not a man who will be able to clearly see and recognize the unjust actions he commits and their consequences.

"Are there any that you would choose to pray for, as I have had my fill of speaking with you, sir? There are more within these families that I must speak with and show the path to their resting world. Granted, most of these loathsome fools will more than likely fall into the pits of hell, before they see the light of God shine down on them. Shall I have at you and you find the answer and report it back to me?" he says, with a smile that appears again, as death has entered his mind once more. This man takes pleasure in ending lives, whether it be for the name of his brother or for the fulfillment of killing within itself.

Friar, it looks as if I will be joining you above quite soon. I pray you, make room for me. May our adventures continue, if I make it to heaven. But then suddenly, my awareness is removed from the moment in my mind to sounds from outside the church doors.

"What, ho! Officers, there are dead men on the steps of the church. Come, we must speak to the friar and find the cause!" a voice from outside loudly calls out. The dead guards of Lord Capulet have been found. Now officers will come and do away with this man for his evil ways. He will now suffer the judgment of the prince who will, without question, introduce this man's neck to the ax.

"It appears as if your life has been granted to you a little while longer, old man. We shall cross paths again, one day soon. When that day arrives, I hope that you have either understood my cause and will side with me or that you have cleansed your soul to make way to heaven. Until then, fare you well." He runs toward the altar and leaves out the side door to the left. He may very well best several of the officers, but by the masses, he cannot beat them all.

His plan is to do away with what remains of each family. If my numbers serve me well, there are not many that still live. I will have to warn them of this, and even more so, inform the prince of what I have heard. He himself will strike down these families, who have nothing to do with the war that all have thought they waged together.

"Juliet? Juliet, my dear?" I say, as I finally stand and walk to where her father lay dead. She lies next to him, looking upon his cold frame, with love and sadness intertwined.

"He is dead and gone, good apothecary. He is dead and gone. I should like to accompany his spirit to heaven. The poor man walks alone, and I still stay within these walls trapped." As I stand there looking upon her grief, officers enter the church, looking around to hold the scene in full awareness, as a couple of them walk toward me.

"Good men, Lord Capulet and his men are slain. The murderer has run through that door just moments ago. If you leave now, you will catch his altered mind and bring him to the prince for his actions. Be aware, he is strong with his sword." The officers run toward where the stranger left, hoping well to catch him. I do not believe they shall find him. This stranger's knowledge of survival and tactics of the kind are well practiced. He shall be a worthy adversary to these men, but by his power, there are not many that will disarm him of his sword.

I hear a noise straight ahead and see the nurse appear from the confessional, cloaked in tears. I had forgot she was there, hiding to listen in on the conversation between Lord Capulet and I. Yet, she has heard it all.

"Good nurse, did you see this man that was here? Do you know who he is?" I ask, in hopes that she can advise me and we leave to speak with the prince of this immediately.

"O', my lord, master Capulet. By the heavens, what evil is this? Juliet, are you here? I cannot believe this has happened. My Juliet, my love, I am here," she speaks to the air, offering support as she knows Juliet will be much saddened by what has happened. The nurse then glances to me, to acknowledge my questions. "Sir, I did not look from the curtain. I was too affrighted by all that I heard. I do not know this man by voice either. What an evil deed is this?" She stands in the row where Lord Capulet lies and looks at him with sad eyes, as tears fall. "Juliet; she must be in full tears. Do you see her? Is she all right?"

"She lays there, next to her father. As one would place as common thought, she mourns for his loss. But we must not let such matters be the same for us. Nurse, go to the prince straight. Tell him all that you heard. Inform him of this man that has killed both Montague and Capulet alike. As the prince looks to strike down each family on this day for the crimes he believes they have committed, we must act and prevent the bloodshed that has not appeared to him as the image he thought. Go now and do this. I shall need to speak with another that knows these families well, so that I may discover who this man is, in that I may offer the prince the name of this killer."

"Juliet, my love, I will be back," the nurse says, but into the air of the church, toward the ceiling, believing that Juliet floats above us. She still does not grasp the information that has been offered to her about how Juliet still resides here and walks the ground as we do.

<u>Chapter Fifteen</u>

The nurse leaves through the front door, as I stand, looking down upon the body of Lord Capulet. I shall inform the nuns of this and have them bring his body down to be with his family members that lay below. O' how each of these families have been tricked and deceived into thinking the other had started the war once again, when it was this man who was in charge of the calendar of their deaths this whole time. I must find out who he is, so that I can report this to the prince and have him brought to justice for what he has done. There is one man that can inform me, as his words still ring in my ear from the impact of their usage and meaning. This stranger spoke of knowing Romeo intimately and even his men. If Romeo were still here, I would have heard his name straight and could have been on my way to the Prince. Since I cannot know if Romeo will return or not, I must find the next solution for my answer. I will go to speak with Mercutio.

"Juliet, my dear, I must go, as I will need to find information to stop this man from what he desires to do. I hope to save the remaining members of your families from certain death. I pray you, keep your heart open with love, as your father has lost his life. There is not doubt in my mind that he now looks upon you, his loving daughter, as you care over him. Even as you both are spirits, his ascent to heaven may not allow him to be seen, but that does not mean he cannot see you."

"Apothecary, I thank you for your words. I will be with him, as there is nowhere else that I need be."

As her words find an end, and as her hopes and desires look to have done the same, I turn and leave down the aisle to the front door. If I am fortunate enough, I shall find Mercutio and speak with him to learn more of this man. I pray that Mercutio's spirit is still on this earth and that he has not departed as Romeo has.

Stepping out of the church doors, I see to the left, in the direction of the graveyard that borders the church, plentiful officers standing around two massive white sheets with red spots scattered on them. They watch upon the bodies of Lord Capulet's guards. These men were as enormous as I've ever seen. Muscle looked to be built upon muscle. How they could have been bested by this stranger, I cannot understand. The stranger may have been quick with the sword, but two men that are not only the size of mountains, but that could move them as well, defeated by one man half their size…it puzzles my mind.

I nod to one of the officers that look up toward me and walk away in the opposite direction, taking me to the market. Mercutio said he would wait there, as he cannot seem to find a way to get into the church. I pray that he is still there. Death of the living, and in Romeo's case, the already dead, seems so spontaneous that if I do not act now upon the desires that may end this war, and even the prince's fatal charge, there will be no one left to continue their bloodlines and halt their certain end. I cannot have this be. The one vision of my mind's eye, the one duty that is owed, is that I must try and do what I can to end this all without all finding their end, for the sake of Juliet. The friar died and Romeo disappeared. Is there coincidence that as we are all tied together, that this happened? To help Juliet fly to heaven, my soul believes that ending this situation will be the answer to it all.

Gathering my mind, I see that I have made it to the market in my quick steps and distracted mind. In my deep thought in pondering the fate of existence, it looks as if my body has brought me here without the need of using my mind for direction. My desire alone knows where I need to be. I will let my fate guide me, as God knows what it is that I am here to do.

It is early still, as many of the sellers of the fine goods still organize themselves for the day ahead. All their attention is on preparing for the citizens who will come to buy their goods—and they will come. I am thankful that their concentration will be placed so finely on their duty, for when I find Mercutio, my conversing with him, as others cannot see him, will make me appear to be mad.

Walking around the area where I saw him last, I do not see him. I remember his features well, as his appearance is sharper than any man, even as a ghost. He looked refined and well dressed, but still held himself as a man that could handle himself in a quarrel or work a field in the countryside. But then, like a sting of sudden cold rain on a warm summer day, my ears hear the shocking tone of Mercutio's voice.

"Are you mad? You cannot think that arranging your stand as so will allow you to sell one thing. Your colors are scattered, your appearance of clothing alone looks as if you slept on the ground wrapped within the rotten fruit from weeks ago, and you place your best items in the front, allowing for them to be stolen before you even open your stand for those who will actually wish to buy such things. How is it that you have survived? You should be as dead as I am!" the wild Mercutio screams.

The voice can be no other, as the words spoken are in the same offensive tone that I myself received upon first meeting him. As I look in the direction of where my ears believe it to have come, I see him. My good fortunes stay with me, and I see that his spirit still walks the earth. And yet, his spirit still offends all that tread on his path, whether they hear him or no.

I walk to him, approaching slowly, as I do not want the merchant to believe I am coming for him. As I am close, and he gains sight of me, I gesture with my eyes to have him come to me. He looks at me and smiles, as if happy to see me. Being a ghost that cannot interact with anyone, it must be a comfort to have the ability to be seen, to speak and to be heard. He does not come from my gesture, so I make it more obvious by waving my arm to him, to have him come closer. Does he not understand what I do? I cannot be too obvious, as I do not want to attract ill attention my way.

"Are you calling me, sir?" the merchant says, as he sees my arm wave.

"No. No, sorry. I was waving away a fly that seemed to enjoy flying upon my head. Please, continue on your day." He smiles to me and moves his attention back to his work. Mercutio, receiving the hint, walks to me. I myself begin to walk away, so that I can find a more private area to speak to him in.

"Where do you lead me, gentle sir? I am not that kind of man. But if it please you to imagine that a man and a ghost can share a moment as you desire, then have at me, but I will be left unsatisfied, which is a devil of a courtesy." He laughs as he speaks, knowing that I am uncomfortable by what he says.

"Please sir, calm that nature whilst I am in need to speak with you. Such things please no more ears but your own. I have news for you and I am in desperate need of information from you as well. If it please you, give me an attentive ear."

"Grand, old man of sagging skin, I cannot offer you an ear, unless it please you to visit my grave and remove it from my cold, dead body. Though, what I can offer you is a place to point your sound."

"The friar is dead."

As I say this, I see the humor that kept a shine in his eye slowly leave, and the softness that I am hoping for comes to his painted face.

"The friar is dead? How? Was it by the way of an accident? Or did another take his life? Who would murder a man of the church? How is this so?" he asks, as he hopes to slip in more humor to lighten the blow of my news, but he is clear in thought that there can be no good voice of humor from this.

"I am here to inform you of this, but even more, and greater, I am here to look closely into your mind and have you offer me the name of the man that has caused all of the bloodshed that we have seen."

"Good sir, I have not seen who it is that has killed all these men, but from the size of each family, there may be too many to name. You lose yourself in your old age," he says with frustration that looks to find the path back to humor.

"I lose nothing. The war is false. There has never been a declaration from either family. I have seen the man who has struck down each of the house of Montague and Capulet. I can swear that I myself have seen him before and recently, too, but it is possible that my mind in my age loses reference of image and cannot bring such memories to its surface. He is not of either household, as he stated himself." Mercutio's stare looks deeply into me, as if I myself were the ghost and he the living being.

"You must explain to me more. How can one man kill all that he has, in the way that he has. This is not of the right fashion."

"I will inform you, lad. First, the friar. His life was taken by a man that even as I have informed you of this master swordsman, had nothing to do with any part of it. He was a man in need of food, that thought the friar and I could provide him with the means to attain such things. As we proved to disappoint him, he collected the spirit of the friar for his payment. The prince's officers shortly apprehended him and his fate rests in the prince's hands. Many would pray for his death, but the prince will decide his fate rightly."

"What a devil was this that would kill a friar? I myself would invade the prince's estate and remove this man's soul from his body with my own hands. Such a thing as that should never be. But now, what is this other matter? What master swordsman are you speaking of," Mercutio says, as his interest is peaked, with a desire to know.

"Mercutio, I witnessed his work with my own eyes. He bested Lord Capulet's guards and entered the church to do the same to Lord Capulet himself. Within his entrance on our scene, I was knocked to the ground by a hit to my head. I then watched as he forced Lord Capulet to pray for the souls of those lost, but to pray more for one that he himself wanted to hear come from Lord Capulet's mouth. This man has lost his brother, and from what it seems, it involves both families. His brother was friend to the Montagues and killed by a Capulet. He seeks revenge from both families for his brother's murder and will stop at nothing to end every life with either name. His rage is fierce, but his skill with the sword is even more ferocious. To best the two guards of Lord Capulet, men that stand as high as a mountain, must mean he possesses skill that many cannot have." Mercutio's eyes are open as wide as I have seen a man's open. He is in shock by what I tell him. "What is it that you are thinking of, Mercutio?"

"It cannot be, but go on. Is there anything more you can tell me about this man," he asks, as his own wonder couples with mine to place us in the same thought as the friar and I have been in together. Mercutio's serious demeanor points our minds in a direction where we can do nothing but find our answer.

"He said he and his brother were never close, but that when one does ill to a brother, their blood does boil and bring destruction to all those who caused such pain. I can understand, but still, a man must have sense to search for meaning in all that he does. He spoke of being more of his books, as his brother was one to never turn a page of any tale. I cannot see how a man, who speaks of such intellect, can be at such a loss of all he has learned."

"Good apothecary, stop. I need not hear more of this." Mercutio, lost in the matter I have informed him of, wears the sadness coupled with disbelief that I have felt within me. I can only believe that he also feels my pain for all that I have heard and places such pain within him. I hope that the man I have described allows him to search his memory and find a name that will enlighten us to the name of the villain to be reported to the prince.

"Mercutio, has anything I have said assisted you with finding out who this man is? Have you come across him in passing? Do you know of whom I speak?" I ask, as his mind looks to have gathered its thoughts and he seems overwhelmed, so that great sadness hangs in his ghostly eyes.

"Good sir, I have come across this man's path, many a time. You need not say anything more. The man you speak of is my brother, Valentine. Everything you have said has described him as if he stood here with you and I."

"You are the brother?" I ask, as amazement once again captures my mind and soul.

"Yes, I am this man's brother. As you know, I was dear friends with Romeo and killed by Tybalt, who is of the house of Capulet. Romeo looked to stop the duel Tybalt and I had engaged in through our foolish and ego-entranced minds. By engaging in our fight, he moved to me and placed me in his arms, stopping my attack but preventing me from defending from Tybalt's striking sword that he did not appear to see. I was murdered in the streets, which is why I believe my spirit is trapped within these same streets, bound into these families' warlike duel. Valentine is a master swordsman and what some would call the opposite of me."

"Good sir, when and where did you see him last? We must find him and stop him from killing the rest of each family. If we can get this information to the prince, we may be able to stop him and save the lives of many innocent people." My urgency runs through me, as my body can barely hold itself together. I am anxious, nervous, and terrified to know that this stranger, now discovered to be Mercutio's brother, Valentine, is tied into this fray as closely as if he were a family member himself.

"The last I had seen or spoke with him was weeks ago on the night of Lord Capulet's grand party. He and I were on the invitation together; *Mercutio and his brother Valentine,* as it read. It did not please him that my name was first on the invitation and he was lightly mentioned after me. It just proved our difference of personality, in that I am a friend with all, and he, a man who is friends with books. I asked if he would like to join me, with Romeo and his men, in attending this grand feast, but he would have none of it. I told him he disrespected our family name, as both our names were on the invitation and we should both pay respects by going. He would have none of it still and waved me off. This was the very night that Tybalt established the direction of his anger to send a death note on Romeo, and bring us to the place we have arrived. If Valentine had come, it would have been likely that Tybalt would not have advanced his hatred so, as all men fear Valentine's skills with weapons of war. Valentine can kill any man with his sword and not allow the other to receive one touch of their sword on him. That is why he wears the rings, one on each finger of his sword hand. They protect his hand in the hilt from receiving a blow that may unsteady his attack or disarm him, and they stand for a symbol of excellence in his craft. He is a wise man and a devil of a swordsman, but lacking the ability to relate with others and even make true and honorable friends. I have not seen him since that night."

"Then, good Mercutio, you must tell me where he stays so that I can inform the prince and have his officers arrest him. He must be captured and brought to justice." Yet, as I ask this question, my mind hangs upon his mention of the rings.

"I admire your bravery and honor, but it will not be so easy. He will not stay at home if he is acting upon such fury against these families. He will find a place to dwell and stay out of sight, one where he will continuously have others keep watch for him, in return for protection or to fatten one's purse."

"Wait, gentle Mercutio. Please repeat what you said. A memory has returned to my aging mind." My brain bends as some of his words strike me to the core.

"I said, he shall not be within our family home."

"No, before that. His sword hand, what was it you said about it?" I ask, as familiarity cripples me about it.

"Yes, his sword hand. He wears a ring upon each finger to defend against the opponent's sword striking his hand to disarm him. It's a brilliant way to defend oneself, though I never cared that he wears these rings at all times. One ring on each finger, each different than the others, and all standing for the craft of swordsmanship he has achieved."

"A ring on each finger... I have seen this man. When I first arrived in Verona, I went to an inn for a drink, before I was to...go to the church. These two men sat at the bar, speaking of the recent murders in the city. One of them wore a ring on each of the fingers of his hand. He was bold in speech and sure of his mind, but this ring on each finger puzzled me."

"That, my dear sir, was more than likely my brother. If I may guess, you were at Il Nascondiglio, were you not? This is where he will likely lodge when he stays within Verona, as he knows everyone there and has contributed to each man's purse. If an officer walked within the doors, or even down the street of the inn with intent to enter there, he would be informed and remove himself well before they got there. He does not hide due to any serious offense, such as murder, but he has started many a quarrel and caused much trouble due to his entitled nature. It is pointless that you tell the prince, as he will run and you shall never have your day."

"This was the place. How ill all is within me that I saw him and listened to the man that has caused so much grief. He spoke of the family war, so lightly and carefree. He was not just informing the man he conversed with but more bragging to the achievement of what he has done."

"Good apothecary, how were you to know? When he is tempered as so, the devil can come through him and support his task. No officer or man of God will bring him to justice. If he did as you said to Lord Capulet's massive guards, then what chance would any of the officers have as well. No man wields a sword as great as his."

He is right. Even if I were to inform the prince, word of the officers coming would alert him and he would be gone for sure. Even so, Mercutio speaks so highly of Valentine's sword that I am not sure that even if I brought justice to him, that justice would prevail. There must be another way. There must be another answer. If God will play a hand in this matter, he will inform me of what needs to be done to stop this man from killing once more.

The nurse will hold the prince's swift hand, I am sure of it, from ordering the demise of each family. But if I cannot stop the murderer himself, then even the prince calling for peace, and each family agreeing, will not stop the bloodshed. If I even engaged the man with a sword myself, my life would surely end, as the inn houses his men and they would sooner take pleasure in seeing my blood fall and life end. I do not have the skill or the youth to challenge him.

Looking to the sky, I watch as the clouds pass across the great, blue canopy. There is a peace in the market before the masses of citizens arrives. The quiet air calms me, slightly. As I stand here, I begin to feel helpless, as there does not seem like there is anything I can do. Though, there must be. My reason for being here cannot be any other than but to end this war, I am sure of it.

"These fools in the market set up their shop so early in the day, that much of their food will rot before someone were to buy it. Look at how those apples there rot in the sun. Does he not know that shade will keep them fresh?" Mercutio looks upon the market, cursing what he sees, as his own anger cannot be contained within him. He begins to yell at the shopkeeper to release his frustration, "You fool! Your cider shall sooner poison those that drink it before it will refresh them. Do you not agree…?"

Hold. Not a word more. That is it. That is what I must do. I reach into my pocket, and as I have placed no other care toward any possession in my life, I feel the vial of poison within my grasp. The poison—the same devil's liquid that killed Romeo. The same liquid that was to take my life within the church. This is how Valentine shall meet his end. I may not have might with the sword, but within the dealings of my trade, as I am an apothecary that has had his day, he will not be a match for my liquid death, as it will dispatch him straight. How will I approach him to use it? How will I be able to achieve such a deed? Why, he said it himself, allowing me such access. And being a man such as he, I know it could work. "Mercutio, I must leave. I am going to side with your brother."

"What? Are you as mad as I thought you were? Side with him, after your rants that filled the air with hatred for all he has done? You are as mad as any man I have met. Go to! May you die a pleasant death, if your wits allow you to understand the day." Mercutio, in disbelief for what I have said, removes hope from his sleeve, believing that I have gone mad.

"Good Mercutio, I bid you farewell. I cannot quickly or easily explain what it is that works my mind to its thought, but I will surely play the theft of life and come upon a path where only God knows if I will live or die. Fare you well. May your stay on this world end as soon as my duty is done, if that be equal to your wishes and desires. Whichever the case, adieu, good Mercutio."

Chapter Sixteen

Walking away from the market, and for the first time since I have been in Verona, I know where it is that I go. My events within Verona started at Il Nascondiglio, and now it looks as if it is where it takes me, as I will look to end these tragic events within the same walls. Valentine has made a pact with the devil to find the power and the will to kill every Montague and Capulet. I have made a pact with God to stop what it is that Valentine has set out to do. At first, I thought it was the families themselves that sought to spill blood and end the other, but as I have learned that Valentine, Mercutio's brother, has set it upon his own fate to avenge Mercutio's death and make each person within these families pay for their hand in his brother's last day, it only changes my focus but not my goal.

Arriving back at the door of the church, I see that many officers still stand out in front, but the bodies of Lord Capulet's guards have been removed from the streets. This is a wise decision; such spilled blood will only cause more panic and unrest. This city has seen enough of such things. From Mantua, I had always seen Verona as a peaceful and loving city, filled with color and love. As I have immersed myself here and seen the dark corners where beauty hides, it has surprised me even as it should not have, that such evils can walk in such a place of amazement.

I feel for Juliet who rests within the church, trapped within the walls and doors, dwelling within the memories of all those that lay dead in the basement. Even as her father was one she had disagreed with and could not find peace with, there was still the deep love in them both that shined through in the end. His thoughts believed in her, and she released that deep emotion upon the care for his life. I have faith in more than all the new belief in the supernatural world I have witnessed, that they will meet again and their spirits will express all that they could not in the living world.

Walking once again, away from the church, to the inn, I prepare my soul for the mask that it must wear. This man, Valentine, is an evil person, who looks to follow his will and murder any that look to stop him. Not having family such as he has, I cannot feel the depth of the emotion that pushes his reason for revenge. My soul has been created to save, not to take lives. Especially concerning my error with Romeo, I more than ever understand the value of life and the purposes behind each moment and decision. Well, life that is not my own. I looked to take my own life in the church, showing no value for my soul and all that I have become. Such thought dishonors my family name and brings shame upon all those spoken to have taken their own lives.

Romeo and Juliet look to have placed that shame in a dungeon well hidden within their minds, as they had more than the act itself driving them, and that their families were the greatest of all families within this city. But God waivers for no name, no rank and certainly does not forgive for the act of taking your own life. Where do I stand with it now? Where does my heart lead me in my existing thoughts on the matter? Only God will know.

In my vision ahead, there it is…the inn…Il Nascondiglio. I have arrived. My blood, like a river over-flooded by heavy rains, makes each part of my body shake. Hold yourself, good man. Do not fall apart upon the doorstep of righteous acts. God, forgive me for what it is my mind prepares to do. You have seen those killed fly upon the clouds of heaven. I cannot allow more to fill your kingdom, when their lives are more needed upon this world. I understand what it is I am about to do, and if my soul shall not make it to heaven, then so be it. My purpose to save the lives of those around me is greater than my own desire to be resting in heaven. This cannot be, that innocent citizens lose their lives and loves from one man's decision. Even as I am the same, one man, I will take the life of one man, and I will spare the lives of many.

Approaching the building, there are men standing outside the door, several steps to the right, speaking. Are these the watchmen for Valentine who will report what is seen in the streets to allow him time to escape? Will they report me as I approach the door, thinking that I myself am someone that can be of trouble? I must not impose fear into my mind, which would sweat to my face, informing of my cause. I have entered here once before, unquestioned, and I shall enter here once again, in the same light. I must turn my inner face, wear my mask, and show that his will is as correct as the killings he has performed for this great city.

The men lock me in their eyes as I walk up to the door, gazing at my appearance. Two and fifty years is nothing for the likes of these men to fear and alert not one pulse in their hearts that I will be of any problem. Not one look or movement of their bodies shows they are the slightest bit concerned by my entrance. I nod to them, and smirk, just as the friar has always done to me. It gave me a sense of acceptance and understanding. They look back to me, smirking with disgust at my gesture. Before they are given the time to act upon the confusion I have given them, I enter the door of the inn.

Walking in, all memories of my previous visit return to the images of my mind. Tables are as they were, a few to the right, with the majority of them all to the left. The far staircase that leads to the rooms above still have a haunting air about them. If I were to dream of a place where demons would walk from the depths of hell to our world, that corner would be where the gates would open.

Fulfilling such dreaded images, my words become action, as Valentine descends from the stairs, walking into the bar. He exchanges glimpses with those he knows and speaks a few words with others, laughing in recognition of their responses. It is clear that his men are present, his protection from the outside world that revolves around him, and he is as safe as the prince within his grand estate. Standing near the door, he has not noticed me yet, but the time will come. I must be ready for when our eyes connect, as he will act upon my sight, or have those around him act on his behalf. That I know who he is and what he has done, will not allow me freedom of time or space while in his presence.

He sits at a table with two other men, who look to have been here long enough that they are struggling to hold their heads up from all the liquid pleasures they have consumed. The day has yet to begin, and these men have already drunken themselves to a point where they cannot function. Or, they continue the previous nights events, not knowing that the night has ended and the day has come. They shall be amusing companionship for Valentine, who has returned from murder and will look to find the bottom of a pint of ale as well.

Yet, this does amaze me equally. He has struck down a man, taken his life from this world just a short time ago, and returns to this place to share in a laugh and drink, as if finishing a hard day's work. This seems out of mind of any that would have rational thought. Revenge must have a hold of him so strong that he does not take to the depths of his heart all that he does. He must not realize the impact such actions leave upon the world, if not on the shoulders of his consciousness. I would not choose to be him when the devil calls for his soul. If the intensity of flames are gathered for the sins one commits, then his fires shall burn so high and fierce that those in heaven will feel the heat upon their feet.

"Good apothecary, come, join me," Valentine calls out, as I looked away for just a moment, which must have given him time to notice me without my knowing. I see several men around him look my way, but then return to their own conversations and drinks. I look to him, firm in face and strong in will. I must not show delay or uncertain stance, as he will feel this and know that I am not natural in my soon to be expressed reason for being here.

I walk to him, passing by several tables, as his resides in the middle of all the tables on the left side of the bar, as if he were surrounding himself for protection. Looking to my right as I walk closer, I see the darkness that surrounds the stairs and feel a slight pull to the darkness. The top where they lead you is as black as night. He must be a demon that has come from the other place, where light does not shine. As I get to his table, I stand and hold myself steady, awaiting for him to question why I am here before I myself prove my reason.

"Good sir, I am not sure how it is that you have found me here, but I commend you in your result. Though, I am not sure it was a wise decision for you to come. You may speak your peace and try to convince me that what I do is wrong, as I greatly assume this is why you have sought me, but be aware, I am not alone in my cause. Look around you; there are men here with hatred for what these families have done as deep as my own. They just do not have the skill or strength of will to take action as I have. You shall have your moment to speak, but I cannot speak to what some of these men may do to you when I am done listening." He looks me deep in the eye, and then turns his attention to the others around him, who have been listening, and gesture to agree that his words are accurate. Murmurs manifest from their forced frames.

"Good sir, Valentine, I am not here to talk you out of what you do. I am here for precisely the opposite of such thoughts." He holds his hand up to me, to bid me hold my voice.

"You know my name, old friend? How did you come across such knowledge? You are wiser than I first thought you to be." His smile holds strong, as it hides his wonder that I spoke his name, which puzzles him, seen through the glare of his eyes.

"Sir, I am wiser than you allowed your mind to believe, but in all respect, I did use such intelligence to do more with my thoughts. I found that your actions are justified. Shall I inform you how I came to such a decision?" I hope that he feeds on these words, instead of my needing to explain how it is that I know his name. It will not be wise to say that I have spoken with Mercutio and he is the one who made me aware. Mercutio's name is not one that should be spoken to him, as I have seen.

"Well, well, well, my good old man. Was it not earlier that you looked to convince me that I was mad? That I was committing sin? And now, I am justified, as you say, in all my actions? O', please inform me on how you came to such a change of decision, as I cannot wrap my mind upon reason that would have an old man as yourself change a mind that is too old to create new thoughts." He laughs and has those around him laugh with him, as he looks at them in what feels like a command to respond.

"After you left and the officers arrived, I informed them as to what happened. I did not speak your name, but that a man outside those of each family has been murdering all those that had fallen. Soon after, several members of each family did come to the church to be informed of the actions. Lady Capulet and others stood, as I spoke of all my knowledge. And yet, soon after, with all I had said and shown, they still spoke that the Montagues were to blame and that all will fall that choose to side with them. It could not be, after everything I had said, that they could still not see clearly and hear what I had spoken to them. Their ignorance outraged me, and it was at that moment that my eyes were awakened. Their lack of awareness to my story and words dumbfounded my mind, and brought me to the conclusion that no matter what any one could say, their deeply rooted hatred will continue on, no matter what is addressed to them. You are right, sir. They will never stop the war that runs in their veins. The only way to prevent innocent citizens, including the likes of your brother, from falling upon pointless bloodshed, is to end the lives of those who cannot see anything otherwise." *These are my thoughts, you murdering, low life pig. I pray they fall into your ears and are believed. It is all that I have to say.* If he questions me more, I may lose belief in this myself, as repeating such a story may be too difficult and cause me to repeat with errors. Speaking too quickly, I forgot upon my brief memory everything I have said. My nerves do not allow my recollections to store such information for long.

"I see. So you are here, good old soul, to tell me that I am correct in my actions and that I may continue with them with your blessing? Am I of sound mind to think this?" He looks at me with piercing eyes. He further tests me. I must keep strong to my will.

"Yes. I am an old man, which we are both clear on. I have lived many years and seen many things. I have seen right and I have seen wrong. I have also myself done things, which may be deemed wrong, but that I hid from others so I would not wear such ill fate on my name. My end may be near, and I may not know of the way this world does turn, but I cannot allow any more false judgment to weigh on me. I was wrong. I am man enough to admit when such things come about. Good sir, you are in the right. As I leave here, I will be leaving

Verona and returning to Mantua, where I will live out the rest of my days knowing that those who deserved their fate received it."

He looks at me once again, weighing my words, judging my body and my face. He looks for hints of falsities that could discredit my stance and allow him the right to end my life. His arm rises from his side, the same arm with the hand that wears the rings that wields the sword that has taken all these lives. He points to the ceiling, as if I should look up, but as there is nothing above us but wooden beams which support this structure, I am well confused.

"Friends, leave us. I should like to speak more with this old man alone." The two drunkards seated at his table slowly look to him and then to each other, and even more slowly stir to remove themselves from the table to make room for me. If I am correct in thought, I believe I have convinced him of my purpose, or in the least, intrigued him to dig deeper into my mind. This victory stays my execution by his sword and allows me the access that will move me closer to my desires.

"I would like a drink," I say. "If it please you, shall I get one for you as well?" Upon the world there is an understanding that nature carries all truth and hope within its flourishing bounty. Life and death walk hand in hand, upon each creature and flower, born of this place. With every drop of this world's will, I pour such outward love into my mind to reflect such truth in my question, as this is the nature of my being here. Should he decline, my task is spent and I have nothing more in hand to do. I will have failed. If God will allow, as I have prayed to save those next scribed on his sword, he will say yes. Please, God, have him speak such a word.

"I would like that very much. I thank you, good old man." My heart, as fulfilled as I feel, beats to extrude itself from my chest, as all shall hopefully be as I desire.

"Is there a drink that you prefer?" I ask, so I can still get a drink to please his liking.

"Request for two ales, one of each barrel. I cannot think which I prefer, but when you arrive back here, I shall decide as I nose the scent of each."

"You are wise once again. I cannot at times decide myself and thus, leave it to my nose to make the decision. I shall return briefly with our ales." I turn and walk to the bar. He wants for me to bring back one of each ale. When I return to the table, he shall decide upon which he will drink by the choice of his nose. What shall I do? Am I to make a guess at which one he will drink? I have only once seen this man drink and cannot recall what it was that he had in his hand when I first saw him here days ago. Shall God direct my hand to pour the poison in the proper cup once they arrive within my sight? How will I decide? Which cup shall house the poison that will achieve my duty?

"Hello, good sir," I say to the bar man as I approach. "May I please request two cups of ale, one from each barrel?" I ask him this and he nods and walks away to fetch the ales. There are men to each side of me at the bar, but far enough away that I should have the ability to pour the poison into a cup. But which cup? I will wait for the drinks to arrive and decide once I see them and nose them myself. Then, a stirring about behind me adds noise to the scene.

"I was going to sit there, you bastard. Stand and remove yourself or I shall remove you for you." As I look back to address the noise, one of the two drunken men that removed themselves from Valentine's table speaks to the other, as they look to plant themselves elsewhere. Their drunken states leave them at a lack of wit, and they argue over one chair, when there are two at their table.

The drinks arrive in front of me, both placed down harshly. This attracts attention from those sitting to each side of me at the bar. This is not attention I should need if I am going to pour the poison into one of these cups. And yet, that is my answer, is it not? I cannot know which one he will choose. There are not many moments like this in my life that I have had, and there may never be moments like this where the fate of all that is good and bad rests in my hand. I have the murderer, Valentine, here before me. He has confessed and still has much to do, in the final acts of his revenge. There may not be time and chance as this for the families or the prince to act in a way of catching this man before he completes his mission. I am all that stands between him and certain death for many innocent people. Thus, I myself must be certain of what I do. I cannot fail. As there is only one chance I have, there is only one decision that can be made.

"I will need payment for these, sir," the bar man says harshly. Returning to my current mind, I had forgot that I would need money to buy these drinks. I reach into my left pocket and there, in the forgotten place, are the forty ducats that Romeo had given me for the poison. I was to place this money in the hands of the church, but as actions came about rather quickly, I had forgot to do so. Thus, this money finds its use in another way that shall still serve its purpose. I place down several ducats on the bar.

"Here is your payment, good sir. Keep the rest for your service." He looks at what I leave and then back up to me. I can only believe that he does not see much offered to him in this way, as his wide eyes are amazed and happy at my gesture.

I reach my hand into my other pocket and wrap it around the poison vial. It rests in my hand and feels heavy, as if it has become stone.

"If you will not move, you canker on the sole of my shoe, I shall move you!" the drunken fool behind me yells, and attacks his friend for such a petty cause. All attention moves to them once again, as they move tables and scream at each other in their drunken foolery. Now is my moment.

I take the poison from my pocket, open the small cork from the top, and pour half of it into each cup, making sure to divide it properly. One vial alone can dispatch twenty men straight, so half is still enough to make his life wilt like a flower during the longest of droughts.

The time has come, where my life has lived its day and now its end walks to me. The decision has been made and the passing moments ahead look to be my last. If all goes as it should, this will truly be my resting place.

Quickly, as order is restored back to the room and the drunkards are separated from each other, I place the empty vial back within my pocket, grab both drinks, and turn to Valentine, awaiting for men to clear a path for me to return back to him.

"These men that you sat with previously do not seem to hold their liquor well," I say, as I approach the table and place both cups down in the middle.

"They are friends since their youth and have never found a way to calmly deal with their issues. If you were to frequent here, old man, you would see this more often and brush it off as we do. Come, have a seat. There is more I would like to learn of you." He pushes the seat across from him out with his leg and I sit, making myself comfortable. My heart has never beat as this, but my course is set.

"Thank you. Maybe when I visit from Mantua, I shall return here and watch as these men break each others heads once again." He smiles and leans himself forward, reaching toward the cups. His eyes stay locked on my own as he does. Does he know? Did he see what I did? Why does he look at me so?

"Well, good man, is there one you prefer of these two ales, as you sniffed them?" he asks, placing his hand in the air, above the two cups, undecided as to which he will choose.

"To my preference, the darker ale pleases me more. It is not as harsh as the lighter ones present themselves to be, which makes my stomach churn. But I am open to either, as I should not judge even a cup of ale I have not had before." He looks at me still, after my answer did not seem to direct his hand.

He grabs the cup with the darker ale and sniffs it. He closes his eyes and does it once again. As he opens his eyes, he places the cup down and picks up the other, performing the same actions. As he opens his eyes, he places this one down too.

"They both have a scent that pleases my desires. But I shall choose this one," as he grabs the darker ale.

"Fine choice," I say as I reach for the other cup and place it in my hand. "I shall open my mind to new experiences and clearer visions once again."

"What shall we drink to, old man? Your health? My health? Or to the inevitable death of every Montague and Capulet?" He raises his cup to the middle of the table, and I raise mine close to his.

"I would say we should drink to each other's health, as such things will allow you to achieve the actions we both desire of you." He smirks at me, pleased with my answer.

"You surprise me, old man. I would not have thought such wisdom could come from one as old as you, who are usually set in their ways, when reason has fled the mind the way youth falls from the skin. To our health!" he says, as we clank our cups. He brings the cup to his lips, eyes locked with mine. I bring mine to my lips, holding his stare. Each cup rests on our lower lips. As I lift my end up, so does he, and we drink a hearty chug from our drinks. As he brings his down, so do I. He places his on the table and scratches his head. I place mine down as well and wipe my lip. He has finished half of the ale in one strong drink. As I look down at mine, I see that I have done the same.

"So, old man, tell me a story. Tell me something wise, as you surprise me the more you speak. I am sure your old bones have done much and seen even more in your life." he says, as he reaches for the cup and holds it in his hand.

"If it please you, I shall tell you a story I know you have longed to hear. Shall I inform you of how I did away with Romeo?" I say, as he leans closer to the table, eyes filled with excitement.

"Yes, that would be grand. Please inform me on how that dog died, as I was not able to take his life myself. That would have been a most pleasing kill for me. He is the most to blame for Mercutio's death. Why my brother would befriend such a fool as this, I will never know. Speak! Tell me the story that will fill my ears with pleasant sounds, as if music of my own heart will play. I have heard rumors, but as you had a hand in his end, you can inform me the best. Speak." He picks up the cup and takes another drink. As I prepare myself to tell him, I take another drink of mine as well and place it back down.

"Romeo had come to me in Mantua, after hearing of Juliet's death, as he had been banned to live the rest of his days there by the prince. He was torn apart in grief and only had one thought in his mind." As I look over, I see Valentine's eye flicker and sweat form on his forehead. "He desired to take his life, as the loss of his true love, Juliet, was too much for him to bear. It is clear to you that I am an apothecary, as he thought to come to me to find a quick way to his end."

Valentine scratches at his throat lightly, as this is when the pressure of the poison will start to build. I feel my eyes begin to burn, and sweat begins to build on my forehead as well. I must speak on.

"He asked me for poison, as strong as I had, to take his life so that he could be with Juliet in her state of death. Now, Mantuan law is strict, but as he had ducats to pay for such poison, and my pockets were bare, I gave in to his request." I reach back into my pocket, grasp the empty vial, take it from my pocket and place it in the middle of the table. My arm begins to shake as I place it down.

"So, he poisoned himself?" he says as his eyes begin to lose the ability to focus, and his head reddens with the clear show of discomfort. I can see the distress that I myself feel.

My heart begins to slow its beat. My head feels as heavy as a stone, and my words will soon not have the ability to leave my lips. The poison is true.

"And…this…is the…bottle?" he says, as he coughs, struggling to hold his head up, concerned at his failing abilities, as his heart looks to be weakening as quickly as mine own.

"No…good sir. This is not…the same vial. But…it was... the same…poison."

His eyes open wide in shock, as the poison has stopped his breath and his heart. As my eyes begin to flicker, I see him start to rise from his chair, shaking at each limb, but then all energy leaves him and he falls to the ground as his eyes close in mid fall.

My head becomes too heavy to hold up. My arms slowly fall by my side. Laying my head on the table, the vial rests below it, pressing to my cheek. I can feel each pounding, slow beat of my heart until the last one comes, as I am aware that it beats no more. My lungs no longer ask for breath. Images blur in my eyes so that a haze is all I see.

Romeo…Juliet…may you both…be… free.

.

Made in United States
Orlando, FL
08 November 2023

38669737R00137